DANCE

"You should be downstairs, dancing," the Earl of Rycote told Caroline, crooking his elbow to lead her out of her chamber.

"Don't be foolish," Caroline said. "Look at me, in this horrid old gown."

"Then we will have to do our dancing here," he said. He held out his arms, moving closer.

Caroline stood rooted to the floor, pinned by the dark eyes looking into hers. Her body felt consumed by an odd, quivering heat.

"You should have known this was inevitable," the earl said.

Caroline could not argue with that. She had known this was inevitable. But she did not know what to do now—as Rycote's arms went around her, and his lips came down on hers. . . .

Miss Caroline's Deception

by

Anne Douglas

A SIGNET BOOK

SIGNET
Published by the Penguin Group
Penguin Books USA Inc., 375 Hudson Street,
New York, New York 10014, U.S.A.
Penguin Books Ltd, 27 Wrights Lane,
London W8 5TZ, England
Penguin Books Australia Ltd, Ringwood,
Victoria, Australia
Penguin Books Canada Ltd, 10 Alcorn Avenue,
Toronto, Ontario, Canada M4V 3B2
Penguin Books (N.Z.) Ltd, 182–190 Wairau Road,
Auckland 10, New Zealand

Penguin Books Ltd, Registered Offices:
Harmondsworth, Middlesex, England

First published by Signet, an imprint of Dutton Signet,
a division of Penguin Books USA Inc.

First Printing, April, 1995
10 9 8 7 6 5 4 3 2 1

One

She must have been a beauty once. Dickon Richardson, Earl of Rycote, could see how her fine-boned face, her straight nose, her chin with a hint of a dimple, might have had the young men gazing with awe and delight, years earlier.

Now she was a painfully thin, lackluster drab who seemed on the brink of exhaustion. Lank locks escaped her black bonnet and hung about her face, which was bent toward her lap. The dark cloak around her shoulders was parted to reveal a swollen belly on which her hands rested, twisting a handkerchief. She was far gone with child.

An elderly woman, undoubtedly a servant, sat beside her on the rough bench in the yard of the Bull and Mouth coaching inn. The servant murmured something and the woman looked up briefly. From a dozen feet away Dickon got the impression she was staring directly at him, though her face was shadowed by her bonnet brim. A trick of the flickering light cast by the torches planted around the yard gave her an unearthly look.

In the chill of the mid-December night the inn yard was surprisingly busy. Passengers, hostlers, coachmen, grooms, and idlers moved hither and yon, producing dozens of little clouds of vapor with their breaths. The din was considerable. The woman and her servant paid no attention; they may as well have been a hundred miles away.

Dickon wondered why a woman in her condition would be traveling with only a servant. Where was her husband? He scanned the yard where he and his widowed older sister, Ruth, Lady Stilton, were about to board the mail coach for a journey up the Great North Road to Durham. No one was paying the least mind to the two women on the bench.

He nudged his sister, a tall, handsome woman in her mid-forties, and asked with some concern, "Should that woman be traveling? Her time could come any minute! I hope she is not bound for Durham. The journey will be unpleasant enough without the prospect of a sudden new passenger in the coach."

"Poor lady," said Ruth sympathetically. "She must have a very good reason to set out all alone at such a time. I do not think she is in much danger of delivering yet, however." Ruth examined the woman's bulk critically. "I would guess her to be about six months gone. But the poor thing! She looks half dead."

"Well, it is none of our affair," said Dickon, drawing his sister away. "Let us find our coach. Damn me, but I do not like this. Taking a public coach to Durham! Let us hope I see no one I know."

"We have had this out." Ruth glared at her brother. "You know Mama would go into a decline if we did not go to her for Christmas, but a post chaise is simply out of the question. The cost would be double what we are paying, and I for one shall be perfectly happy in the mail coach. You too should be watching your pennies, my boy."

"Pah!" said her brother. "Who knows what riffraff will be on the mail coach? A gentleman would hire a post chaise."

"We are practicing economy," Ruth reminded him sweetly. "It will do your consequence no harm this once, Dickon. Is this our conveyance? I do believe it is. Let us get in before it fills."

Dickon followed without enthusiasm. His duties at the War Office, useless as he believed them to be, had been so unrelenting of late that he knew he had to get away or go mad. It had taken every bit of cajoling he could muster to beg some time off to spend the holidays in Durham with his mother. He had hinted, though not actually claimed, that his poor mama was in the grip of some deadly malady and was calling for him. At least it was true she was calling for him; they had not seen each other in nearly a year.

And now he had agreed, under duress, to ride in the mail coach. The weather was bad and threatened to get worse. He disliked long coach journeys in any case, but he was too rolled up to afford the luxury of a post chaise. The War Office did not pay well. The short holiday he had so looked forward to was not beginning in an auspicious manner. He shivered despite his greatcoat, and swore softly to himself.

Ruth permitted her brother to assist her into the splendid black-and-red coach, which had but one other passenger so far; an elderly man in clerical garb. Dickon made sure their luggage was being loaded by the guard and climbed in after her.

A few minutes later they were joined by the mysterious mother-to-be and her servant. Observing her close-up, Dickon estimated her to be well into her thirties, perhaps even older. Certainly years older than his own one-and-thirty. His heart sank. Dammit, another complication. He hoped she and the old woman were bound for a nearby town. He was in no mood to act the gentleman and fuss over some fool stranger who knew no better than to undertake a journey on a bitter December night when she was so near her time.

She climbed clumsily into the coach, helped from behind by the servant, who made soothing noises as she pushed her mistress up the step.

The woman sat in the corner, motioning her maid to the middle next to the cleric, who occupied the far corner. They faced Dickon and Ruth, who had the forward-facing seat to themselves. The coach was meant to hold only four inside, as was usual, and Dickon thought briefly of riding on top, but decided against it. He had paid the fare for a seat inside and had no wish to brave the cold wind. The three opposite him were all small and slender; the mystery woman's bulk was all in front, not at her sides, and they did not seem crowded.

"Would you not prefer to face forward, ma'am?" Dickon asked courteously, looking at the woman. Her head was down and her black bonnet obscured most of her face. The head rose and the vacant eyes looked through him. The woman brushed aside a lank strand of hair and bent her head again. "No," she said finally. The voice was low-pitched and melodious, but Dickon had never heard such utter despair in a single word. "No, I thank you," she said. The head did not rise again. A handkerchief came out of her reticule and the woman began a methodical shredding of its lace border.

Dickon exchanged glances with his sister. Ruth's eyebrows rose. She discreetly shrugged her shoulders.

The guard glanced in and collected their tickets before mounting into his place over the boot. He seemed surprised to find five persons, not four. After a pause he grunted, remarked "Top's full," and slammed the door. With a blast on the horn, the coach pulled out of the yard promptly at eight of the clock, bound for Edinburgh by way of Durham.

The road was in fairly good repair but the ride was miserable. Sleet began to fall before they were clear of Islington, and the coachman, trying to keep to schedule, did not slacken his pace until the horses had skidded alarmingly several times. Thereafter he held them to a walk until the next change. Dickon knew four horses never walked well together. Their slow, uneven plod had him grinding his teeth. He would have preferred to walk himself had it not been so cold. The coach grew stuffy, and he opened a curtain to get a breath of air, only to draw his head in abruptly when he found himself pelted with sleet. He tried to doze, but his feet were too cold. He grumbled to Ruth, who bore the discomfort stoically. Occasionally, he looked across at the pregnant woman. She seemed oblivious to everything around her and continued to pick at her handkerchief.

The coach made short stops for mail and changes of top passengers as well as of horses. Dickon got out as often as possible to stretch his legs. The cleric left the coach at Biggleswade; now it held only the four of them inside. As the night gave way to a gray, gloomy day the sleet changed to a sullen rain, and the coach picked up speed.

The short stops for meals left Dickon and Ruth only minimally fed. The pregnant woman and her servant did not alight for refreshment, but stayed in the coach. The woman hardly moved. Dickon wondered whether she was asleep or unconscious and gave the servant a questioning look; she stared back blankly. He gave up.

"Damn me," Dickon remarked as he and Ruth worked the kinks out of their muscles on the way into yet another small inn. "She hardly seems alive. Should we do something?" he said, frowning.

"What can we do?" she answered. "If she needs help, surely she will call for it. That servant does not seem to be worried."

"She has not eaten a thing," said Dickon. "If I were to take a pasty to her, perhaps? If she refuses it maybe that woman with her will eat it."

"Why not?" Ruth asked. "It seems a friendly thing to do. I doubt she can get in and out of the coach without a deal of trouble. That may be why she stays in the coach."

"Or she is hiding from someone and does not wish to be discovered," said Dickon.

"Do you think so? Why should she do that?" Ruth's eyes widened as she was struck by a new thought. "I know what it must be! She is unmarried and her father is furious with her at the prospect of a babe on the wrong side of the blanket. Do you think that could be it? Though in all truth I cannot see what man would be attracted to her. Poor thing. We shall probably never know."

"I doubt any father would wait this long to vent his spleen," said Dickon. "Nevertheless, I intend to take her a pasty."

"Make it two," said Ruth. "Remember the servant."

Dickon and Ruth had time for pasties, washed down with ale, before the coach was ready to leave. He carried two still-warm pasties in a paper to the coach. Neither woman inside had moved.

"A bit of refreshment for you, ma'am," he said as he held the paper before the woman's nose.

"Oh!" she said. She looked him up and down. She swept a glance around the interior of the coach, her eyes coming to rest on her companion. "Pasty, Dossie?"

"Oh, thank you, Miss Caroline," said the servant. "But you first! You needs it more than I."

"Take them both," the woman directed.

"But Miss Caroline! You ain't had a bite! You'll waste away!"

"I dare not eat," said the woman. She sighed, a long, hopeless sigh. "Take them both, Dossie." She resettled herself in the corner of the coach and closed her eyes.

"Yes'm," said Dossie. She ate them both, noisily.

They were behind schedule because of the sleet, and the new drivers—they changed every third stage—did everything in their power to make up for lost time. The mealtime stops, which should have been forty minutes, were cut to twenty, then fifteen. Dickon, who had a healthy appetite that was not being satisfied, muttered imprecations to himself while Ruth pretended not to hear. The women across from him paid no attention.

The pregnant woman suddenly came to attention as the coach pulled into Wansford for a change at the Haycock, an inviting inn of gray Cotswold stone. She murmured something to her servant, and the two climbed awkwardly out of the coach.

"You heard the servant address her as Miss Caroline," Ruth pointed out in a low voice while the women were away. "That makes me think I was right. She is a poor, misguided wretch whom some man took advantage of, and now she must pay the penalty with a babe out of wedlock. Horrid! The man should have married her."

"Yes," Dickon agreed. He was more puzzled than ever. Despite her bedraggled appearance, the woman had an aura of respectability about her. He could not see her as a light-skirt. He knew, however, that even the most circumspect ladies got carried away on occasion, with unfortunate results. Perhaps she was one.

Ten minutes later the two women were back, looking less gloomy. The younger one even glanced shyly at Ruth as she settled herself in her accustomed corner.

The early December dusk had fallen and they were still some distance from Durham when Miss Caroline shifted uncomfortably and let out an "Oh!" of surprise. Dickon and Ruth immediately sprang to attention. The servant Dossie was dozing next to her mistress and did not appear to hear.

"May I be of help, my dear?" Ruth offered. "Is the baby coming?"

"Oh, no, not yet," said Miss Caroline softly. She kept her face averted. "Not for months yet."

"Are you sure? Sometimes they come early, you know. Is this your first?"

"Oh, no." She grimaced. " 'Twill be the fourth, I believe. Or is it the fifth? It is so hard to keep tr—" Miss Caroline slumped over in a dead faint.

She did not want to wake up. Someone was rubbing her hands; someone else was patting her cheeks. Why could they not leave her alone? She kept her eyes closed in hopes that they would give up and let her rest, but the gentle ministrations continued. From a long way off she could hear the voice of old Dossie, not her usual soothing voice but one laced with anxiety.

"Miss Caroline! *Miss Caroline!* You must wake up, ma'am. We are in the coach yet! You cannot give out on me now." The old woman's voice rose in panic. "What am I ever to do?" she wailed.

Caroline opened her eyes. Dossie was rubbing her hands while the kind lady in the opposite seat was patting her cheeks and occasionally smoothing her forehead. Thank heaven no one had offered salts. The very thought of them nauseated her.

"I am here," she said weakly. "Never mind. I shall be quite all right." Finding herself lying across the entire back-facing seat while her loyal maid crouched on the floor, she attempted to sit up.

"Just lie still," the lady sitting across told her. Caroline turned her head and caught the eye of the gentleman with her. Such a handsome gentleman! But that meant nothing. She had thought Walter handsome once too. This one's tall, straight body, broad shoulders, thick brown hair, and wide brown eyes could well hide a perfect devil. At the moment he hardly looked devilish. He looked badly frightened.

"Ruth," said the gentleman. "She is not about to—to—is she? Shall I stop the coach? Oh, God."

"Hush!" Ruth hissed. "I do not believe the babe is about to come. Are you having pains, madam?" she asked Caroline.

"No," said Caroline. "I certainly should be able to tell by this time, should I not?" She looked toward her bulging belly with a frown. "I just feel a little weak. I am sure it will pass."

"Not if you don't eat," the servant muttered.

"Where are you bound?" the woman named Ruth asked.

Should she tell them the truth? Best not, she decided. She was so tired it was hard to think straight. The tale she had carefully fabricated beforehand for just such a situation was buried in her mind somewhere but she was unable to summon it. She did know she must not leave a trail that Walter could follow, and it was possible these people could be questioned.

"We go to my sister," she lied. "In Durham."

"Your husband?" Ruth asked.

"Dead," said Caroline. She frowned as old Dossie let out a gasp. "Dead these two months."

"But your—your other children!" Ruth cried in distress. "Do you mean you left your other children behind?"

Caroline covered her face with her hands. She never should have mentioned them! Never, never. "They are in good h-h-hands," she cried. "I h-h-have no worries about them." She tried to compose herself, but it was too much. "Oh, what is the use?" She turned away from the others, making herself as small as possible as she lay on the narrow seat. She hid her face in the leather squabs and sobbed.

Dossie bent over her, swaying as the coach swayed, and

patted her arm. "There, there, my pretty," she said. "'Twon't be much longer. Just a little farther, luv. Come, now."

The babe had stopped its thrashing and Caroline felt more comfortable physically, if not emotionally. It felt so good to lie down, even if on the seat of a mail coach rattling northward at great speed. She decided to remain where she was.

Still the memories came crowding back. If she had not happened to overhear Walter . . .

She had determined to have a civilized discussion with him about their future and had dared to seek him out in his private study, a room where she was not welcome, before dinner the previous day. The door was slightly ajar, and she stopped, her soft slippers making no sound.

" . . . will be another damned girl, I have no doubt," Walter was saying. "The bitch cannot seem to give me a live son, no matter what I do. I have reached the end of my rope. I thought surely she would die in childbirth by this time, but no! The babes die, yes, but does she? Never! Whines around like a sick cat, looks the veriest drab so I can hardly bear to touch her, let alone get another child on her!

"Look here, Fenland. Will you help me? I'll make it worth your while. She is near six months gone now, which means she may deliver any time—it was four months once, as I recall—and if it ain't a *boy*, and it ain't *alive*, I tell you, it's the end. A carriage accident . . . or fall from a horse . . . no help at hand . . . bleeds to death . . . something can be arranged, can it not? Then after a suitable interval I can find me a docile young thing who will give me an *heir*."

Caroline, horrified, did not wait to learn whether James Fenland was willing to help stage her death. Having met Fenland, she had no doubt he would enjoy helping. She turned and remounted the stairs as fast as her ungainly body would allow, roused Dossie, who was napping in a chair in Caroline's chamber, and set her to packing a few necessities. Together they stole down the servants' stairs and out of the house through the busy kitchen. The staff, in the midst of preparing dinner, looked at them curiously and went on with their work. Caroline took with her the few pounds of pin money that was all she had, and her cache of jewelry, which she hoped to pawn or exchange for coach tickets.

Where should they go? As they rode in a hired hackney toward the Bull and Mouth, the starting point for mail coaches headed in many directions, she conferred with Dossie. No one in Caroline's own family would welcome them, she was certain. Dossie's sole suggestion was the family she had worked for before coming to Caroline five years ago, the Fincasters of Durham.

"Treated me like one of the family, they did," Dossie assured her. "Mistress Fincaster, she was always takin' in strays, you might say, and Mister Fincaster, he never seemed to mind. Said she was doin' the Lord's work. You don't mind mornin' prayers, do you, Miss Caroline? Mistress Fincaster sets great store by prayers. I've told you about her, haven't I? She'll take care of you if you can stand bein' prayed over."

That seemed to Caroline to be a small price to pay for a safe refuge. "You are certain the Fincasters are yet in Durham?" she asked. Assured they were at last report, Caroline agreed they should head for Durham. Then what? She refused to think ahead. It was sufficient for now to get away from Walter.

Two

Caroline lay supine on the coach seat for the remainder of the journey to Durham. In truth she did not feel too well, though she did not believe the babe was coming. She had had plenty of experience in gauging when a baby was due, she thought ruefully. She offered to make herself smaller to permit Dossie to sit at her feet, but Dossie demurred. The pair across from her, who she had learned from their conversation were Dickon and Ruth, brother and sister, last name not mentioned, moved more closely together and made room for Dossie. Caroline closed her eyes.

Now that their journey was nearly at an end her courage almost failed her. What would Dossie's old employers, the Fincasters, think of an unknown woman, six months gone, asking for help? Dossie had not seen them since coming to work for Viscount Carroway's bride-to-be five years before. They might not even remember Dossie.

She thought of her own family. Henry would be five-and-twenty now. He had been married for three years and already had two children. They had once been close but she had not seen him for many years; he was engaged in his own pursuits and seemingly gave little thought to his only sister. She had never met Henry's wife or children. They, as well as her parents and six other brothers, were in Bedfordshire, not all that far from London, but Caroline had never been able to travel—it might endanger her pregnancies. They wrote occasionally, but had never visited since Caroline's first miscarriage. She believed she could understand. There was no joy in Viscount Carroway's household.

Caroline tightened her hands into fists and tried not to

think of the other restrictions her frequent pregnancies had placed upon her. No horseback riding. Daily "rests" whether she wished them or not. Doses of a dozen tonics Walter had heard would ensure healthy babies, seemingly several new ones for each pregnancy. A succession of shapeless gowns, much like the one she wore now. A complete lack of social life, for fear of her becoming "overstimulated." Worst of all, Walter's detached businesslike attempts to make sure she was again with child, attempts that resumed with distressing frequency only too soon after she had delivered or miscarried. Twice she had delivered, only to lose the infants later.

Ruthlessly Caroline put her memories aside. No matter where she found herself, she was determined to lead a more normal life once this fourth babe was delivered. She had no hope it would live, but if by chance it should, she would find a little cottage somewhere and with Dossie's help, she would raise it herself, never letting Walter know of its existence.

She feared all her plans were mere dreams, but it was the first time she had been able even to dream of a life other than the horror her own had been since her marriage. She fell into a doze, and the worry lines in her face faded a little.

Dickon looked at her in the dim light of the closed carriage. He was right. She must have been beautiful once, and in repose she was very nearly beautiful again. He berated himself for his first selfish thoughts, his complaints that her presence might disrupt the coach trip. If this woman was having difficulties, it was up to him to help. He was the only man in the coach, and it behooved him to act the gentleman and do whatever he could. But what a puzzle! He had no idea how to begin.

"Miss Caroline! Wake up. We're to Durham." Dossie gently shook Caroline's shoulder. "Powerful cold it is, too. If you will stand by our bits and pieces, I'll see if I can get us a hackney."

Caroline reluctantly opened her eyes. It was pitch-dark, but the inn yard was well lit and bustling with people and horses. "What time is it?" she asked.

"Near two in the morning," said Dickon. "Is no one meeting you? Where is your sister's home?" he asked, puzzled.

Caroline had momentarily forgotten her story of going to a sister. "What?" she asked groggily.

"Your sister. Is no one meeting you?" He jumped from the coach and held out his arms to help her down the step. A chill wind whipped at their clothes. Caroline turned her head to keep the blast from striking her in the face and found herself staring up into Dickon's eyes. Dark eyes, almost black. They held nothing but warmth and sympathy. So different from Walter's habitually cold glare.

Caroline pulled herself together and looked away. "We are not expected," she said. "That is—not on any particular coach. We did not know which one we would take in time to inform my sister. We shall hire a hackney to take us there."

"At two in the morning? How far is your sister's? Perhaps you would permit my sister and myself to take you up. My mother's coach is yonder." Dickon indicated a glistening black-and-yellow coach parked a short distance away.

"You must let us," Ruth echoed. She waved to the coachman, who yawned, stretched, and began to move the coach toward them.

Caroline looked at Dossie in confusion. She had no idea where the Fincaster home lay. She had never been in Durham in her life. "I—I'm sorry, I am so tired I cannot think straight," she said. "Dossie, would you be kind enough to direct them?"

"Yes'm," said Dossie fearfully. She looked around as if to get her bearings. "I ain't never been around town after dark, y'see, but as I recall, the Fincasters live north—you go to the cathedral, and then north—"

"The *Fincasters*?" Ruth and Dickon cried in unison.

Caroline and Dossie looked at them in surprise.

"You surely do not mean Nell-on-her-knees, do you?" said Dickon. "She cannot be your *sister*. She is old enough to be your mother!"

"You—you know them?" Caroline inquired hesitantly.

Why could not this pair let them go their own way? She bit her lip.

"We know of them," said Ruth. "Dickon, that was not a kind thing to say about this lady's relative. Mrs. Fincaster's godliness is well known in Durham. She does nothing but good works. And no one has a bad word to say about Mr. Fincaster." She looked daggers at her brother.

"Sorry," Dickon muttered. "Let us not stand around in the cold." He noticed Caroline's shiver. "Do climb in Mama's coach and I will tend to the luggage. We can sort this out on the way." He took Caroline's arm and gravely escorted her to the waiting coach before returning for their luggage. It had been piled on the ground as the mail coach readied for departure toward Edinburgh.

He remembered the small portmanteau Caroline had by her when he had spied her in the London inn yard. It lay among his own things. So few belongings! Why had she not brought a trunk if she was to stay in Durham indefinitely? The garments she wore were of good quality, if drab, but then he reminded himself she was in mourning for her husband. Still, Caroline presented a mystery. He wished he had some answers.

Once their combined luggage was firmly strapped on top, the coachman, unbidden, started off. Caroline paid little attention. She was too tired and miserable to inquire where they were going. She preferred to lie back on the comfortable squabs and let someone else make the decisions. Dickon, however, pounded on the trap door and asked the coachman if he knew where the Fincasters lived.

"Y'goin' *there*?" said the man, his voice full of disbelief.

"There first," said Dickon. "Then home."

"Yessir," the coachman answered. He turned at the next corner.

Caroline did not hear. She had fainted again.

"Miss Caroline! *Miss Caroline!* Oh, whatever shall I do?" Dossie was on her knees once more, chafing her mistress's hands, looking woefully into her unconscious face.

"We should be at the Fincasters' soon," Dickon assured

her. "Since you are expected I feel certain they will be able to make Miss Caroline comfortable. They would have a chamber all ready for her, would they not? But I still do not understand. Mrs. Fincaster cannot be her sister, surely." He believed with the coachman's help he could carry Miss Caroline inside, should she not recover consciousness. He amended that. Even if she should recover consciousness.

"Her sister?" Dossie's voice betrayed her confusion. "Miss Caroline has no sisters, sir. One of eight, she is, all the rest of 'em big, strappin' boys. Oh-h-h-h . . . " Dossie clapped her hand over her mouth in guilt. "What am I sayin'? . . . I mean to say, sir, Mistress Fincaster is like a sister to her. Yes, that she is." She looked defiantly at Dickon, who returned her look with a glare of his own.

Dickon opened the trap and shouted at the coachman. "Forget the Fincasters', John," he directed. "Straight home."

"Very good, sir," the coachman answered. He swung the coach deftly around another corner. Traffic was almost nonexistent at this time of a cold December night, and he sent his team at a spanking pace.

"What are you doing?" Ruth demanded. "Dickon, have you gone mad?"

"Something havey-cavey here," he said. The maid was still murmuring over her charge, and the coach rattling over the cobbles nearly drowned out his lowered voice. "She can stay at Ryfield tonight—for what is left of the night—and we can deliver her to her friends in the morning."

"Bring in a complete stranger—and in her condition—in the middle of the night? Mama will have a fit!" Ruth said in a harsh whisper. "We must take her to her sister, or her friend, or whatever Mrs. Fincaster is," she finished lamely.

"All in good time," said Dickon. He smiled. "To tell truth, I have no wish to spend hours with the Fincasters answering inane questions to which I have no answers, assuming we can rouse them from their beds. I am cold and tired and wish to seek my own bed. Surely you feel the same." He looked beseechingly at his sister and swept a lock of hair out of her eye.

"Oh, very well," said Ruth. She glanced toward Caroline. "Is she conscious yet?" she asked Dossie. When told she was not, Ruth sighed. "We are taking you home with us," she explained to the maid. "You may go on to the Fincasters' tomorrow if you wish. I should not wish to awaken them now, and our own home is so much closer."

"Oh, ma'am! Thank you, ma'am," said Dossie, obviously relieved to pass on the responsibility.

Within ten minutes they were approaching Ryfield. The big, square, stone house was dark except for a candle in a front window and a torch fastened outside the front door, its flame tossed fitfully to and fro by the wind. Once the coachman had halted, Dickon jumped out, assisted Ruth and the maid to alight, and summoned the coachman to help him with Caroline. She seemed semiconscious, though her eyes were closed; small moans came from her lips.

The coachman looked at her thoughtfully in the flickering light of the torch. "We'd best 'urry before she 'as it," he said as Dickon eased her out of the coach. The coachman helped settle her in Dickon's arms and followed closely in case of difficulties. Awkwardly, Dickon climbed the steps to the door, where Ruth had already knocked.

Though the lady was thin as a post, Dickon was panting by the time he reached the door. This unborn babe must weigh at least three stone, he thought. Mayhap twins or even triplets were in her future?

"At last! My chil—" began a plump, white-haired woman in a mulberry-hued wrapper. She must have heard their arrival and had been standing at the door, Dickon thought. His heart sank. He had hoped to have their guest settled somewhere before his mother was awakened.

"Who in the world is *that*?" Lady Rycote asked, peering closely at Caroline.

Dickon took a better grip on his burden and motioned the coachman toward the stairs at the back of the broad reception hall. "All in good time," he told his mother. "First we must get her to bed. Where do you suggest? The blue room? Is it made up?"

"Yes—no—the fire is laid, but—good God, boy, is she about to deliver?" Lady Rycote was frantic. "We cannot have—not in the blue room! Take her to Benjamin's old room."

Caroline had fully recovered consciousness in time to find herself being carried in Dickon's strong arms. This felt so right, so comfortable, that for a moment she made no effort to move. She watched curiously as the plump, white-haired lady gesticulated and shouted, until it suddenly came to her that *she* was the subject of this hubbub. At the same time she realized her savior was beginning to weaken. He had let her sag, and he hitched her up again with an almost inaudible grunt.

"You may let me down now, if you please," she said. "I beg your pardon for my vapors. I am certain I can walk."

Dickon released her, carefully setting her on her feet, but kept a protective hand on her arm.

"We could carry 'er in a chair, my lord," the coachman suggested.

"The very thing!" Dickon replied, beaming. He reached for one of the straight chairs lining the walls of the reception hall. He and the coachman gave Caroline no time to protest before they had her seated in the chair. One on each side, they grasped seat and back and lurched toward the staircase. He beckoned two sleepy, hastily dressed footmen, hanging in the background, to help them.

Lady Rycote had not waited. Anxious to get this creature out of sight, she had started up the stairs ahead of the men with their burden. Suddenly she turned and ran down again, brushing past them so abruptly they nearly lost their hold on Caroline and the chair. "Must get a lamp," she explained. She looked around wildly. Spying the candle burning in the window, she snatched it and passed them on the stairs once again. "There," she said triumphantly. "This way."

"Mama, I know as well as you where Benjamin's room

is," Dickon protested. Their burden seemed heavier by the minute.

Lady Rycote was able to keep her wits together long enough to reach the chamber formerly occupied by her younger son. She set down the candle and drew back the coverlet of the big, high bed.

"Put her here," she said unnecessarily. As the men laid Caroline carefully on the bed, Lady Rycote seemed to notice Ruth and the maid Dossie, following behind, for the first time.

"Oh!" she said, "Ruth, of course. Welcome, dear. You have a new maid? Send her down for Redding, will you, to make up the fire."

"She does not know Redding," Ruth said in a faint voice. Explanations would have to come later. "I will go myself." She darted out of the room, leaving Dossie standing open-mouthed.

"Let me make Miss Caroline comfortable," Dossie murmured to her ladyship. She looked at the coachman, who was too fascinated to leave. "Would you get her bits and pieces, sir? The portmanteau, it is, atop the coach." She moved to the high bed and smoothed Caroline's forehead. "There, there," she said, "Let old Dossie make you comfortable. Can you sit up for me to get them clothes off?"

Now aware the maid must belong to the strange woman and not to Ruth, Lady Rycote left her to it. She suddenly realized with horrible clarity who this creature must be. That Dickon should bring his mistress, so far gone with his child, to his mother's house! And at Christmas! She glared at her elder son.

"Dickon," she said in icy tones. "I despair of you. We will go to the sitting room and you will try to explain yourself. I do not care if it takes all night. That you should do this to me!" She marched blindly out of the room.

"But Mama! She is ill—we must not—" Dickon rushed after her. Fortunately, lamps had been lit in the passage. In her present state his mother would not have noticed, he felt sure.

"She will keep. That woman seems to know what to do

for her. For your *Miss* Caroline. Why in God's name bring her *here*? Oh, Dickon." Lady Rycote sniffed.

As they descended to the first floor, Dickon striding angrily after his mother, they met Ruth starting up.

"You come too," Lady Rycote said sternly to her daughter. "You are obviously a party to this—this—oh! Come along." She grasped Ruth's arm. Ruth, looking mystified, offered no resistance.

"And a Happy Christmas to you too," Ruth muttered as they headed toward the sitting room.

Lady Rycote permitted Dickon to pour himself a much-needed glass of brandy before she lit into him. Ruth asked for and received one as well, despite her mother's raised eyebrows.

"Just who is this *Miss* Caroline and why in heaven's name did you have to bring her here?" Lady Rycote demanded. "Your father would turn over—"

"Never saw her in my life until the Bull and Mouth in London," Dickon cut in. "Is that not so, Ruth?"

Ruth nodded. "She and her maid happened to board the mail coach with us," she said. "We do not even know her name, other than Caroline. She has told us only that her husband died—two or three months ago, was it not?—and she was on her way to a sister's here in Durham."

"Likely story, I must say." Lady Rycote's lip curled. "What did she do, act ill and throw herself on your good offices? And you two idiots fell for it. You can be sure there never was a husband. Why did she not go to this 'sister'?"

Dickon and Ruth looked at each other in dismay. Ruth shrugged and sipped her brandy. Let Dickon explain if he could. He was the self-appointed white knight, not she.

"Oh, I believe there was a husband," said Dickon, stretching his arms above his head. They had felt pulled from their sockets in the climb up the stairs. He rotated his shoulders, then picked up his glass and swallowed a healthy slug of brandy.

"Why?" his mother asked. "You have no proof. Did that

maid say so? Probably too loyal to her mistress—you note I said *mistress*—to tell the truth."

"This is her fourth babe," Dickon said quietly.

Lady Rycote stared at him in shock. She was unable to utter a word.

"We learned she intended to go to the Fincasters," Dickon continued. "She seemed to have no idea where they lived, and of course Nell-on-her-knees cannot be her sister. We had taken her up, but when she fainted I decided she must come here for the rest of the night. She does not seem well, Mama. She can go to the Fincasters tomorrow—or should I say later this morning. You would not turn her out now, surely."

Lady Rycote bowed her head and played with the sash of her wrapper. For a long moment she said nothing. Then, raising faded blue eyes to her son, she blinked back tears.

"I misjudged you, and I am sorry," she said. "If what you say is true, then naturally we must do all we can for her." She straightened and threw back her shoulders. "Fincasters! I cannot believe it. Nell, I do not doubt, would pray over her during her labor, but never lift a finger to help her. Whyever would she choose to go to the Fincasters?"

Lady Rycote suddenly was struck with a thought. "Dickon!" she cried. "Is this Miss Caroline of good family? We cannot have a member of the servant class sleeping in Benjamin's chamber! Tell me, is she quality?"

"I believe she must be," said Ruth. "All we have to go on are her speech, of which we have heard precious little, and her clothes. She is in mourning, of course, but I would venture to guess they are fine. Then, too, she has a maid."

"Anyone can hire a maid," said Lady Rycote, becoming more agitated. "What if she is some jumped-up tradesman's widow?"

"Mama!" Dickon roared. "Enough! What can it matter? She is not to live here. We are merely sheltering her for the night." He downed the remainder of his brandy in a single draught. "I shall inquire of her maid how she does and then I am for bed. God! When was I last in bed?" He stalked out.

"I was only asking," Lady Rycote said in a small voice. She rose and went to Ruth. "Oh, my dear, I am so happy you have come. I suppose we should look in on our guest, see that the trundle is out for her maid, and then we too should seek our beds. Do sleep late tomorrow, dear, for I know you must be tired." She hugged her daughter, and together they climbed the stairs.

They found Dickon, who had planned only to ask after their guest's welfare, sitting on a straight chair pulled up to Caroline's bed. The chamber was gloomy. Gloom was what Benjamin, the room's previous occupant, had seemed to enjoy most during his boyhood; the big, dark pieces of furniture, the brown-painted walls and heavy brown hangings were exactly to his taste. He had enjoyed shutting himself up there to read horror stories when he should have been at his lessons. Now Benjamin was a captain in the army on the Peninsula and living his own horror stories.

What a dismal place Benjamin's room was for this poor stranger, Lady Rycote realized for the first time. The gloomy surroundings were enough to give the most optimistic soul the megrims. Now that she had some sympathy for Miss Caroline's predicament, she chastised herself for having the woman put in such a chamber. But of course the woman would be leaving in a few hours. To make up for her earlier discourtesy, Lady Rycote approached the bed with a welcoming smile, Ruth at her elbow.

"And how do you feel, Miss Caroline?" Lady Rycote said brightly. "Better, I hope?"

Dickon frowned at his mother and exchanged a glance with his sister.

"I believe we should call this lady by her proper name," he said. "She tells me she is Mrs. Makepeace. Is that not right, madam?"

"Yes," said Caroline. She hoped she could remember to answer to Makepeace, which had been her grandmother's maiden name. "Yes, that is right," she continued. "I must thank you for your very kind attentions. You, I am told, are the Dowager Countess of Rycote? Your daughter is Lady Stilton, and this gentleman is the earl? I fear we did not exchange identities in the coach and I have only now learned who you and your family are. That you should take in a complete stranger in the middle of the night is beyond anything. I shall not inconvenience you further—in a few hours Dossie and I must go on to my sister's—but meanwhile, I am most grateful." She gave Lady Rycote a tired smile.

Lady Rycote's face grew grim at the mention of "sister."

"You are not about to bam me with the tale of Mrs. Fincaster as your sister," she said. "Not Nell-on-her-knees."

Caroline looked confused. She had been caught in a lie, but her weary mind refused to produce a more likely story. Out of her memories of years of embroidering the truth for Walter's suspicious mind, she dredged a solution: If you cannot provide a believable answer, change the subject. Not infallible, but worth trying.

"Oh!" she cried, clutching her stomach. "A pain! I wonder . . . "

Lady Rycote was immediately all business. "Dickon, send a footman after Dr. Francis. Ruth, see that someone in the kitchen sets water to boil, and have Redding collect some clean cloths. I will remain here and do what I can. Mrs. Makepeace," turning once more to Caroline, "you are not full term, are you?" When Caroline shook her head, Lady Rycote looked worried. "I hope we can prevent . . . you do not want a miscarriage . . . oh, dear. We will do what we can."

Caroline felt lower than a worm's belly at setting all this in train for nothing. "Should we not wait to see if more pains come?" she asked in a weak voice. "This may mean nothing. I do have these pains now and then."

"Best to be prepared," Lady Rycote announced in a brisk tone. To her son and daughter, hovering nearby to hear the final decision, she directed, "Go!" They hurried out.

"Now," said Lady Rycote, settling in the bedside chair Dickon had vacated. "I am told this is your what? Fourth? Surely your babes come more easily now. You must not worry, my dear. We are doing all we can. Tell me. Where are your other children? Such a marvelous family! You must miss them. I hope they all lived?"

Desolation gripped Caroline. She turned her head away from Lady Rycote and murmured, "No. None of them."

Tears came unbidden as she thought of the long, anxious years of trying to birth a live, healthy son for Walter. Of the two babies born alive, one had died in her first few weeks. Only Charles, her third, had survived. How Walter had rejoiced! Nothing had been too good for little Charles. He had a wet nurse—Caroline was not permitted to nurse, for fear she would not be able to become pregnant again while nursing—as well as a nanny, and a maid to do the bidding of both nurse and nanny.

Then, in his eighth month, little Charles had been found lifeless in his cradle one morning. Walter's wrath had been terrible to see. He sacked the nurse, nanny, and maid, but seemed to believe the fault was wholly Caroline's. He accused her of stealing into the nursery and smothering the baby in a twisted revenge on himself and his need for an heir. Caroline was sure he would have done her bodily harm had she not been four months gone with her fourth child.

Now here she was, temporarily in the home of kind strangers, but soon to move to the home of other strangers. Would they care for her? The remarks about "Nell-on-her-knees," dimly heard, did not auger well. Three months to go before the babe would be full term, if all went well. The future had never looked bleaker. Still, whatever befell her, she would not go back to Walter.

Lady Rycote, shocked, reached for Caroline's hand and held it in a warm clasp. Her other hand went to Caroline's abdomen.

"I can feel him kicking," she said cheerfully. Then her manner became serious. "My poor dear, what trials you have had. To lose those babes, and then your husband too! Almost too much to be borne. Of course, this one is likely to be your last, now that your husband is gone. We will pray the babe survives."

Caroline scarcely heard her, so immersed was she in memories and in fear of the future. She continued to weep.

Dossie, who had been resting on the trundle bed, rose

and came to her mistress. "There, there, Miss Caroline," she crooned. "It ain't your time yet, is it? Seems like you should of had some more pains by now."

"No more pains," Caroline said between sobs. Suddenly, her eyes widened, and she grimaced. "Oh! They are starting!"

Within minutes the pains became regular and more frequent. Ruth arrived with a pile of clean cloths and reported hot water would soon be on its way.

Dickon came in to report that Dr. Francis had been sent for. Caroline, clad in a worn night rail taken from the portmanteau, stood near the bed, one hand holding tightly to the back of the chair placed there. Her face was calm though her eyes still held tears. Lady Rycote, Ruth, and Dossie were engaged in yanking the covers off the bed and replacing them with the cloths Ruth had brought. This was no place for Dickon now. He retired to the library with a bottle of brandy.

Bloody hell, he thought. One would almost think it his babe they awaited, the way everyone was carrying on. He was so weary he could hardly keep his eyes open. He removed his neckcloth and boots, ran his fingers through his hair, and stretched his legs before him. Soon he dozed, his brandy glass still half-full.

Soon after the dawn of another gray, cold day, Dickon was awakened when Ruth touched his shoulder. She looked exhausted, her hair coming out of its pins, her eyes red and puffy. A bloodstain marred her skirt.

"It was a boy," she said. "It did not survive. Mrs. Makepeace is as well as can be expected."

Three

When Caroline awakened she found Dossie hovering over her, looking worried.

"Some nice thick broth for ye, Miss Caroline," said Dossie. "Best to have some afore it gets cold." The maid reached back to help Caroline to a semi-sitting position and plump up her pillows.

It took Caroline a moment to realize where she was. She looked down at herself. No more bulge in front. She could see the ridge in the bedclothes made by her toes. It was all over, again. She felt empty, useless, a weak vessel unable to accomplish the task for which the Lord had created her. It was a feeling she had had so many times that it had become unpleasantly familiar. Months of inactivity, of utmost care, of nourishing foods, of tonics and nostrums, of prayers and pain, hope and despair, and the result? Another failure. Each time it hurt a little more.

"I'm so tired," she said faintly. "What time is it? Surely we must be leaving for the Fincasters."

"You ain't goin' anywhere until you 'ave this broth," said Dossie, bringing a steaming bowl to the bed. The rich aroma was so enticing Caroline wanted to swallow it in one gulp. She reached for the bowl so eagerly she nearly tipped it over.

"Not so fast!" Dossie cautioned, pulling back. "We're goin' to do this proper." She returned the bowl to the tray it had occupied, a tray decked out with a plate of very thin, buttered bread, a damask napkin, a cup of tea, several pieces of silver flatware, and a fragrant hothouse orange blossom in a tiny vase.

The brown draperies had been opened and Caroline glanced out the window as Dossie settled the tray on her lap. Gray and gloomy out, as she expected.

"It must be morning," said Caroline between spoonfuls of broth. "What a day. I do hope the sun peeps through before evening."

"It's past midday," said Dossie.

Caroline started. "Midday!" she cried, rescuing the bowl before it slid off the tray. "Why did no one wake me? We must be off to the Fincasters!"

"No'm," said the maid. "I'll fetch milady. Said to get 'er when you woke." Dossie scuttled out of the room.

Caroline, ravenous, finished the bread and butter, drank the tea, and looked sorrowfully at the empty broth bowl. Would it do to ask for more? But she was so tired. She would have liked to lie down again, but was hampered by the tray in her lap. She sat slumped, waiting, her thoughts in chaos. Another pregnancy got through. Another crushing disappointment. Never again. But what to do now? The thought of moving to the Fincasters' house did not appeal.

Lady Rycote and Ruth entered together, smiles pasted on their faces.

"How are you feeling, my dear?" Lady Rycote asked. "Were you able to take some nourishment? Ah, yes, I see you were." She removed the tray to a nearby table.

"I am feeling pretty well," Caroline answered. "I believe I could manage to travel to the Fincasters if someone were to help me down the stairs. I do not wish to impose on you any longer. You have been so kind!" Giving the lie to her claim of well-being, she sank back on her pillows.

"You shall do nothing of the kind," said Lady Rycote. "You must rest and recover. Meanwhile, my dear, I must bring up a sad subject. Where do you wish the little babe to be buried? No doubt you will want him to join his little brothers and sisters and your husband in some family graveyard, or perhaps in your churchyard? You are in no condition to take care of the matter, of course, but I am sure Dickon will be pleased to handle it for you. You need only tell him where."

Oh, God, Caroline thought. What now?

She turned on her side so she could study Lady Rycote more closely. She saw a pleasant, friendly woman who seemed genuinely eager to help, now that she knew Caroline was not Dickon's mistress. Caroline had heard enough on their arrival to understand the lady's confusion as to her identity.

Next she looked at Ruth. Ruth was a tall, stately woman with a few streaks of white in her brown hair. She had been nothing but kind and caring since they had first been thrown together in the coach.

"If you will kindly summon the earl, I will explain," said Caroline.

Ruth rang for a footman and sent him to find his lordship. Lady Rycote looked at Caroline, then peered into the empty bowl.

"You are so thin," she said. "I shall have more broth sent up within the hour. Mercy! Have you been starving yourself, child?"

"Oh, no," said Caroline, wondering how Lady Rycote could remotely consider her a child. She felt a hundred years old. "I had not eaten recently, because I tend to become ill in a coach. Mama knew never to feed me before a coach journey."

"But you must have left your mama some time ago," said Lady Rycote. "Did you not outgrow this—this problem? Most children do."

"I had not taken a coach journey since my marriage, so I do not know. On this journey I was taking no chances."

Lady Rycote seemed perplexed. She was about to open her mouth when Dickon walked in.

"Good morning," he said to Caroline, moving to the bed to give her a warm smile. "Or rather, good afternoon. I hope you have had a good rest since . . . "

"Yes, indeed." She smiled and gave him a keen glance. He looked even better than she remembered. His coat of dark-blue superfine was adorned with brass buttons, his pantaloons fit like gloves, his neckcloth was tied just so, his boots were polished, and his abundant brown hair was tamed and neatly combed. She knew almost nothing about him, but she was going to have to trust him. That came hard. She had little trust of men.

Caroline cleared her throat and addressed the three members of the Richardson family who had been so kind to her.

"I see that I must confide in you," she began. "I fear I have not been entirely truthful with you."

Lady Rycote looked interested. Ruth looked surprised, and Dickon looked sympathetic and—warm?

"I was betrothed at sixteen, married at seventeen," she said tonelessly. "I come of a family whose women are considered 'good breeders.' When the man who became my husband—I will not reveal his name, but we will call him, ah, John—was looking for a young wife who could give him children, he looked my way. I am one of eight and the only girl. My mother lost but one babe in nine pregnancies. I was so flattered at John's attentions—I considered him handsome, and he was a most persistent suitor—that I agreed at once to marry him when he proposed. My parents believed him a splendid catch."

Caroline drew a long breath and continued. "What I did not know until after we were married was that John was desperate for a son to succeed him. Oh, I know"—she saw that her listeners were ready to interrupt—"that is a common situation. But the women of John's family are *not* good breeders. He was the only surviving child of his mother's six pregnancies. He must have decided to waste no time in making sure he had an heir. I had my first child at seventeen. I have been carrying a child much of the time since. I still have not given him his heir."

"How long were you married?" Lady Rycote asked.

"Five years," said Caroline.

"Oh, my dear." Lady Rycote gasped. "Then you must be two and twenty."

"Yes," said Caroline. "You are surprised? I know I look older. It has not been an easy life."

Not an easy life? What more could a woman ask, or expect? Dickon frowned as he considered her statement. It seemed to him that her life probably had been as easy as most. Perhaps she had suffered from childbearing complications she had not mentioned. Perhaps her husband had been cruel to her. Or perhaps—this seemed most likely—she had had to nurse her husband through a long and debilitating illness and then, finally, lose him.

"Was your husband ill long?" he inquired gently. "It must be difficult for you to go on alone. Have you no family of your own?"

Caroline hesitated. "That is what I must set straight," she said finally. "He is not dead. He is very much alive."

"Then why is he not with you?" Dickon demanded. "Has he cast you out? Or have you left him? My God, woman, why are you not together?"

"I—I . . . " Caroline could control herself no longer. She buried her face in the pillow and sobbed.

Ruth went to her immediately and tried to comfort her. "You are safe now," she said softly. "Tell us what happened to bring you to Durham. Please, Mrs. Makepeace."

In halting phrases Caroline told of eavesdropping on her husband and hearing his decision to have her done away with and replaced should she not birth a healthy boy.

"I knew I had to get away," she said. "The problem was, where? Dossie worked for the Fincasters before she came to me, before my marriage, and she assured me they were godly folk who would take me in. There was no time to write them. We simply took the mail coach with the intent of coming upon them unannounced. I would be there now if not for—for your kindness. I believe we should go there directly. We must not impose on you."

"You may stay here as long as you like," Lady Rycote said firmly. "I would be grateful for your company. These two," she indicated Ruth and Dickon, "will be returning to London after Twelfth Night. My other son, whose room this is, is fighting on the Peninsula.

"May I say something about the Fincasters without causing offense? Nell-on-her-knees is indeed godly, but she believes in the sanctity of marriage. Should she learn your husband is alive, nothing would do but you must go back to him. 'Whom God hath joined together, let no man . . . '

You know how it goes. My dear Mrs. Makepeace, you must not go to the Fincasters."

"But—" said Caroline.

"Is your name truly Makepeace?" Dickon wondered.

"No, but that is what you may call me," she said. "Or Caroline. Why not call me Caroline?"

"We shall all call you Caroline, if that is your pleasure, and if you promise not to seek out the Fincasters," said Lady Rycote.

"At least until I feel stronger," Caroline agreed. "Then we shall see."

"Stronger! That means more broth!" Lady Rycote decreed, pulling the bell rope.

Then she remembered. "I dislike bringing it up again, but you must tell us where you wish the babe to be buried," she said in a hushed voice. "Dickon, will you take care of it?"

"Certainly," he agreed. "What are your wishes, ma'am?"

"I do not seem to be able to think," Caroline mourned. "What do you suggest?"

Dickon thought for a moment. "The village churchyard," he said. "The vicar has his living from us. He will be pleased to do it. A quiet ceremony, don't you think? A few prayers over the coffin."

"Yes," she agreed. "And another small headstone." She pondered. "It could say only, 'Infant Makepeace' and the date. That should not cost so very much. I have a little money—and my jewels—"

"Not to worry," said Dickon. "We can discuss it some other time when you are stronger. I go now to see the good vicar." He gave Caroline a quick salute and departed. She could hear his heels thundering down the stairs.

"I wonder that you have lost so many babes," Lady Rycote mused as she smoothed Caroline's covers. "You must have had the best doctors. Had they no ideas? I fear it is the lot of all of us to lose some—I lost two, but kept three, and Ruth here lost three, poor girl, but has three fine sons, all grown now.

"I meant to tell you what Dr. Francis said, but there has been no opportunity until now. The little fellow seemed to have something wrong with his lungs. Of course he was premature, but Dr. Francis did not believe he would have lived even if you had carried him a full nine months. I trust Dr. Francis implicitly. He received his training at Edinburgh. Do you know of anyone in your family with lung trouble? Did your other babes show signs of it?"

"No," said Caroline. "No, no lung trouble that I am aware of." She wondered whether anyone in Walter's family had weak lungs. She knew little of Walter's relatives. He had a connection in Kent whom he visited regularly—without Caroline—but no brothers or sisters, and his parents were dead.

"It was just a thought," said Lady Rycote. "Now, here is your broth. Then you must have a nice, long sleep and regain your strength. Ruth and I plan to go with Dickon to fetch the yule log tomorrow, and if you are able, we shall have you carried downstairs to admire it." She helped Caroline sit up and arranged the tray Redding had brought on her lap. "Tell your maid when you are finished and someone will come after it," she said, and left with Ruth.

Caroline was able to get down only half her bowlful. Dossie took the tray away and Caroline gratefully settled herself for sleep.

This interlude away from the War Office was not going at all the way he had expected, Dickon thought with a rueful chuckle as he changed into riding clothes. He intended to confer with the vicar at Brancepeth, the village near Ryfield, and he meant to ride there. This business of sitting at a desk all day, going over indecipherable battle reports and trying to make sense of widely differing views before presenting them to his superiors, had his brain in a spin and his muscles slack. He needed fresh air and action to clear the cobwebs.

He was pleased he could do something for Miss Caroline, as he continued to think of her. Odd how a worn-looking stranger could get under his skin so quickly. Naturally, it was only the sympathy that any right-thinking person would have for a woman in her situation. Why, she was younger than he! He never would have believed her to be only two-and-twenty. He thought of the husband, whose name was not John. Had she loved him in the beginning? Was it not to be expected that she would increase with child after bouts of lovemaking? It had never before occurred to Dickon to look at the woman's side on the issue of conjugal rights. He had only to bring Caroline's image to mind; her strained, worried face, her over-thin body, her bouts of tears, to see what a man's power could do to an innocent woman.

That gave him plenty to think about as he repaired to the stables, hailed a groom to saddle a horse, and set out for Brancepeth. The sun was low on the horizon, turning the departing clouds in the east to rose and violet. There should be time to get to Brancepeth and return before full dark.

The arrangements were quickly made. The short graveside service would take place in the morning and the headstone was ordered. Dickon explained as few of the circumstances as he thought prudent and bade the vicar keep the burial quiet. There was bound to be talk, Dickon knew—all the servants must be whispering about the strange woman and the premature birth at Ryfield—but he hoped it would be minimal and would die down soon.

He was within a half-mile of Ryfield on his way home when he met a lone horseman, obviously in a hurry. The galloping horse had passed him when its rider pulled to a sudden halt. "Dickon!" the rider cried in amazement. "Is it really you?"

"Harry!" Dickon turned to greet his old friend Sir Henry Wadsworth. Much laughing and as much back-slapping as was possible to manage on horseback ensued.

"How goes it at the War Office? Have you managed to rid us of Bonaparte yet?" Wadsworth asked.

"Dullest job in Christendom," said Dickon, pulling a face. "Why did I let the family talk me out of buying a commission and work for the War Office instead? There's Benjamin in the Peninsula, making no end of a name for himself—not a scratch on him, last we heard—and I am stuck in London shuffling papers. God, it is good to get away from them! Ruth and I are here until after Twelfth Night. Where are you headed? Why not come along for supper? We have much to catch up on."

"Wish I could, but I'm escorting Maddy to dinner at the Packenhams' and I shall be late as it is."

"So it's Maddy now, is it? I take it you mean Miss Curtis? So that's the way the wind blows!"

"She has accepted me, and we tie the knot come May," said his friend. He turned his horse, ready to resume his journey.

"My congratulations!" Dickon shouted as Wadsworth nudged his horse and rode off. "Come by when you can and tell me all about it."

So old Harry was stepping into the parson's mousetrap. He and Maddy Curtis would have a good life, Dickon mused. The man had a fine estate and was firmly in control of it. Dickon had to compare it with his own situation. Ryfield was not prospering, and he doubted it would until the war was over and he could return to Durham to run it himself. Between his infrequent visits he wrote regularly to his steward, Fetter, and to his mother with advice and instructions, but what could he know of day-to-day problems when he was stuck in an airless office in London?

Dickon breathed deeply of the crisp December air and wished only for the day when he could return to his beloved north country to stay.

Four

Dickon, Ruth, and their mother were the sole mourners at the brief graveside service held next morning for Caroline's baby. They had hoped no one in the neighborhood would even be aware of it, but the knot of small boys watching curiously from a distance told them otherwise. Soon all Brancepeth would know, and then all Durham would know. In time probably all Cumberland and Westmorland, not to mention Northumberland and Yorkshire, would know as well, Dickon thought sourly. He had no use for gossip.

He had reason to feel sour, as it turned out. Not three days later, he learned from Ruth, who had had it from Redding, who had heard it in Brancepeth, that all and sundry believed it was his bastard who had been buried in the Brancepeth churchyard under the name of "Infant Makepeace."

"Curse it! Do those dolts think I would bring a mistress—particularly a mistress about to give birth—to my mother's home?" Dickon shouted. He slammed his fist on the mantelpiece of the library, where he stood glowering at Ruth. "At *Christmas*?"

"Calm down," Ruth ordered. "Christmas has nothing to do with it. If a child is to be born at Christmas, that is when it will be born. I fear Mama's first, mistaken conclusion about Miss Caroline must have been overheard by who knows how many servants. You know how they will talk. It was a story too good not to tell, even though I am sure most of them now know the truth. Good heavens, Dickon, this will not affect you. It is Miss Caroline I worry about. Her reputation will be in tatters."

Dickon swallowed his anger and spoke in a more normal voice. "How can that be? No one knows who she is—not even we know!"

"True, as far as it goes. But as long as she is here, the reputation of Caroline Makepeace will be in tatters. I doubt she is concerned at the moment with the reputation in London of Mrs. Caroline Whatever-it-is. That woman has disappeared."

"So what would you have me do?" Dickon demanded.

Ruth wrinkled her brow. "I hardly know," she said. "You, of course, will deny any connection with Miss Caroline or her babe. If Mama takes Caroline to her bosom as she seems to be doing, that should set the rumors at rest. No mother embraces her son's fancy woman or their by-blow."

"If Caroline would only trust us," Dickon mused. "If she would only tell us who she is—who that devil of a husband is . . ."

"Why are you so concerned?" Ruth asked curiously. "The husband has done nothing wrong. I mistrust her tale of his plans to do away with her; it sounds so much taradiddle to me, an excuse she has invented to explain her leaving him. What decent man would act so? As for her loss of so many babes—these things happen. Look at Queen Anne. She birthed seventeen children and lost them all."

"But that was a hundred years ago! Surely in this modern day and age—"

"Dickon, childbirth has not changed." Ruth stared at her younger brother. They were twelve years apart; their mother had lost two between them and considered herself fortunate to be able to raise these two and Benjamin to maturity. Dickon knew this as well as anyone; it was common knowledge that only about half the children born in England survived infancy. Why was he so incensed at Caroline's husband's attempts to get an heir?

"That husband of hers must be a brute," said Dickon. He reddened and looked away from his sister.

"I do believe I begin to see," said Ruth triumphantly. "You are jealous!"

"Jealous? Whatever of? If you think I have lustful thoughts about that poor creature in Ben's chamber, think again! My God, she would not tempt the most lecherous man on earth. I feel nothing but pity for her."

"Possibly," said Ruth, smiling. "Possibly. I believe you are jealous of her husband. You have your own heir to think of, and you—"

"Enough!" Dickon roared. He swept out of the room.

As he climbed the stairs to his chamber he thought about what Ruth had said. He certainly had no designs on Miss Caroline; she was a pitiful creature with no looks left and seemed capable of no emotions other than fear and distress. As for her husband—he stopped. What would it be like to get a woman with child, again and again and again? The process would be pretty damned wonderful, no doubt. He felt warm all over at the thought.

Obviously Miss Caroline had not thought it wonderful at all. Dickon had never dealt with a woman who took no pleasure in lovemaking. Was Miss Caroline an ice maiden? Or could it be that the husband whose name was not John—Dickon thought of him always as Not-John—had never taught his young wife how pleasant lovemaking could be?

Dickon resolved to believe the latter. Foolish husband, to overlook such a rewarding task. Miss Caroline was an emotional young woman, much as she tried to suppress the evidence, and surely would have enjoyed the marriage bed had she been treated tenderly.

Now if *he* instead of Not-John had been her husband . . .

Dickon planned to ride to the village, but before he changed clothes it would be only polite to see how Miss Caroline fared. He knocked on her door. Dossie opened it and told him Miss Caroline was asleep. Disappointed, he went on to his own chamber.

By Christmas Eve Caroline was feeling almost well again. Lady Rycote believed she should remain in bed, but

Caroline knew the longer she lingered, the weaker she would feel when she finally arose. She had been through this before.

"I shall dress and come downstairs," she announced when Lady Rycote appeared in her chamber after breakfast. "I have eaten a monstrous breakfast without spilling any tea on my night rail or butter on the sheets, but it was not easy! Please, my lady, let me eat properly at a table again!" She smiled and climbed out of bed before Lady Rycote could stop her. "See?" she said as she walked across the room to find a dressing gown in the wardrobe. "I can walk perfectly well. I promise to hold on to the banister as I go down the stairs. Dossie, will you help me dress?"

"Oh, very well," said Lady Rycote, outmaneuvered. "You may come and admire the yule log. But you must not venture outside yet. On that I insist!"

Less than an hour later, Caroline, wearing one of the shapeless, dull dresses that were all she had, her hair tied back with a black ribbon, her face pale but her eyes bright, went slowly down the stairs. She held on to the stair rail, but her chin was lifted. To Dickon, standing at the bottom, she looked like a bedraggled queen.

Caroline glanced down and saw Dickon in conversation with a strange young man who stared at her with unfeigned interest.

"Who in the world is that?" asked Harry Wadsworth in a tone meant only for Dickon's ears, but Caroline heard him.

Dickon did not hesitate. Smiling up at Caroline, he held out his hand as she approached him. "Caroline, may I introduce you to my old friend and neighbor, Sir Harry Wadsworth? Harry, this is Mrs. Makepeace, an old and dear friend of my sister's come to spend Christmas with us."

"Mrs. Makepeace," said Harry. He bowed and regarded her gravely. "Are you all right, madam?" he asked, taking in her pale face.

Before Caroline could open her mouth, Dickon said smoothly, "Mrs. Makepeace has been ill. We are delighted that she is able to come downstairs for the first time this morning." Turning to Caroline, he asked, "Will you not join us for a late cup of tea, madam? I have just ordered a pot in the breakfast room."

"Thank you, I will," she agreed. She wished to know what other fabrications Dickon had in mind—old friend of Ruth's, was she?—before she put her foot in her mouth.

Settled in the cheerful breakfast room, where a footman soon brought tea and hot scones, Caroline tried to relax. She felt uncomfortable with Sir Harry Wadsworth's obvious curiosity. Afraid she would be unable to lift the heavy teapot, she let the footman pour for her and then stirred much too much sugar in her cup.

"So you are an old friend of Ruth's," Sir Harry began. "In London, I trust?"

"Y-yes," said Caroline. "In London."

"Then you know of her boys, of course," he went on. "How is young Alfred? I thought he might come to Durham also, but then there was that trouble . . . "

Caroline sent Dickon a terrified glance.

"He is perfectly well now, and will spend the holidays with George and his wife," Dickon said calmly. "I do not believe you have seen him since he recovered, have you, Caroline?"

"No," said Caroline. "No, I have not." She stirred her tea with unwonted ferocity. In her heart she thanked Dickon for his smooth control of the situation, but she wondered how long it could last. She lived in mortal fear of saying the wrong thing.

"I was never quite sure what happened," she ventured, looking at Dickon. "Ruth never told me."

"She did not? She must have believed you knew," said Dickon. Addressing Sir Harry, he continued, "You no doubt heard that Alfred was thrown out of Gentleman Jackson's after an altercation. 'Twas nothing to do with him. It was some other lad, and poor Alfred happened to be in the way. He was knocked down and they feared at first he had a broken bone, but 'twas only a sprain and he is right as rain now."

"That *is* good news," Sir Harry said heartily. "Alfred is a good lad. So tell me, Mrs. Makepeace, are you—"

"I just remembered that you have not yet admired the yule log we went to so much trouble to drag in," Dickon interrupted. He smiled at Caroline and rose, setting his teacup aside. "May I escort you on a gala inspection? Come along, Harry, you may look at it too."

Somewhat taken aback, Harry rose also. "Delighted," he said.

Caroline breathed a sigh of relief and permitted the two gentlemen to escort her to the fireplace in the great hall, where an enormous log was burning brightly.

"It is beautiful," she said in hushed tones. "It reminds me of my childhood. Oh, my! I did not realize how I missed having a yule log."

"You mean, you have not . . . " Sir Harry began. He was stopped by a warning frown from Dickon. "Sorry," he said.

"I must find Lady Rycote—she wished me to—to—I must go," said Caroline. She dared not spend another minute in the company of Dickon's friend, who was entirely too inquisitive. "Excuse me," she said quickly, and fled toward a hovering footman who could lead her to Lady Rycote.

"Very well. Now you may tell me the truth about that *drab*." Sir Harry looked at Dickon with amusement. " 'Tis told in the village that you got her with child and then had the temerity to bring her to your *mother* for her delivery! I cannot stomach that. That ain't your way, Dickon. Who is she?"

Dickon poked aimlessly at the burning yule log. "A friend of Ruth's," he said. "I had never met her until she came up in the coach with us. I know very little about her."

"Friend of Ruth's, eh? And you share a house with Ruth in London, do you not? Odd that you had not met." He gave Dickon a knowing smile.

"You do not believe me? You think that I—"

"I am almost inclined to believe you, only because that poor thing is not to your usual taste. Gad, Dickon, she is not the sort a man would look at twice. Is she one of Ruth's

'causes'? Some poor creature she took pity on? I understand she gave birth to a babe, but lost it. That must have
been a jolly time at Ryfield. How did your mama take it?"

"Mama took it in her stride," Dickson said proudly.
"And no, Ruth is not 'taking pity' on her. Ruth is her
friend. There has been some difficulty—she had nowhere
to go, I am told—but I do not know the circumstances."

"You mean you are not telling," said Harry wisely.
"Very well. The mystery of the year, right here in Durham,
and your lips are sealed. Where is Mr. Makepeace?"

"I have no idea," said Dickon, stiffening.

"*If* there is a Mr. Makepeace," Harry persisted.

"You were telling me of your thoughts on the incursion
of mining on agricultural land," said Dickon. "Do you expect it to affect you directly?"

"Pah," said Harry. He laughed. "Mystery visitors who
give birth in other people's homes are much more titillat-
ing, are they not? As for the mines, no, I do not expect one
in my pasture in the immediate future. Come along,
Dickon. You were going to entertain me with a visit to the
stables to see what sorry horseflesh remains there. I
promise not to mention Mrs. Makepeace again . . . for the
present. Shall we go?"

Caroline found Lady Rycote in the morning room going
over her mail. Lady Rycote looked up with pleasure at her
visitor.

"Do join me," she invited. "Will you have a cup of tea? I
have just sent for some. It helps calm me when I see the
size of some of these duns. I cannot think what the trades-
people are up to! I do beg your pardon. You cannot be interested. But sometimes I get so angry!" She swept a pile of
bills to one side and thumped a heavy leonine paperweight
on the pile.

"No tea, thank you," said Caroline hesitantly. "I have
just had tea with his lordship and his friend. And dear
madam, I was hard put to know what to say when the friend
quizzed me. Thank heaven his lordship came to my rescue!"

"He did? I must admit surprise. Ordinarily, my dear Dickon is blunt to the point of embarrassment," said Lady Rycote. She looked critically at Caroline. "My dear, have you no other gowns? Now that you are no longer increasing, you do not need all that—that extra fullness. Surely you own some—shall we say—more shapely gowns?"

"No." Caroline shook her head. "When would I have worn them? The intervals when I was not increasing were so short as to make it foolish to go through the fittings and all—and of course I went nowhere, so it did not matter."

"You went nowhere?" Lady Rycote tut-tutted. "In London? But there is so much to see and do there! Surely your husband let you visit friends—go shopping—go *somewhere* between babes. That is, of course, if you were well enough." She looked kindly at Caroline.

"My husband did not believe I was well enough," Caroline said, and sighed. "And to tell truth, I would hardly deliver—or lose—one babe and recover, before my husband would make sure I was once again with child." Her face was bitter as she remembered.

"It was as if he kept you in jail!" Lady Rycote said indignantly. "Did you never rebel?"

"Rebel? Against John? I had no choice." She smiled a moment. "I did escape once. He traveled regularly to Kent to visit a connection of his—some sort of cousin, I believe. He always tried to schedule it for a time I was safely increasing. One time, several years ago now, he left for Kent when I was in my third month and feeling, for once, quite healthy. Unbeknownst to him, I had Dossie summon a hackney and we went shopping! I bought a new bonnet, and a pair of lavender gloves, and a beautiful silk fan with roses painted on it, and a shawl—it was beyond anything! I had them all put on my husband's account. We were away from home nearly an entire afternoon! Oh, that was heaven."

Lady Rycote's heart went out to this young woman whose idea of heaven was a shopping trip to buy a few fripperies. What a monster her husband must be. To think that Caroline had lived a virtual prisoner, nothing but a brood mare, for five long years was insupportable. "Were you found out?" she asked. "But of course you must have been, when your husband received the bills."

"Yes," Caroline admitted. "I intended that he would. That is why I had my purchases put on his account. I wished to show him I was not his slave, with no mind of my own." She sighed. "I fear it was useless. I had no opportunity to wear any of those things, for what use are lavender gloves or painted fans when one goes nowhere, sees nobody but servants? My husband confronted me when he received the bills, and—and—I do not wish to talk of this." Caroline turned her head to hide the tears that welled up unbidden.

"Oh, my poor dear," said Lady Rycote. She went to Caroline and put her arm around the young woman's shoulders. "He did not hurt you, surely?"

"Not physically," said Caroline, her voice unsteady. "I was three months gone, remember—four months, by the time the bills came in—and he never touched me when I was known to be increasing. He retrieved everything I had bought and burned them in the fireplace. He did not return them! Oh, no! He burned them, and made sure I watched. Everything but the fan, that is. I had hidden it in a safe place, and I told him it had been broken and discarded. I have it with me." She raised her head in a gesture of defiance.

"Bravo!" Lady Rycote clapped her hands. "My dear, I am so glad you have found us. You shall never return to that monster. But tell me, what did that rascal Dickon say to his friend? I must know what stories we are telling."

"I am an old friend of Lady Stilton's," Caroline answered. "Now, dear madam, you must tell me all there is to know about Lady Stilton. I must appear knowledgeable when questioned."

"My pleasure," said Lady Rycote. She rang for a servant. "We shall have more tea. A pox on those bills." She looked distastefully at the pile under the paperweight. "Let me tell you about Ruth, my only daughter and the best one could ask for."

As Lady Rycote recounted her daughter's life history, her happy marriage to Lord Stilton, her three sons, her widowhood, and numerous anecdotes along the way, Caroline began to relax. Walter and her life with him seemed far away and long ago. Though still a bit weak and tender, she felt more cheerful than she had in years. Her fear and anger toward Walter, mixed with guilt that she had broken her marriage vows and left him—was it really true that he wished her dead?—began to recede. Lady Rycote had been horrified at her tale, and she valued Lady Rycote's opinion. She had been justified in running away. She smiled at her hostess and forgave her for making Ruth into a goddess come to earth.

Ruth had spent most of Christmas Eve at the home of one of her old friends, taking trifles for the friend's children and a plum pudding made by Mrs. Wright, Ryfield's justly famous cook. Now she was home, full of good cheer and tales of her friend's children's escapades, ready to help distribute the holly, evergreens, and mistletoe about the house.

"We shall decorate before dinner," Lady Rycote told her daughter as Ruth warmed her hands over the yule log, "and we shall spend a pleasant evening after dinner inventing a past for Mrs. Makepeace."

"We shall?" Ruth was mystified. "Is that not her prerogative?"

"Naturally she will be present and be permitted to say aye or nay," Lady Rycote answered. "I believe we all should be present so that we are aware of the same set of 'facts,' or should I say the same fancies? I should tell you now that Dickon already has told his friend Harry that Mrs. Makepeace is your old and dear friend. I have prosed on about you to Mrs. Makepeace for half the day, I vow, and she must know as much about you as I do, if she can remember it all. Now we must turn the tables and learn about *her*. Naturally most of it will be for your benefit, for I am not expected to know much, having just met her. Dickon, the wretch, has denied knowing her until your journey."

"He has not given anything away, has he?" Ruth asked anxiously. "Knowing Dickon . . . "

"Caroline tells me he behaved admirably, saving her from great embarrassment."

"Remarkable! I look forward to a most unusual Christmas Eve. Now where have you stored the greenery? We must get started or dinner will be late."

Dickon was somewhere about the estate with Sir Harry, but Caroline, summoned by a footman, joined Ruth and her mother to help twine greenery around newel posts, over family portraits, and along fireplace mantelpieces. Holly wreaths became crowns for the pair of Grecian busts mounted on pedestals in the great hall. Caroline tilted the wreath on the marble head of a handsome Grecian youth and pronounced it properly rakish. She was chosen to hang the final touch, the bunch of mistletoe, on the base of the chandelier near the front door, which she did amid much merriment as a stolid footman held the ladder steady.

Dickon appeared in time for dinner, minus Sir Harry. After the meal his mother told him of the evening's plans and they all repaired to the library.

"Miss Caroline, you look done in," Dickon commented as he showed her to the most comfortable chair before the fire. "Have my demon mother and sister worked you too hard on your first day out of bed? Mama, how could you?"

"No!" Caroline cried, rising from the chair she had just lowered herself into. "It was not that way! It was lovely. I enjoyed every minute of it. I *needed* that, your lordship. I am a little tired, but I have had the most beautiful, the most—the *friendliest* day I have had in many years." She looked around at the three people before her. "You have brought me back to life," she said, sniffing to prevent the tears. "I can never thank you enough." She sat down.

Dickon broke the embarrassed silence that followed. "Speaking of life, shall we now invent yours?" He smiled warmly.

Some of the suggestions that followed were outrageous,

particularly those offered by Dickon, who seemed to be in an outrageous mood himself. He was all for presenting Caroline as a foreign princess in disguise, or an heiress who had lost her memory and still did not know who she was ("Then how do I know I am an heiress?" Caroline demanded.), or a babe abandoned on the Isle of Mull who had grown up and was searching for her parents in Durham (No Scots accent," said Caroline. "And why would I look in Durham?").

Caroline laughed until she was hoarse. Dickon caught her eye and laughed with her. Why, he is doing this to cheer me, she thought. How different he is from the haughty, stiff gentleman of the mail coach journey.

Once the laughter had died down and the company had caught their breaths, they became serious. It was decided that Caroline was a widow temporarily without means until the provisions of her late husband's complicated will could be carried out—there would be unnamed difficulties, perhaps a search for a missing heir. Meanwhile her devoted friend Ruth, knowing how devastated Caroline felt at the loss of her husband, had invited her to Ryfield for a change of scene. The unexpected loss of her child was but one more cross for her to bear. Her previous history of childbearing need not be mentioned.

"What if someone asks your plans for the future?" Ruth wondered.

Caroline colored. "Unfortunately, I have none yet," she said. "I shall make some, never fear. I do not intend to abuse your hospitality. Now that I am feeling stronger—"

"You will do nothing of the kind," Lady Rycote said with determination. "I have begged you to remain here as long as you wish. When these two are gone," she said, gesturing at her son and daughter, "I shall be all alone and I should deem it a pleasure to have your company."

"I thank you, Lady Rycote," Caroline replied, "but I must make my own way. Dossie and I have been conferring, and when we have come to a decision, I shall let you know."

"You are never going to Nell-on-her-knees, are you?" Lady Rycote recoiled in horror. "You promised!"

"I think not," said Caroline. "Not unless all else fails."

"We shall not fail you, my dear," Lady Rycote assured her. "Do, I beg of you, consider staying here."

"Again I thank you. I shall let you know."

James Fenland cursed roundly as the mail coachman, gripping the gold sovereign Fenland had given him, climbed onto his perch and prepared to leave. Had no one noticed where Lady Carroway had gone? After days at the Bull and Mouth in London, he had finally learned that a drab woman, far gone with child, had boarded a mail coach to Durham. Now he was in Durham, it was Christmas Eve, he was tired, hungry, cold, and dispirited, and no one knew anything. Worse, a misty rain had begun to fall.

He returned to the inn, where the smell of wet wool and roast beef overpowered the piney fragrance of a few limp garlands hung in the common room in a futile effort to provide Christmas cheer. Fenland sat down and ordered his dinner, then checked his pockets. A few more sovereigns dispersed in hope of information and he would be out of money. Next time he would offer them shillings. Carroway would never know.

What if Lady Carroway had bought a ticket for Durham, but had left the coach somewhere short of Durham? Hell, if that were true he would have to search half of England. He had to find the particular coachman who had covered the final stage before Durham on the right day—and which was the right day?

Fenland scratched his thinning hair. He was a man of forty, a man so ordinary-looking that no one paid him the least attention; no one could pick him out of a crowd. He knew that was why Carroway valued him. By God, when he finally got out from under Carroway's thumb, he would show the world he was no ordinary man. He would wear embroidered waistcoats and diamond stickpins . . .

Damn Carroway anyhow! Why did he want that dull creature back? He should be glad she had fled. Now Car-

roway could start looking around for a biddable chit. Assuming Lady C. would not return, Carroway would be perfectly justified in taking a new bride. Perhaps a bit
irregular, what with no proof of Lady C.'s death, but irreg-
ularity had never bothered Carroway. He would get around
it somehow.

Fenland dug viciously into his beef. Another day or two
in this Durham hell hole and he would be late getting to
Kent, where a shipment was due before New Year's, and
where the weather was mild compared to this bitter north-
ern climate. Why anyone should choose to live north of
London was beyond him. He snatched at his flagon of ale,
which splashed over his right hand. Damn. Ale all over his
coat sleeve.

A group of carolers tuned up outside the inn. Fenland
glared sourly at the delighted smiles of the common room's
occupants.

Christmas. It sickened him.

Five

Caroline awoke on Christmas day ready to climb mountains. When Dossie pulled open the heavy brown draperies and she discovered that the sun was shining, her enthusiasm heightened. So the sun did shine in Durham!

She tumbled out of bed and splashed cold water from the ewer on her face. She felt a slight lingering weakness in her legs. Perhaps she had overestimated matters. Perhaps she was ready to climb hills, not mountains. Mountains tomorrow. It was Christmas, and she was in the bosom of a kind, caring family. What more could she ask for?

"Help me dress," she directed Dossie. "I am starving, and after breakfast I shall take a walk. Such a glorious day! Would you care to walk with me, Dossie?"

"Walk, Miss Caroline? Wotever for? Oh, beg pardon, ma'am. It's for you to say, but why walk when we don't 'ave to?"

Caroline, pulling on her stockings, looked up at the elderly woman, who was frowning at the rusty black dress of Caroline's she held in her hands. No, a walk would be no treat for Dossie, whose joints were not what they once were.

"Never mind," Caroline said. "Someone else may be willing to walk with me, or I could go alone. But think, Dossie! I am free! I can go where I wish! No one has me locked in, or pregnant, or—"

"They says you are not to go outside," Dossie remarked.

"Oh, pooh! That was before I recovered. I am now perfectly well."

" 'Twill be on your 'ead," Dossie muttered darkly. "Go eat your breakfast."

Caroline ate an orange, a bit of fish, and three eggs, all washed down with tea, despite Lady Rycote's warning that an enormous Christmas dinner with Norfolk turkey was only a few hours away.

"I shall walk off my breakfast," Caroline announced. She nipped a piece of dry toast from the rack to munch on her walk and started upstairs to get her cloak.

"Hold!" Dickon called after her. "Where do you think you are going?"

"For my cloak. Does anyone else wish to walk? It is such a splendid day!"

"So it is. An excellent idea. Does anyone else wish to go? Mama? Ruth?"

The ladies looked at each other. "Church," said Lady Rycote reprovingly. "Are you not going to church, Dickon? There will be a beautiful service in the cathedral, you may be sure, and you have not been home for it in several years."

"True, but for all the good folk know, I am in London and will not be missed. We cannot leave Miss Caroline here alone, now can we? Yet I do not recommend letting her show her face in the cathedral—or anywhere in Durham, for that matter. Who knows that someone may not be searching for her? You and Ruth go, Mama, and I will stay home and amuse our guest."

The two ladies looked at one another again, gave slight nods, and agreed.

"Get your cloak and bonnet and change to sturdy shoes," Dickon directed Caroline. He looked down at her soft slippers. "You do have sturdy shoes or boots?"

"Ah, no," she replied. "I have not had need of them."

"Perhaps some of Mama's . . . I shall search."

Ten minutes later Caroline was in the great hall, sniffing delightedly at the pine garlands. She wore the rusty black gown, the dark cloak, her black bonnet, and some very worn white kidskin gloves. Her feet were still shod in soft slippers. When she did not find Dickon waiting, she sat in

one of the chairs lining the wall and made faces at the
solemn Grecian bust wearing the tipsy holly wreath. Lady
Rycote and her daughter passed her on their way to their
carriage, and she bid them Godspeed.

Ten minutes after that, Dickon, out of breath, appeared
from the back of the house. In his hands were worn, scuffed
half-boots, their toes permanently bent toward the sky.

"Mama's would never have fit you," he said apologeti-
cally. "I had to rally the servants, and such to-do! They are
all working on dinner, and you would think I was some
ogre to be interrupting puddings and sweetmeats and—and
the turkey! You have never seen such a turkey! Here. These
are from Esther, who is one of the kitchen maids, I gather.
While no one was looking, I stole these for us."

Proudly, Dickon held out his hand and showed her his
stolen goods. Four sweetmeats clung firmly to the fine
linen handkerchief in which he had hidden them. He looked
abashed. "We may have to eat them directly off the cloth,"
he said. "See if these boots will do."

The half-boots were too wide, but of about the right
length. Caroline said they would serve beautifully and
clumped along behind Dickon as they left the house.

Despite the sun, it was cold, with a fresh breeze. Caroline
fastened the frogs on her cloak, thinking how long it had
been since the frogs met around her middle. The old white
gloves provided little warmth: she had had them since before her marriage, and some of the fingers had come unstitched, been mended, and come unstitched again. She
wished she had a muff.

Dickon was striding eagerly down the drive ahead of her,
drawing in great gulps of fresh air, when he apparently realized he was setting too fast a pace. He stopped and waited
for her.

"Sorry," he said. "I tend to forget you are a recovering
invalid. You look so—so *well*. You have color in your
cheeks, your eyes are bright, your smile . . . " He smiled at
her, and she noted his eyes were bright as well. They stood
still for a moment, gazing at each other, and Caroline felt
an odd sensation rising in her. She looked away.

Dickon broke the spell when he noticed her gloves. Gad, did that Not-John husband of hers refuse to let the woman have a decent pair of gloves? Not wishing to embarrass her, he asked, "Why not put a hand in my greatcoat pocket? I will keep it warm for you. Then after a time we can change places and I will warm the other hand."

"If you wish," she said timidly. She slipped her left hand into his right coat pocket and found his right hand waiting to clasp it. Its warmth penetrated the barriers of their gloves. "That is better," she admitted.

Once they had adjusted their pace—with her hand buried in his pocket, they had to go in step—they swung along the graveled drive, feeling the sun on their faces. Or more accurately, on his face.

"Stop," Caroline said suddenly. "My bonnet is in the way." She withdrew her left hand and untied her bonnet strings.

"You must have something on your head!" cried Dickon. "You will catch your death!"

"Watch me," she said, giving him an impish smile. Ruthlessly she bent the stiff, deep brim of the bonnet back on itself, replaced it, and retied the strings. It resembled a slightly askew nun's coif.

"It will never be the same," she said in feigned despair. Then she broke into laughter.

Dickon, startled, laughed as well. He grasped her left hand with his right and put them firmly back into his coat pocket. They continued down the drive, munching sweetmeats.

They were out more than an hour, long enough for her right hand to have a turn at warmth in his pocket, and for her to understand what Ryfield, asleep in its winter quiet, meant to the Earl of Rycote. He became quite lyrical when he recited some of the improvements he wished to make, the livestock he wished to raise, the fish he wished to tease up out of the waters of his stretch of the River Wear.

"What is stopping you?" she demanded as they halted for a few minutes on the riverbank. A slender rim of ice bordered the dark, flowing water. "Why should you be in London when you so obviously wish to be here?"

"I am tied to a desk in the War Office," he said grimly. "All my own fault. I had wished to buy a commission and go to the Peninsula, but the family rebelled. Said the heir must not be put in danger of his life. Ha! So Benjamin went instead, and I volunteered—*volunteered*, mind you—to do my bit in London. I would trade places with Benjamin in a minute. I expect to die of boredom or lack of fresh air long before the war is over."

"Which will be soon, God willing," Caroline said. She could understand his dilemma. Coming from rural Bedfordshire, she had disliked the noise, the smells, the crowding, the dirt of London. Rural Durham was not like Bedfordshire, but to him it was home.

An unattached gentleman, however, should find no lack of entertainment in London.

"Do you not find much to amuse you in London?" she asked. "My husband seemed to. He was at his club, or at the races, or the theater, or playing cards . . . I assumed a gentleman never ran out of things to do in the city."

"True, if one has the blunt," he said, lobbing a stone across the river. "Because I cannot be here, the estate is not doing as well as I could wish. I am not one to lose what I have at cards."

"Oh!" she said, suddenly realizing what a burden she and Dossie must be to a family worried about money. She had believed those at Ryfield to be very comfortably off, if not wealthy. "I had no idea. You must not let Dossie and me impose upon you any longer. As you can see, I am perfectly well now—I will set Dossie to packing—"

"And go where?" Dickon removed her hand from his pocket, holding it tight, and grasped the other hand. His dark eyes bored into hers.

She tried to pull away, but his hands held her immobile. She looked down at her toes, the shabby, turned-up toes of the half-boots belonging to a kitchen maid. "I . . . I do not rightly know yet, but I assure you I am working on it. I believe I could be a governess, or a shop-girl, or a housekeeper—yes! I could be a housekeeper. I have run my own home for five years." She looked up at him defiantly.

"Run your own home? And just how many dinner parties have you given? Balls? House parties? Musicales? Routs?"

"None," she admitted, her voice low. "We did not go out in society and we did not entertain, of course, for fear I would be overstimulated and some harm would come to the babe."

Dickon muttered an oath under his breath. He turned, placed her right hand in his left pocket, and started back toward the house. "You are going nowhere," he said gruffly, and squeezed her hand.

Caroline vowed she had never eaten so much at a single meal in her entire life. They sat at table for two hours as more and more dishes arrived from the kitchen, each seemingly tastier than the last. By the time the sweetmeats appeared at the end, Caroline had given up. Dickon caught her eye and winked.

A vast ennui settled over the diners once they had had their fill, so they went to their respective chambers to sleep it off while the staff had their own Christmas dinner. Dossie was eating with the servants, so Caroline had her chamber to herself. She removed her slippers—the half-boots had been returned—and lay down on the bed to think.

It was imperative that she and Dossie get away. She was a burden to the Richardson family, but what was more important, she feared Dickon might be forming a *tendress* for her, and that would never do. She was a married woman. Even if she were free, she would never marry again. All men wanted heirs, and she shuddered at the thought of more pregnancies. Besides, what was the use? She was unable to bear healthy children.

But where to go?

She was still racking her brain for ideas when she fell asleep.

* * *

One by one the family woke and wandered downstairs, where cook had set out a cold collation and tea. Despite groans and protests, they found themselves nibbling on turkey, bread and butter, nutmeats, and tea. Afterward, Lady Rycote brought in a basket of wrapped packages and wished the others a happy Christmas.

Caroline was upset at having nothing for any of the others, but they brushed aside her apologies and watched eagerly as she tore open the one package with her name on it. From all three of them, it was a bonnet of warm pink wool with a shallow brim. Caroline was so touched she almost wept.

"How did you know?" she cried. "You could not have done this—found this—since our walk today! Oh, if you only knew how I hate that old black bonnet, but it was all I had."

"Once we learned you were not a widow in mourning, the idea just came to me," Lady Rycote explained. "I noticed immediately that the black one did nothing for you. Pink, you know, is the color for someone who has been ill; it makes you look better. 'In the pink,' you understand? I had it made up for you days ago." She smiled fondly at Caroline.

"Oh, thank you!" Caroline cried. She tried it on; it fit to perfection. She tied the bonnet strings into a perky bow and pirouetted around the drawing room.

"I am acting like a schoolgirl," she said, halting her whirls. "Do pardon me. I must look a sight, in this dreadful black dress and a beautiful new pink bonnet." She sat down circumspectly. "Are you not going to open your packages?"

Amid murmurs the others opened theirs. They were all small gifts of little value but much sentiment. Caroline looked on, entranced. Walter had never held with the custom of exchanging gifts at Christmas, and she had not been part of a Christmas celebration since leaving her parents.

The remainder of the evening was spent in packing gifts for the servants for Boxing Day tomorrow. They got such utilitarian items as aprons, hats and caps (no pink bonnets!

Caroline noticed), shawls, and mufflers. The farm workers, who did not live in, got food.

At last it was done. The four repaired to the great hall to check on the yule log, still burning brightly and admire once more the swags of greenery decking the hall, before retiring.

Caroline turned to go upstairs to bed, but found her arm caught by Dickon. Gravely he steered her the length of the hall, past the Grecian busts, until she stood under the chandelier near the front door.

He glanced up at the mistletoe she had hung, then down at her face. His hands were on her shoulders. Gently he pressed his lips to hers, a feather touch that lasted only a few seconds, then drew away. "Happy Christmas, Miss Caroline," he said. "Remember, you are going nowhere."

Dazed, she looked at him in confusion, then fled up the stairs to her chamber.

Caroline knew she must somehow acquire a proper wardrobe. Whether she obtained work of some sort or not, she could not continue to wear only the dark, shapeless gowns that were all she owned. Now that she felt well again, she begged Lady Rycote to let her visit Durham to see what she could find.

"I have my jewels, which surely would bring enough to pay for a few gowns," she explained at breakfast the day after Boxing Day.

Dickon, who was busy with a plateful of kippers, looked up. "You evidently forget that you are attempting to remain incognito," he said. "What better way to alert any searchers that you are in Durham? You have been fortunate so far— two weeks, is it not?—but the danger is far from over." He frowned, considering. "Should you wish to sell your jewels, I will be glad to take care of it for you. I could do it today; I have a few errands in Durham. You realize you are not likely to get their true worth. As to gowns, I beg to decline. Mama, what do you suggest?"

Lady Rycote glanced from Caroline to Ruth, who was just arriving for her breakfast, and back again. "Not at all the same size," she mused. "Nor am I. You are still too thin, child. One could put two of you in one of our gowns. I believe we shall have to take your measurements and provide them to our seamstress. We can explain that you are too ill to come yourself. But oh! You will not be able to choose your fabrics! That is the best part of ordering new gowns."

Caroline had visions of silks and satins; muslins and dimity; warm, soft wools and velvets; bolt after bolt in dizzying confusion. The visions were heady, for she had not been inside a dressmaker's shop in nearly five long years—not since she had chosen her bride clothes under her mother's supervision. Since then a dressmaker had come to her, bringing only the dull brown, gray, and black—usually black—bolts that were deemed serviceable if not stylish. Walter had made it clear that frippery was not to be tolerated; what was the point when she went nowhere, and had no figure? Besides, she was in perpetual mourning for lost babies. The bride clothes were still in her wardrobe in London, hardly worn, for they did not fit a lady who was increasing.

At her crestfallen expression Lady Rycote said soothingly, "You shall tell us what colors you like, and what fabrics, and we shall follow your wishes. Shall we not, Ruth? It will be such fun, ordering gown after gown!"

Caroline was still dubious. What harm could come to her if she was driven to town in a closed carriage and visited only one establishment—with only a moment in public view to alight and reboard? No one looking for her would be in a dressmaker's shop.

She would think on it. "That is most kind of you," she assured Lady Rycote. "I will get my jewels for you, your lordship, once I finish my eggs."

Dickon was amazed at the hoard she brought him. Spilling out of a leather bag were necklaces, rings, a tiara, and a number of pins, all of gold set with diamonds, rubies, emeralds, and pearls. This hoard did not match with a miserly husband who kept his wife a drab prisoner. For a moment he wondered what game she was playing. She had given them one story, then changed it; was her second story false as well? He toyed with a diamond brooch and frowned.

Caroline seemed to sense his uncertainty. "You wonder where these came from, do you not? I assure you they are truly mine, all given to me by my mother. You recall I am the only girl in my family. My parents were so pleased at my marriage to a p-p-peer"—she hesitated; she had not meant to say that—"and they wished me to make a good impression when we went out in society. These were, you might say, part of my dowry." She looked defiantly at Dickon.

Lady Rycote caught the word "peer" immediately. "So you are truly *Lady* Makepeace, rather than plain Mrs. Makepeace?"

"I am neither, as I have told you," Caroline said. "Shall we continue to refer to me as Mrs. Makepeace? I am becoming quite accustomed to it."

"But your husband is titled?" Lady Rycote persisted.

"He is. That is all I am prepared to say."

"I just *knew* you were a lady," Lady Rycote murmured.

"You did?" said Dickon. "Somehow I failed to get that impression." He grinned at his mother, who turned beet-red.

Dickon returned from Durham jubilant. He had been able to sell Caroline's jewels for sixteen hundred pounds—nothing like their true worth, he explained, but still more than he had hoped to get. He had felt lower than the low, having to dispose of Caroline's only valuables, family jewels that undoubtedly meant a great deal to her. Had he sixteen hundred pounds available he would have "bought" them himself and then returned them to her, but he had nothing like that much to spare.

He was surprised to discover that she had little sentiment for her jewelry, or that if she did feel more strongly, she covered it well.

"Sixteen hundred pounds!" she repeated when he told her. Her eyes sparkled at the bank notes he held out to her.

"Think of all the gowns! A riding habit! A new cloak! Half-boots! Bright colors! I vow I shall never wear black again, no matter who should die."

" 'Tis a shame you must give up your family jewels for a few gowns," said Dickon.

"Pah!" she said. "What good are they to me? Do you see me as a governess wearing a diamond tiara? An emerald necklace on a housekeeper? A housekeeper dressed in my rusty black, at that? No, I have no regrets." She beamed.

Caroline had her hands on the bank notes, looking at the most money she had ever seen at once, seemingly trying to take in the fact that it was all hers. Dickon reached out a hand and laid it over hers. "You are not leaving us," he said.

She raised her eyes to his. "Do you not see?" she asked. "I am as much a prisoner here as I was in my husband's house. Please do not misunderstand me. I love it here; Ryfield is beautiful, even in the dead of winter, and you and your family have been all that is kind. Still, I am a prisoner, and I must leave."

She gathered her bank notes and walked out of the room. Dickon did not say a word. A prisoner at Ryfield? It sounded near heaven to him. He was beginning to think it would be even closer to heaven if Mrs. Makepeace dwelt there as well.

In the end Caroline did not go with the other ladies into Durham, despite the temptation. She had not been giving proper attention to her uncertain future, nor had she created a disguise to wear to throw off possible followers. She chastised herself. She had been so caught up in enjoying the company of her hosts, in becoming part of the day-to-day life at Ryfield, that the danger of being found out by Walter or someone in his employ had seemed far away. Letting Lady Rycote and Lady Stilton choose her gowns seemed a small price to pay for safety.

Today they had departed in the shiny Ryfield coach, taking with them Dossie, who knew Caroline's tastes in gowns. Dossie had been present when Caroline chose her bride clothes, and even if that had been five years ago and styles had changed, Caroline believed Dossie would know best what she liked. Besides, she found it restful not to have the elderly maid fussing around her for a few hours. Dossie was not persuaded that Caroline was entirely well and constantly begged her to rest—almost as if Caroline were back in London and six months gone, she thought wryly.

Caroline stared at her hair in the looking-glass of the gloomy chamber. She believed some new growth had appeared; she certainly hoped so! Her hair had always seemed too thin during her pregnancies and she had often wondered whether she would be reduced to wearing a wig. Now, should it be growing in again, she certainly did not wish to cut it to change her appearance. Perhaps a wig after all, if she could just stuff her own hair under it . . .

The new gowns would help. Oh, yes, the new gowns would help! No one would believe it was really she if she appeared in something handsome, well-fitted, colorful. She resolved to examine her new wardrobe with that in mind, and seek the advice of the Richardsons. They always seemed eager to help.

"This is Mrs. Cutter's." Lady Rycote indicated to Dossie the small shop in front of them. Its bow windows, polished to a gemlike brightness, revealed dozens of bolts of fabric of every hue. "Mrs. Cutter is not so dear as that jumped-up French person in the next street, but her gowns are every bit as fine. Is that not a good name for a seamstress? Mrs. Cutter?" She smiled at Dossie.

"Yes, ma'am." said Dossie solemnly.

Once inside, they were invited to wait, as Mrs. Cutter was busy with another customer. Dossie shifted nervously from one foot to the other and appeared afraid to examine the bolts of cloth as both Lady Rycote and Ruth were doing. She was looking at the floor when Mrs. Cutter ushered her customer out of the fitting room.

The customer gave a shriek when she caught sight of the maid, and flew to her side. "Dossie Carter! Whatever are you doing in Durham? I thought you were with some titled

lady in London! How do you do, my dear? I trust the good
Lord has been watching over you."

"Mrs. Fincaster! Oh, ma'am, it is good to see you. And
'ow is Mr. Fincaster, ma'am? I've thought about you so
much. Been near five year, ain't it? I'm fair to middlin',
ma'am. Got a bit of a creak in me joints, is all."

"Are you visiting here with your mistress?" Mrs. Fincaster asked. She spoke in a hearty voice that filled the little
waiting room. Mrs. Fincaster's friends called her hearty;
others compared her to Gabriel blowing his last trumpet.
Tall and commanding, she seemed to take complete charge
of Mrs. Cutter's shop. Before Dossie could think of an answer, Mrs. Fincaster waved an airy hand at Mrs. Cutter and
boomed, "I shall return for the final fitting on Wednesday
next. I trust that is satisfactory?"

The cowed Mrs. Cutter mumbled that Wednesday was
indeed satisfactory. Dossie meanwhile moved quietly to
Lady Rycote's side and whispered, "Wot shall I say,
ma'am?"

"Oh, dear," Lady Rycote said mournfully. "Tell her
that—let me see—you are between positions and are visiting a member of my staff who is a friend of yours? No, that
will never do; she will know you have no old friends
among my staff. Perhaps you *thought* one of your old
friends was on my staff. Quickly, think of someone it might
be! And of course we took you in temporarily after you'd
made such a long trip." Lady Rycote frowned. She was
afraid Dossie was not a quick thinker. "Do you wish me to
explain for you?"

"Oh, would you, ma'am?"

Lady Rycote, with Dossie trailing behind, approached
Mrs. Fincaster with a welcoming smile on her face. "Nell
Fincaster! How long has it been? You are looking uncom-
mon well. And how does Mr. Fincaster?"

"Lady Rycote!" Mrs. Fincaster bobbed a curtsy, a ludi-
crous attempt for one as tall and ungainly as she. "Ah, I am
well but Mr. Fincaster ain't. We pray over him nightly and
hope that the good Lord will see fit to spare him. It is, of
course, in the Lord's hands. Is Dossie with you?"

"Yes indeed," Lady Rycote said brightly. "Ruth"— she called her daughter over—"you remember Mrs. Fincaster, do you not? Ruth is here for the holidays, as is my elder son Dickon," she explained to the woman, "Benjamin, as you no doubt know, is on the Peninsula."

"Delighted to see you, Mrs. Fincaster," Ruth said, putting on her most charming manner. "I am sorry to hear of your husband's illness. Has he been ill long?"

"More than a month," said Mrs. Fincaster. "Can't keep his food down. Wasting away, he is. I get the girl—Patsy, it is—to fix him some good broth and it comes right up again. Then one of the girls—Sarah, most likely—has to clean him up, and clean up the bed, and change the bedclothes, and it's all been for nothing. The only time he feels comfortable is when Sally or Ella wipes a wet cloth over his forehead while the other one—Ella, or Sally—reads to him from the Bible. They've got to the 'begats' last I heard."

"But you are not there with him?" Lady Rycote asked.

"Much as I can be," said Mrs. Fincaster. "I got all those girls to look after. Doing the Lord's work, you know. I tell you, you would not believe the stories those girls tell of what they was doing before they came to me. 'Twould curl your hair, it would."

"How many girls have you? Your wards are all girls, I take it?"

"Got seven girls at the moment. Just sent two of 'em out to work. You don't need a biddable kitchen maid, do you, your ladyship?"

"I believe not," said Lady Rycote, "but I will certainly keep you in mind. Where do you get your girls?"

Mrs. Fincaster launched into a detailed recital of the backgrounds of all seven, then the backgrounds of the two for whom she had found positions, explained that the Lord had sent them to her, and suddenly stopped. "What's Dossie Carter doing here?" she asked.

"Maybe the Lord sent her to us," Ruth murmured under her breath. Lady Rycote frowned at her.

"She is on loan to us while her mistress is abroad," said

Lady Rycote with a straight face. "In Italy, is she not,
Dossie? Her mistress is one of Ruth's oldest friends."

Ruth hastened to corroborate. "We have been friends
since I married and moved to London," she said. "Dossie
had such fond memories of her years in Durham with you
that she wished to see it again, and see you, too, of course,
dear Mrs. Fincaster. When I learned that, I suggested she
accompany us. It has been in the nature of a homecoming
for her, has it not, Dossie?"

Dossie had been listening to all this with her mouth
open. She appeared ready to take flight any moment. When
Ruth addressed her, she could only look sheepish and say
in a small voice, "Yes, ma'am."

Mrs. Cutter, who had been hovering in the background,
now asked Lady Rycote how she could help her.

"We need a number of gowns," said Lady Rycote, "for a
friend who cannot come herself because she is ill. I have
her measurements right here. Lady Stilton and I will choose
the fabrics."

"You want me to tell you what I think she'd like?"
Dossie awoke from her stupor, determined to be useful.

Lady Rycote and Lady Stilton looked daggers at the
maid, who did not realize for a moment what she had done.
Mrs. Fincaster meanwhile, lingering by the door, heard
every word.

"Someone is ill at Ryfield?" she asked. "Might I be permitted to offer prayers on her behalf? Tell me her name and
I shall do so this very day. Or even better, with your per-
mission I shall call in person to do so."

"Very kind of you," said Lady Rycote, "but unnecessary,
I believe; she is mending nicely. I know how busy you are
with your ill husband and seven girls to look after. I would
not dream of putting you to so much trouble."

"If she does not prosper then you must call on me," said
Mrs. Fincaster, acknowledging defeat. "And now, Dossie,
will you not walk with me to my carriage? These ladies do
not need you, and I must hear how you are getting on." She
took the bemused Dossie by the arm and propelled her out
the door.

Lady Rycote and her daughter exchanged glances. They could only hope Dossie had the good sense to keep her mouth shut about Miss Caroline and why they were in Durham, but it did not look promising.

"We might as well choose some fabrics," Ruth said, smiling at Mrs. Cutter. "What do you think of this blue poplin?"

James Fenland believed there might be hope after all. He had finally found a coachman who remembered a woman far gone with child, traveling with a maid, who had disembarked at Durham some two weeks back. Fenland was so ecstatic he gave the man three shillings. The only difficulty was, the coachman had been unable to tell him where the woman and her servant had gone.

"They was with two others, gentry, it looked like," he said. "Got in a private coach. No, don't know whose coach. They all looks alike, don't they? I unloaded 'em and went on north. Had to keep on schedule, you understand."

The coachman could not even remember whether the "gentry" they were with were two men, or a man and a woman. He bit on the shillings, decided they were genuine, and sauntered off.

Fenland had to believe Lady Carroway was still in the vicinity. Where to look? He bethought himself of Lady Carroway's appearance the last time he had seen her, and slapped his knee. Of course! The drab would want new gowns. No, that was not right either. She was more than six months gone with child; the new gowns would have to wait. Even so, he would bet his last sovereign that she would want at least some ribands and frills; it was what all women wanted. Then again, if she was so far gone she would not be shopping in the streets of Durham. Or would she? Considering how long Carroway had kept her penned up, she might be eager to get out, whatever her condition.

He decided to wander over the town and keep an eye out for a woman far gone with child. He could think of nothing better to do.

This became tiresome after a time. He was continually

jostled by women trailed by maids carrying baskets of he knew not what. They paused to look in windows filled with ribands, or shoes, or hats, or books, and he had to steer around them on the narrow walkways. God, what he would not give for an ale! The afternoon was young yet, however, and doggedly he walked on.

His attention was caught by a tall, awkward woman with a carrying voice who was conversing with an elderly woman, one who seemed of the servant class. They were standing by a shabby carriage, and the tall woman handed a parcel up to the coachman as he watched.

"My dear," the tall woman said in ringing tones, "what in heaven's name are you doing in Durham? If you are in trouble, you know you need only come to me. Why did you not come when you first arrived? You must have reached Durham before Christmas—I'm sure his lordship and her ladyship were here for Christmas."

"Yes'm," Dossie said mournfully. "I was 'opin' to come sooner, but I 'ad to wait—didn't want to ask for the coach—I couldn't do that, now could I? 'Ow was I to get there?"

Fenland's eyes opened wider. By God, wasn't that old biddy the servant Lady Carroway had taken with her?

"Here!" he yelled. What was the old biddy's name? Dossie something. "Dossie!" he cried.

Dossie recognized him immediately. Filled with terror, she did the only thing she could think of. "Take me with you!" she begged Mrs. Fincaster. "Quick, ma'am! I must get away!" Without waiting for an invitation, she climbed into Mrs. Fincaster's coach.

Mrs. Fincaster followed and sent her coachman on his way. "Now," she said sternly. "Tell me what this is all about."

"'E's a bad man," said Dossie. She shook with terror, and leaned out to see if Fenland were following. He was lost in the crowd.

"A bad man? In what way? Now, Dossie, you know there is always hope. You will come home with me and we will pray for that man's soul. I will have my seven girls pray as well, and Mr. Fincaster too if he is able. You have not answered my question. What are you doing in Durham?"

"It's like 'er ladyship said." Dossie was determined not to let anything else slip. She had done enough damage. "They was kind enough to let me come to Durham with 'em while my mistress was away. I can't tell you no more." She wrung her hands.

When Dossie did not return, Lady Rycote and her daughter became uneasy. Ruth offered to dart out and see if she was still talking to Mrs. Fincaster, though they did not know where Mrs. Fincaster's coach might be. After nearly an hour of conferring with the seamstress, Ruth left in search. No Fincaster coach presented itself. Their own coach was empty except for the coachman, waiting patiently on his perch. He had not seen Dossie.

"We shall simply have to visit Nell-on-her-knees and inquire," Lady Rycote decided. "I have a feeling Nell is trying to worm the truth out of Dossie. Heaven help us if she has succeeded. It will be all over Durham."

They had ordered three gowns for Caroline, one in a soft blue poplin, one in a pink wool very like her new bonnet, and a muslin print of bright yellow-and-white flowers with green leaves and green braid around neck and hem. They were simple but stylish. A blue cloak and a bright green riding habit were added when Lady Rycote learned the whole would cost far less than Caroline's sixteen hundred pounds. New boots were deferred to another day; both ladies were anxious to find Dossie.

They found Mrs. Fincaster's home with little trouble; the woman was widely known in Durham. She and her husband lived on the north edge of Durham in a big, old, shabby house of stone turned gray with time and soot. It was not known what they lived on. Fincaster had been a clerk of some sort, not a well-paying post. Some said Mrs. Fincaster had inherited money.

Lady Rycote, with Ruth at her side, climbed the steps

and knocked. The door was soon opened by a slovenly girl of about sixteen summers. "Yes?" said the girl.

"May we see Mrs. Fincaster?" Lady Rycote asked.

"She's prayin'," said the girl. "Old Mr. Fincaster, he's sinkin'. You want to wait?"

"We will wait," said Lady Rycote. "Do you know whether she brought an elderly servant, Dossie Carter by name, home with her from town?"

"That who she is? Aye, she's here. You want to see her?"

"Indeed I do," said Lady Rycote, summoning her most imperious air. "Tell her Lady Rycote is here."

"Dunno if I can interrupt durin' prayers," the girl said uncertainly. "Mrs. Fincaster, she won't like it. Wait here, ma'am."

The girl wandered off, leaving the two ladies to twiddle their thumbs. The entry hall boasted no chairs. It was papered with a pattern that had once been red roses, now faded to a feeble tan. The table and a coat rack showed evidence of hard use. A strong smell of cooked cabbage permeated the air.

Eventually, they heard a disturbance and looked up to see Dossie hobbling down the stairs as fast as her ancient legs would carry her.

"Oh, ma'am!" she cried. "Oh, thank the Lord you're 'ere! Miss Caroline and me, we've got to get away! 'E's 'ere! 'E's found us!"

"Who is that?" Lady Rycote tried to calm the terror-stricken servant. "You mean Miss Caroline's husband?"

"Oh, no, not 'im. No, it's that 'orrid man of 'is! Oh, wot 'ave I done?"

Six

Amid much weeping, Dossie poured out her tale of meeting up with "that 'orrid man" as Lady Rycote's coach raced toward Ryfield. It was some time before Lady Rycote was able to learn the straight of it, so upset and self-recriminating was the maid. Lady Rycote was fast losing patience.

"Who might the 'horrid man' be?" she demanded, breaking into Dossie's wails. "Do get a hold of yourself, Dossie."

Dossie sniffed and wiped her eyes with a sleeve. "Oh, your ladyship," she cried, "it's 'im that is friends with 'is lordship. The one that was to cause the accident to 'er ladyship, you remember? 'Is lordship must of sent 'im after 'er ladyship. Why did I go along with you to the mantuamaker? I should of known. I should of known!" She broke into fresh sobs.

Lady Rycote, once she had straightened out Dossie's various "ladyships" and "lordships" in her mind, looked appealingly at Ruth. "Do you believe this 'horrid man,' whoever he is, will put two and two together and track Miss Caroline to us? I cannot see how he would connect Caroline with us; he did not see you or me," she said, sighing.

"No, but that is not to say he will not learn of our connection through Mrs. Fincaster," said Ruth, a worried frown on her brow. " 'Twould be but a few moments' effort for him to learn the ownership of that old coach. Everyone in town knows Mrs. Fincaster's coach. We should have sought out Mrs. Fincaster and tried to ensure her silence. Oh, fiddle. Why did we not?"

"It was not the most opportune time," her mother said

dryly. "With Mr. Fincaster at death's door, I doubt she would have been in any mood to listen and I could not blame her. And you must remember that gaggle of girls. Who knows how many saw Dossie arrive? Even if they did not, they will know about it. You may be sure the 'horrid man' will get it out of one or another."

"Mr. Fenland," Dossie said. "That's 'oo 'e is, Mr. Fenland."

"What do you know of Mr. Fenland?" Lady Rycote demanded.

"Don't know much," said Dossie. " 'E's a friend of 'is lordship's, 'e is, always 'angin' around and drinkin' the master's brandy. Seems like 'e's workin' for 'is lordship, but 'ow can that be, for 'is lordship 'asn't got anyone workin' for 'im—apart from the servants, o' course. Mr. Fenland, 'e don't act like no servant." Dossie looked perplexed.

"Caroline will know more," said Ruth as the carriage turned into the Ryfield drive. "Oh, dear. We must tell her at once."

Caroline and Dickon were taking tea together in the morning room when the three distraught ladies returned. Hearing their excited voices in the hall as they turned over their wraps to a footman, Caroline felt a vast relief. The time alone with Dickon had put her on edge. Barely holding on to their tempers, they had discussed what Caroline should do next. Dickon could see no reason for her to do anything; was she not safe, well, and happy where she was? She'd suddenly begun to see him as one more man who expected her to do his bidding, no matter what her feelings. She did not like the look in his eye. The more he tried to reason with her, the more adamant she became. She had decided to throw herself on her brother Paul's mercy, at least for the time being. Walter would be sure to look for her at her parents' home, but he had never bothered to keep track of all her brothers. She supposed the two or three youngest were still at home, but the others would be married, with homes of their own. If she could induce Paul to keep her whereabouts a secret, she should be safe with him and his family for a while.

"I will stay only until you and Lady Stilton return to London," she told Dickon. "You may leave me off with my brother in Bedfordshire, and beyond requesting that you deny all knowledge of me should anyone inquire, I will ask nothing further of you.

Dickon, she could see, was thoroughly exasperated. "Your brother!" he burst out. "That will be the first place for Not-John to look! I will not have it!"

"Your lordship," she said, slowly and carefully, "it is not for you to decide." She put down her cup and gave him her full attention. "I beg of you, let me do as I see fit and let us part as friends. I can never repay you and your family for all—"

They were interrupted as three very agitated women burst into the room.

"Oh, Miss Caroline!" Dossie sobbed, running to her mistress and awkwardly clasping her hands. " 'E's 'ere! That 'orrible Mr. Fenland's 'ere! Wot are we goin' to do?" She stared at Caroline with red-rimmed eyes.

Caroline jumped up and looked fearfully toward the morning-room door. "Here?" she asked, appearing ready to flee. "In the house? How did he get in?"

"No, no," Lady Rycote assured her. "But in Durham, Dossie tells us." She explained the circumstances as Dossie had told her. "We have to hope he will not be clever enough to seek out Mrs. Fincaster and learn from her or her girls of your connection with us, but I fear it is a vain hope." She sank into a chair by the fire. "Ring for more tea, would you, Dickon? I vow, I am near frozen. Nell-on-her-knees is consumed with curiosity already. What monstrous luck, that she should be in Mrs. Cutter's shop when we arrived."

"I shouldn't 'ave gone with you," Dossie mourned. "Oh, Miss Caroline, I shouldn't 'ave. It's all my fault!" She started to sit down, then caught herself. "Beg pardon," she said weakly. "I'd best get upstairs."

"No, stay," said Caroline. "We will need your help. Are you certain it was Mr. Fenland?"

"Oh, yes, miss! Couldn't mistake 'im! 'E called me by name. 'Dossie,' he yelled. 'Orrid man, he is." Dossie retreated to a corner of the room, unwilling to seem to mix with her betters.

"We must leave at once," said Dickon, taking in the four frightened faces. "Ruth, how soon can you be packed?"

"But you are to stay past Twelfth Night!" Lady Rycote cried.

"Mama, think. We lack our own coach; we must take the mail, and we must do so before this Fenland can learn that Miss Caroline bides with us. Otherwise he has only to haunt the coaching inn to find us. He may be doing so now! He must know that Miss Caroline will learn from Dossie that he is after her, and that she will wish to flee. Gad! When is the next mail coach south?" He looked wildly at his audience.

Nobody knew.

Dickon ran his fingers through his hair in distraction. He heaved a great sigh and looked at Ruth. "I believe the only answer is a post chaise," he said, "whatever the cost. I will send a footman—"

"No!" Caroline cried as a servant entered with fresh tea. "You shall do nothing of the sort. This is my problem. Dossie and I shall go alone. You must remain with your mother until Twelfth Night. Dossie, you may go up and start packing. Oh, my new gowns! Did you order them? What a pity! I shall have to leave without them." She glanced down with loathing at the dowdy gray gown she wore. Then her chin rose and she looked squarely at Lady Rycote.

"Tell me their cost and I shall leave enough with you to cover them. Perhaps you can have them sent to me when I am established somewhere. We should have enough left over to pay our passage."

"When are the gowns to be ready?" Dickon asked his mother.

"Some in a sennight—some in a fortnight—oh, I do not

rightly remember," Lady Rycote answered. She poured herself a cup of tea with shaking hands. "My dear," she said with an affectionate look at Caroline, "even after the dresses, you will have at least six hundred pounds left. That should see you nicely to . . . where? Where do you plan to go?"

"To my brother Paul," said Caroline. "In Bedfordshire. I can hope he will give me sanctuary. I should have gone there rather than coming to Durham—I have been such a burden to you—"

"Why did you not?" Lady Rycote asked sharply.

Caroline faltered. She did not wish to admit her misgivings about her possible reception at her brother's home. It had been years since they had had anything to do with each other. She had always felt closer to George, the oldest, but George was the heir. She did not trust his viewpoint on the subject of heirs. Paul, as second son, might look at her situation differently. Or so she hoped.

"Paul would have room for me," she said with more confidence than she felt. "His family is small. Why did I not go there? I hardly know. We have not seen each other in many years. I have not felt close to my own family, unfortunately. It . . . it seemed best to get as far away from London as possible." Caroline choked back tears. She must take charge of herself, whatever these kindly people offered.

Dickon's temper rose. Leave Caroline with an uncaring brother? A brother as likely to turn her over to her husband as to hide her? Was she to disappear forever into Bedfordshire, so he—and his mother and sister, of course—would never learn what had happened to her? It was unthinkable. Why did he care? He refused to delve into his reasons. He felt angry and confused.

"Paul be damned!" Dickon burst out. "We shall hire a post chaise—whatever you say, Ruth—and be off, down to London. You must know that Not-John will visit every one of your brothers in his search for you. You shall be safe with us, in the house Ruth and I share."

"B-but if Mr. Fenland learns from Mrs. Fincaster . . . he will search you out in London, once he knows of our connection . . . I should be no safer than at Paul's," Caroline pointed out.

"I beg to differ," said Dickon. "Fenland—and Not-John—will believe London to be the last place you would go. Hiding under their noses! By the time they have visited your parents and all your brothers, Ruth and I will have found a secure place for you. Perhaps a new name—a new identity—"

"I am sure 'John' will have visited my parents and brothers already," Caroline said quietly. "He will not have sat by and let Mr. Fenland do all his dirty work for him. By this time he will know I am not with Paul. If I go there now, I should be safe."

"Humph!" said Dickon. He was determined to avoid Paul and any other brothers at all costs. He would take charge of this flight, and they would *not* travel through Bedfordshire. "We shall not take that chance," he said. "Ruth, were you not going to pack? I shall send the footman to inquire about a post chaise, and pack myself." He set down his teacup with a clatter and pulled the bell rope.

Caroline tried to control her growing anger. What right did Dickon think he had to tell her where to go? The man was a bully, a pig-headed bully. Unfortunately, she had little choice. "Oh, very well," said Caroline. "I cannot like this. Surely we could go by way of my brother's. Bedfordshire is not out of the way. I am sure I could find his house—now, let me see . . . "

"Do you mean you do not know his direction?" Dickon roared.

Just then a footman entered, and Dickon, calming himself, charged him with engaging a post chaise as quickly as possible.

"Now," he said, once the footman had gone, "tell me where this brother lives." He frowned at Caroline.

"Near to Sandy, I believe," she answered. "Or is that Charles? You must know that I have never been there, or to the homes of my other brothers. They have all grown and married and settled since my own marriage, except for the youngest, of course. They are still at home—or at school, I have no doubt."

"We shall not take the chance," Dickon said firmly. "We shall go directly to London."

"But—"

"Please get your bits and pieces together. Mama, perhaps you could ask Cook to fill a hamper for us; we cannot wait upon supper. I must pack." Dickon shooed the women out of the morning room and headed for his chamber.

What could Caroline be thinking of, prattling on about going to Bedfordshire when *he*—and Ruth, of course—offered a haven so much more secure? *He*—and Ruth, of course—would keep her safe. There was no accounting for the fancies of females, he thought in distraction as he stuffed a shirt into his bag.

Caroline, Ruth, and Dickon sat disconsolately in the drawing room, awaiting the return of the footman sent after the hiring of a post chaise. Their packed bags sat in the hall. Lady Rycote flitted about like one possessed, asking whether they had enough food in the hamper, whether they would stay at an inn or drive all night, whether it would not be better to delay their departure until morning, whether they would like a nice cup of tea before leaving.

"Enough, Mama!" Ruth cried at last. "Do please sit down and control yourself. We are three adults who are perfectly able to look after ourselves." She half rose from her chair when she heard the sound of a carriage outside. "Ah, Moffatt must have returned."

The man heard in the hall a few minutes later was not Moffatt, however.

"The earl is expecting me, I believe," came the voice of Sir Harry Wadsworth. "Am I in time for supper?"

The ladies' eyes all turned accusingly on Dickon, who pounded his fist on the chair arm. "Damn!" he said forcefully. "How could I forget?"

Sir Harry, with the ease of long acquaintance, did not wait to be shown into the drawing room. He strode in, all smiles, until he took in the group of tense people staring at him. He looked nonplussed.

"A rip in my waistcoat?" he asked, examining his clothing with a weak smile. No one spoke. "No? A death in the family? Why is everyone looking daggers at me?"

"Sorry, old fellow, forgot you were coming," said Dickon. He drew a great breath. "I suppose there is nothing for it now but to tell you. Harry, damn you, you must swear never to breathe a word of this. Understand?"

Before Harry could answer, Dickon rose and stood before his friend, looking him straight in the eye. "Can I trust you?" he asked.

"Fine way to treat a friend you invited to supper," Harry groused. "Of course you can trust me. What about?"

Hurriedly Dickon sketched their dilemma. "We only await Moffatt with word of a post chaise and we are off," Dickon concluded. "There is no time to waste."

Caroline watched Harry's face as the tale unfolded. Expressions of surprise, alarm, sympathy, and finally excited eagerness chased each other over his countenance, but he said not a word until Dickon was through.

"Ha! Always thought there was more to 'Mrs. Make-peace' than met the eye." said Harry. "Now look here, Dickon. You ain't taking a post chaise back to London. I won't have it. Too easy to trace. You are taking my traveling coach. It hasn't left my stables in near a year; I have no need of it. Your Mr. Fenland will never connect it with you. You want John Coachman as well? You shall have him. And horses, of course. Begging your pardon, but I don't see any prime goers in your own stable, so take mine. All to be returned, to be sure, but no hurry."

Dickon straightened his shoulders and looked steadily at his friend. "We have our own coach, thank you," he said, hurt. "I did not suggest it because it would only be in the way in London. Yours would be no better."

"Climb down from your high horse, Dickon," said an exasperated Harry. "We all know you have a coach, a perfectly splendid coach, bright-yellow and black, bearing your crest, and recognized from one end of Durham to the

other, right? *My* coach is black, not so new, not so old, hard
to distinguish from a hundred others. That is why I thought
of it. Do not be a dunce, Dickon."

"Harry," Dickon replied, grabbing his friend's arms. "I
cannot let you do this."

"And why not, may I ask? You would do the same for me,
and have done as much in the past. What are friends for?"

Dickon could hardly believe it. Harry would do this for
him—not really for him, but for Miss Caroline, whom he
hardly knew, because Dickon wished to help her? But it
was the answer to a prayer. A privately owned coach would
be much harder to track down than a post chaise. The Ryfield coach was too easy to spot.

"I accept," Dickon said before he could change his mind.
So when Moffatt finally returned to report he could obtain
no post chaise before the morrow, Dickon dismissed that
idea altogether.

"Sir Harry's generous offer deserves a celebration," said
Lady Rycote, breaking into the chorus of questions and ex-
clamations Sir Harry had produced. "And supper! You cannot set out unfed. I must notify Cook immediately." She
bustled out.

Harry and Dickon, however, wished to waste no time.
They left almost immediately for Harry's home, Brancebridge, to get the coachman, coach, and horses. When Lady
Rycote returned from the kitchen she found only Ruth and
Caroline, still dazed at the speed with which all this had
been decided. Dossie was upstairs restoring Benjamin's
room to rights.

"Oh, dear madam, I cannot like this plan," Caroline told
her. "Here I am, still virtually a stranger, and now not only
your family, but Sir Harry as well, insist on going to a deal
of trouble for me. You have only my word that I am in danger of my life; how do you know I am not bamming you?"

"But what about Mr. Fenman, or Fenland, or whatever
his name is?"

Caroline shivered at the mention of his name, Lady
Rycote noticed. If she'd needed any further proof that Caroline was not making this up, here it was. The young

woman's fear was palpable. Her husband must be a monster indeed.

Lady Rycote smiled and said, "Do not try to spoil these young men's adventure, my dear. I have not seen such enthusiasm on Dickon's part in years, and he and Sir Harry are two of a kind. They *need* something to stir them up. I vow, if Sir Harry could, he would be with you every turn of the wheel, plotting and planning your next step.

"Now, while they are gone, do come to supper. It will be a rather hasty one, I fear, but you will need your strength." She urged them into the breakfast room, where a cold supper had been laid out.

Caroline, who had thought herself too excited to eat, found she was ravenous. As she helped herself to another slice of turkey, she decided she would look upon their coming flight as an adventure, just as the Earl of Rycote seemed to be doing. Flying in a borrowed coach near the length of England in mid-winter! With the Earl of Rycote in command, she had no qualms. If only he were not so bullheaded. She would do her best to steer him toward Bedfordshire, though she had no illusions about her chances. At any rate, he seemed determined to save her—although just what he was saving her for, she wished she knew.

The coachman Sir Harry provided, Elias Stackpole, was a short, stout man whose head seemed to grow directly from his torso without benefit of a neck. His conversation consisted mostly of grunts as he, Harry, and Dickon loaded the luggage on top of the coach. Harry, caught up in the excitement, rode back to Ryfield so as not to miss the departure. He burdened Elias with instructions and admonitions while Dickon settled the ladies and Dossie in the coach. Heated bricks had been provided for their feet, for the cold was intense. Clouds of steam issued from the horses' nostrils.

"Do we dare take the Great North Road?" Dickon asked Sir Harry as he wrapped a muffler around his neck. "That is sure to be Fenland's first thought, once he learns we have flown."

"True, but I give you a day at least ahead of him," said Harry. "Surely he will come to Ryfield first, once he learns of your connection with Mrs. Makepeace. He will not be prepared to follow immediately. We do not know whether he has his own carriage, or how he got to Durham; he may have to make arrangements to hire a rig. And why is he to think you would go down to London again? My advice would be to start south with all haste."

Dickon's own reasoning had been similar. With it confirmed by his friend, he made sure all was in readiness, kissed his mother goodbye, and climbed into the coach. At a signal Elias cracked his whip and they started out, the women still calling their thanks and farewells through the window until they were well out of earshot. Ruth quickly closed the curtain to conserve what little heat the coach held.

Dickon rubbed his cold hands and smiled expansively at his companions, who looked silently at him in the dull glow of the single lamp. "So, here we go again," he said. "The same foursome as a few weeks ago, the same road, if in reverse, but how different it is now! Now we are friends, and we are united in a single purpose. I, for one, am starved. You ladies have eaten, but I was too busy. Dossie, would you hand up the hamper? Anyone else for a bit of cheese? No? Turkey? A tart? Then I shall indulge."

Dickon, in splendid fettle, made a good meal while the ladies watched. Conversation was desultory as one by one they fell asleep.

Dickon had just settled himself for a nap when he felt the coach lurch, drop, and halt. They seemed to be in a ditch.

Seven

R uth was the first to be awakened by the sudden halt. "Where are we?" she asked drowsily. "Why have we stopped?" Then she noticed that her side of the coach was higher than the other side, where Caroline sat, and that she was sliding slowly along the seat, aimed toward a pile-up with Caroline. Dickon, opposite her, was similarly sliding toward Dossie, who sat opposite her mistress.

"Dickon," Ruth said, "that fool coachman has got us in a ditch."

"Yes," said Dickon. "How clever of you to notice. Help me get this door open, will you, and I shall see what the trouble is."

Getting the door open was no easy task, for they had to fight gravity as well as a firm latch. Dossie, meanwhile, had come to, only to find the Earl of Rycote repeatedly sliding her way despite his efforts to move up and away toward the door he was fighting to open. Dossie, apparently fearing she would be crushed, screamed.

Caroline, awakened and taking in the situation at a glance, groaned. "Hush, Dossie," she ordered. "You are not harmed. See if you can help me get the door open on this side."

Caroline, with Dossie's fumbling help, soon had the door on her side unlatched, but it would open no more than a foot. Its lower corner caught in the side of the ditch, which was liberally thatched with tall, winter-browned grasses. She was unable to close it again as great tufts of wet grass worked their way between the door and its frame.

Dickon and Ruth were still shoving at the opposite door to little avail when the voice of their coachman inquired.

"All right in there? I'm comin' quick as I can." A muffled curse, and the topmost door was pulled open. Elias's head appeared.

"You'd best get out until I can get the coach righted," he said. "But take care! There's a good six or eight inches of water in the ditch. Here, sir, let me help you." He reached an arm in to Dickon, who clambered to the door sill, crouched, and jumped, landing at the far edge of the ditch unscathed.

He had no time to congratulate himself before he felt his feet slipping from under him on the wet, grassy slope of the ditch. Wildly he reached for a hand-hold on the coach; he was able to brace himself in time, but a small splash and a numbing cold told him he was now standing in water.

"Hell and damnation," he muttered. He shook his head, which was hatless. His beaver was too tall to wear comfortably in the coach and he had set it atop the food hamper. "Elias, help me get the ladies out."

The ladies were remarkably in control; only Dossie seemed on the verge of hysteria. Ruth was helped out first, with only a surprised, "Oh!" when her feet inevitably sank into the water in the ditch. Caroline first handed out Dickon's hat, then struggled to bring up the food hamper before she permitted herself to be hauled out. She had removed her flimsy slippers, which she tucked into her reticule, and came out in stocking feet. Soon they were soaked halfway up her calves.

"The hot bricks slid out the other door," she reported as Dickon pulled her up the grassy slope to safety. "I think they had lost all their heat anyhow."

Dickon surveyed their predicament. The horses stood quietly, now and then blowing and snorting. They were half on, half off the road, but clear of the ditch. The coach had slewed as if executing a tight turn, but the stretch of road visible in the coach lamps was straight. How had it come to be in the ditch?

"Explain, please," Dickon said sternly to their coachman.

" 'Twas another coach, your lordship. Didn't you hear it? Comin' hell-for-leather, no lanterns, no torches, no nothin', like he owned the road. I could *hear* 'im, but I couldn't *see* 'im till the last minute. I tried to get over, let 'im have 'is way, but I never saw that damned ditch, sir, I swear I didn't. No moon, sir, and it's powerful dark out, as you can see. Now if you'll just move aside, I'll get us out of here."

Elias climbed atop the tipped coach, urged his horses forward, and nothing happened.

"Bloody hell," he muttered. He tried again. The coach moved a few inches, then rolled back.

"Ditch is too damned slippery," he announced. "Your lordship, do you think you could . . . ?"

Gamely Dickon waded once more into the ice-cold water of the ditch, put his shoulder to the coach, and at a signal from Elias, pushed with all his might. It took three tries— each time the coach moved a bit, then settled back—before the ditch finally yielded its burden and the coach rolled up and out onto the road.

The huddled, chilled passengers reboarded. While Elias retied the shifted luggage on top, the ladies cleaned off as much of the grass clogging the doorway as possible until they could get the door to latch, and Dickon distributed carriage rugs he had taken from the coach's small boot. He thanked his lucky stars he had thought to ask about them when readying the coach with Harry.

"We shall have to stop at an inn for the night," he told the ladies. "I had hoped, if we held to an easy pace, we could keep going, but wet as we are, we will all catch our deaths."

"What time is it?" Ruth asked.

Dickon pulled out his watch and peered at it in the feeble light of the interior lamp, which miraculously had not gone out. "Past eleven," he reported.

"Where will we find an inn at this hour?" Ruth demanded.

"I do not know, but the first inn we see shall have our business." Dickon pounded on the roof and when Elias drew up, he directed the coachman to stop at the next inn, whatever it should look like.

Twenty minutes later they pulled into Darlington. Dickon roused himself, stumbled on numb feet to the door of the small inn when Elias had stopped, knocked up the landlord, who was readying for bed, and bespoke two chambers. Neither had a fire going. By the time fires had been lit, and the tired travelers had spread their wet clothing on chair backs to dry and sought their beds, it was one in the morning.

Sharing a chamber with Elias, for he found it too much trouble to arrange otherwise, Dickon had waited until the coachman had made sure the horses were well taken care of. He sat by the fire with a welcome bottle of brandy at his side, warming his feet.

Once the weary Elias appeared, Dickon pressed a brandy on him. "Sit a moment," he said. "How did you come to volunteer for this journey?"

Elias gave a rueful laugh. "Thought it might be a lark," he said. "I was glad to come when Sir Harry asked. Things get dull at Brancebridge."

"Whatever else this journey may be, I do not believe it will be dull," said Dickon.

A good night's sleep and a bountiful breakfast next morning had the travelers in a more hopeful mood. The inn was busy as numerous buyers and sellers of wool and cotton cloth conducted their business over eggs and lashings of tea. Darlington was becoming an important center of the textile industry, and the inn was, apparently, a favorite of those in the trade.

Eavesdropping on nearby conversations, Caroline was struck by how little she knew of the lives of most of the English. She was accustomed to measuring cloth in ells; no one around her spoke of ells, but rather of dozens, scores, hundreds of bolts. There was much haggling over delivery dates, discounts, quality, what was likely to sell, problems with workers' wages. The thought of absorbing so much information made her head swim. Yet these men talked of nothing else, and even seemed to enjoy it.

"Is this all they talk about?" she asked Dickon in a hushed voice, indicating with a nod the two men conducting a heated argument nearby.

Dickon listened for a moment. "Arguing over the price of raw wool," he reported. "It is down, as I know to my sor-

row. With the war and the American blockade, we cannot
sell our woolen cloth overseas so it is piling up in the ware-
houses. The Ryfield shear this year was up, but we got precious little out of it." He frowned and tapped his fingers on
the table.

"So you are in this too!"

"Of course. Wool is an important crop at Ryfield."

"But your work is at the War Office!"

"Just so. Jack of all trades and master of none. I must try
to stay abreast of wool prices, and mutton prices, and
grains, and potatoes, and horses, and the latest cultivating
practices, and crop rotation—all that and do my duty at the
War Office."

Caroline looked at Dickon with new eyes. Heavens
above, how could one man do it all? On her walk around
Ryfield with Dickon, she had listened with interest to his
plans for the estate, but she had pictured him as a sort of
gentleman farmer, watching all his plans unfold while he
rode carelessly over the estate or sat in his study counting
his receipts. Here, she realized, was no dilettante. But because of her, he had left Ryfield nearly two weeks earlier
than he had planned.

"When do you expect to get back to Ryfield?" she asked.

"Who knows?" Dickon grimaced. "When will the war be
over?"

They left Darlington soon after breakfast, heading south
on the well-traveled road. It was cold, but there was little
wind. A watery sun peeked out at intervals. After a pause
for luncheon, Dickon elected to join Elias on the box, and
drove much of the afternoon. He explained to the ladies
that he was out of practice on the ribbons.

They reached York before full dark and put up at a pleasant inn. Dickon obtained a private parlor for their supper,
then sat in the common room over a brandy while the ladies
refreshed themselves.

He looked up to see Ruth beckoning to him. "I would
like to talk to you," she said. "Join me in the parlor." She
led the way.

"Yes?" Dickon asked when they were settled by the fire

and a young woman had brought Ruth a pot of tea. "A problem?"

"It may be too soon to say, but I think we are doing very well," said Ruth. "Why are you looking so worried? You have no reason to think we are being followed, do you?"

"It is not that," said Dickon. He wondered that Ruth had noticed his worries, which he had tried to hide. She knew him too well. "I fear we lacked the time to plan this very carefully. We have but the one team of horses, with no arrangements made for changes on the way. There was no time, nor for that matter, any spare teams to place in advance. We cannot count on hiring job teams without delays and setbacks. Who would make sure Harry got his own back?

"But that is only one of our problems. Ruth, I am not at all certain we have enough blunt to stay at decent inns every night, what with five people to feed and bed down and the horses to be cared for. I would put the cost on tick, but these innkeepers have never heard of me; they will not be willing to extend me credit. When I called for rooms here and gave my name as the Earl of Rycote, the creature at the desk looked at my signature as if I had just invented it and said, 'That will be five pounds, please, plus a guinea for the parlor.' Damn!"

"Five pounds seems a little excessive."

"So I thought, but who among us is willing to travel all over York looking for a better bargain? Not I."

"You forget," said Ruth, warming her hands on the teacup, "Miss Caroline still has six hundred pounds or more, and I am sure she will be happy to share. After all, we are doing this for her."

"No!" Dickon set down his brandy and gripped the arms of his chair. "She will need every penny; that is all she has for the indefinite future. I will not hear of it."

On his high horse again, Ruth thought. When would her brother learn that his way was not the only way; his decisions not infallible?

"What is your alternative?" she asked. "For heaven's sake, Dickon, be reasonable. Meanwhile, I have a bit with me, certainly enough for another night's lodging if we are careful. Then I shall speak to Miss Caroline. As for the horses, I have no suggestion other than to do as we have done, going only as far as they can carry us, and hope for the best. Hardly like the mail coach, is it? We would be in London by now if we had taken the mail coach."

"Perhaps." Dickon stretched his weary muscles and poured himself another tot of brandy.

Their financial situation had occurred to Caroline as well. That night as Dossie prepared both ladies for bed—Dossie had offered to act as maid to Ruth too, considering she had no maid with her—Caroline brought it up.

"Is the earl paying for this?" she asked Ruth. "He refuses to say anything when I ask him. I cannot permit this."

"It is his stupid pride," said Ruth. "A man as near to the edge as Dickon cannot afford to have pride, but try to tell him that." She gave a rueful chuckle. "He does not mind borrowing from me—we do it all the time—but from you? Never. Yet he admitted to me this very evening that he lacks enough to get us to London. I have some money with me, which he shall have, but he will take none from you."

"Then I shall give my money to you and you can give it to him."

"Much like the loaves and fishes, eh?" said Ruth, smiling. "I believe it might work. I shall show great surprise when I discover yet another few pounds hidden away in my reticule or the hem of my cloak or whatever. Bless you, Miss Caroline. If the horses hold up, we may get to London yet." She edged Dossie aside—the maid was brushing Caroline's hair—and gave the younger woman a hug. "Sorry, Dossie," Ruth apologized.

"London for you; Bedfordshire for me," said Caroline firmly.

"We shall see," said Ruth.

It rained throughout the following day, a cold, driving rain that turned the road into a quagmire. Despite voluminous coats and mufflers Elias was soaked to the skin. He was shivering violently when they stopped for a midday meal. Dickon ordered him to toast himself before the inn's common-room fire and plied him with restoratives, delaying their departure by nearly an hour. Finally, Elias pronounced himself ready to drive again and climbed onto the box, urging the freshly watered and fed horses onward, but Dickon did not like the looks of their coachman. He called a halt for the night at Doncaster.

Again Dickon and Elias shared a room. Normally the coachman would have bedded down over the stables, or in a lesser room intended for servants, but Dickon found it simpler for them to share. He rather liked Elias, who was intelligent and willing. He had known the coachman for years but had never exchanged more than a few words with him at Sir Harry's. The last two evenings they had enjoyed a discussion of horses in general, Sir Harry's horses in particular, and had been racking their brains for the name of a long-gone stallion in Sir Harry's stable that had had a perverse habit of kicking over feed pails left within reach.

Now Elias, filled with good stew, wrapped in numerous blankets, lay in bed sniffling. "Agamemnon," he said.

It was only nine of the clock and Dickon was glancing at a newspaper as he sat before the fire, a brandy at his side. "That's it!" he cried. "Agamemnon! How could I forget? Thank you, Elias."

He turned a page of the newspaper. A dispatch from the Peninsula caught his eye. Nothing new there. Skirmishes. Somebody had advanced. Somebody else had retreated. He'd heard it all before.

"Agamemnon," came from the bed.

"Right," said Dickon. He noted the Prince Regent had held a ball at Carlton House. The room was quiet except for crackling from the fire. When he folded the paper, the rattle seemed too loud. A noise from the bed caught his attention.

He rose and went over to peer at the coachman, who was breathing stentoriously through his mouth. His face was red. His eyes were closed. He shivered, and the pile of blankets shook with him.

"Oh, my God," said Dickon. "He's come down with the ague."

He rushed out of the chamber, ran down the stairs, and demanded the innkeeper send for a doctor.

"Elias is in no condition to drive us," Dickon told the ladies, who had been summoned to the private parlor he had hired earlier. "Do we leave him here and go on, or do we wait here a day or two? I can drive, of course, if need be. I have seen no sign of anyone following us. Surely we have escaped Mr. Fenland, but I would feel better if we were in London, not in Doncaster. Should we take a vote?"

There, he thought. They cannot accuse me of making all the decisions, riding roughshod over their own wishes. He looked at Ruth, then at Caroline. Dossie was in the ladies' chamber.

"Go," said Ruth, just as Caroline said, "Stay."

"We cannot just abandon him!" Caroline cried. "Who would wish to be ill, alone in a strange town, with no one to care? That is monstrous! Yes, you can drive, your lordship, but what if it rains and you too catch the ague? Then what would we do? I vote we stay."

"And what are we to do in Doncaster for days on end?" Ruth asked. "It has never been my desire to spend time in Doncaster."

"We could visit the racecourse," Dickon suggested. "Even though there are no races at the moment, the grandstand is a sight to behold, or so I have been told. Or perhaps you would wish to go along the High Street and view the Mansion House. I know little else about Doncaster, I confess."

"And where did you learn this much?" Ruth asked tartly.

"From the innkeeper, of course. He is proud of Doncaster. He has every right, just as we are proud of Durham."

"But Durham has a cathedral!" said Ruth.

"That it does, and St. Cuthbert as well, but not every town can be so fortunate," said Dickon. He gave his sister an amused look. "I can see I shall have to vote to break the tie. I vote we stay for one more day and see whether Elias will then be fit to travel. We can take another vote tomorrow night. Ladies, I bid you goodnight."

Dickon had had Elias transferred to a chamber of his

own, a small servant's chamber under the eaves, for Dickon did not wish to catch the man's malady. He hired a daughter of the innkeeper's, a young woman of about seventeen, to keep an eye on Elias and see that he was fed and took his medicine. This was all costing extra, and he was relieved to learn that Ruth had discovered she had more money with her than she had first realized. At least he had not had to go to Miss Caroline for money! Dickon carefully noted every shilling so he could repay his sister.

The next morning the rain had let up. After breakfast Ruth and Caroline, accompanied by Dossie, explored Doncaster's shops, and Caroline was able to buy a pair of sturdy half-boots. That, she decided, was enough to make Doncaster worth the visit.

Dickon went off alone. If he visited the racecourse grandstand, he did not mention it.

By evening they were fidgeting to be gone, but Elias was no better.

"One more day," said Dickon at supper in the private parlor. "Only one more, and then we shall leave, with or without a coachman."

By midmorning of the next day, the coachman seemed on the mend. Elsie, the girl who was looking after him, tried to report this to Dickon, but the earl was out, no one knew where. Elsie therefore sought out Lady Stilton. She and Caroline were in their chamber, taking turns at looking out the window when not trying to read. The weather looked like snow, Ruth reported as she frowned at the lowering gray clouds.

"Your man says as how he's feeling better," Elsie told them when she had been admitted. "Wouldn't swaller his draught though. Says it's worse 'n the ague." She giggled.

"Thank you, Elsie." Ruth smiled and gave the departing girl a coin. "Caroline! We must find Dickon and tell him. If Elias is able, we might yet leave today. Oh, why did Dickon have to go out? I have no idea where to look for him." She rushed to the window again as if to conjure him up on the street outside.

"I will step outside and see if I can see him anywhere," Caroline offered. "He may be back already and having a drink in the common room before dinner, for all we know, though surely Elsie would have looked there." She gathered her cloak and bonnet, preparing to depart.

"No!" Ruth demurred. "You will go nowhere alone! It is too dangerous. I will go with you. Dossie, you remain here should the earl come looking for us. We shall be right back, but just in case . . . " Hastily she tied her bonnet strings and threw her cloak about her.

Dickon was not in the common room. The innkeeper, when queried, denied having seen him. The ladies fastened their cloaks, smoothed their gloves, and stepped outside, where they were greeted by a remarkable sight. Four men, two women, and a child, a howling toddler trying to pull away from the woman who held his hand, were bearing down on the inn. Behind them a pair of porters struggled with a mountain of luggage. "Make way! Make way!" one of the porters called.

Ruth and Caroline looked beyond the group of travelers, wondering what had brought them here without coach or carriage, only to see a thin wisp of smoke rising in the distance. "Fire!" someone shouted, and everyone in the street, except for the arriving group of travelers set off at a run. As they watched, the wisp of smoke grew, and spread, and became an ugly, black column. "It's the White Horse!" a man near them yelled. He raced toward the conflagration.

Ruth and Caroline were so caught up in the excitement that they paid little attention to the arriving travelers, who had reached the inn entrance and were attempting to get inside. Their way was blocked as what seemed to be the entire population of the inn tried to get out in order to see the fire.

Jostled and pushed to one side, the two ladies held on to each other to wait until the passage was clear. Caroline, standing behind the taller Ruth, almost missed the unremarkable man who was one of the arriving travelers. It was James Fenland.

Eight

Had Fenland seen her? Caroline thought not, or he would have given some sign—probably would have grabbed her on the spot, she thought fearfully. She stood perfectly still, clutching Ruth's arm in a death grip and looking down at her feet, face averted, until she was certain Fenland had passed inside with the others.

For a moment they were alone, the inn having emptied of its avid fire watchers and the travelers, with their luggage, having gone inside.

"Ruth!" Caroline managed a hoarse whisper. "That was James Fenland! He is here! Whatever shall we do?"

"Oh, my God," said Ruth. "Are you sure? Which one?"

"Oh, yes. We cannot go inside; he will be there. *You* can go inside, of course, for he does not know you, but then you will not recognize him either. He was the second man; did you notice? Not likely. He is not noticeable. Only Dossie and I know what he looks like—I pray Dossie does not come downstairs!—but—but I cannot stand out here all day!"

All Caroline's bravado, all the healing she had done in the weeks since she had fled from her husband, dropped away as if it had never been. The old, hopeless terror came back with a rush. She felt paralyzed. Her attempt to escape had been futile from the start. Walter, as always, would win. She was Walter's chattel, his possession to do with as he wished. Had she to do it over, she never would have married him, but she had made her bed; now she must lie in it. That adage struck her with fresh horror; the thought of lying in bed with Walter sickened her.

Oh Lord, where was Dickon?

Ruth saw the hopelessness in Caroline's face, and though she had no quick solution, she was not ready to give up.

"I'll wager that wherever Dickon meant to go, he is now watching the White Horse burn," said Ruth, giving Caroline's arm a reassuring squeeze. "All of Doncaster must be there. Shall we walk a bit closer? We might see him."

Caroline nodded. Anything that would take her away from the Three Feathers—the inn that now contained James Fenland—was preferable to standing there. She held tight to Ruth's arm as they moved down the street.

Acrid smoke filled their nostrils as they neared the chaotic scene. Flames leapt ever higher into the air. Doncaster's fire company had retreated once it was evident they could do nothing; their efforts now were directed toward wetting down neighboring buildings to prevent the fire's spread. A ring of spectators clogged the street, shouting information and rumors to each other. Ruth and Caroline learned that the fire was said to have started in a bed chamber when a drapery, too near the fireplace, had caught. It had been discovered when an arriving traveler had been shown to the bed chamber. This traveler and other new arrivals had been sent to the Three Feathers while the White Horse staff attempted to put out the fire with water from the chamber's water jug, a feeble attempt that was too little, too late.

The White Horse's stable, fortunately, had not caught, but the ostlers and grooms were taking no chances. In the midst of pandemonium they were attempting to lead the horses to safety, an effort the horses were violently opposing. The neighs and squeals of frightened animals, the yelling of the men, the whoosh of the fire, punctuated with crashes as floors and roof gave way, were the background sounds of a scene from hell, Caroline thought. She pulled at Ruth.

"Let us get away," she begged. "We do not belong here."

"I was hoping to find Dickon . . . " said Ruth, standing on tiptoe to search for her brother. "Oh! There he is!" She pulled Caroline after her as she shoved her way through the crowd.

Dickon, filthy with soot, his hat missing, a bruise on his cheek, limped toward them at Ruth's hail. "What are you doing here?" he demanded. "This is no place for you!"

"What are *you* doing here?" Ruth retaliated. "Were you in the White Horse? What happened to you?"

Caroline was appalled as she took in his appearance. Dickon could have been killed! She was shocked to discover how important he had become to her.

Dickon explained that he had gone to the White Horse stables in hopes of hiring spare horses. The White Horse was a posting house with a commodious stable, a much better prospect than the smaller Three Feathers. At the cries of "Fire!" he had run into the inn to help evacuate patrons or help save valuables, whatever was needed. He had stayed a bit too long, he remarked with some embarrassment, and had narrowly escaped when a beam came crashing down next to him, scraping one foot. Thank heaven for sturdy boots, he said, holding out his left foot. The boot was scraped and dented.

"Let us go back to the Three Feathers," he suggested. "I need a bath!"

Ruth and Caroline looked at each other.

"Dickon, James Fenland is at the Three Feathers," said Ruth.

"The devil you say! Are you certain? Did he see you?" Dickon stopped their progress and turned to face the two ladies, looking at them with concern.

Caroline told him of her glimpse of her husband's man. "I am sure he failed to see me," she said, "but how can I avoid him? We must return—to get Dossie, and Elias, and our belongings—where could I hide? Even if I made myself scarce, there is Dossie—she knows nothing of this." She paused a moment, her voice catching. "I might as well give myself up and be done with it," she murmured, her head drooping. She scuffed at the ground with her toe, numbly noting the half-boots that had been such a happy find the day before.

"Miss Caroline!" Dickon's fingers gently raised her chin until she was looking directly at him. "That is not the Miss Caroline we have come to know. *She* is determined to live her own life as far from Not-John as is possible. *She* is not one to give up easily, particularly when she has friends who will go to great lengths to keep her safe." He smiled and dropped his fingers. "Oh, my, I have spread soot all over your chin. Come. We will manage. I wonder how Elias is today?"

"Better!" said Ruth. "That is why we set out to look for you. Can we not leave Doncaster?"

"I hope so," said Dickon.

Caroline, warmed by the touch of those soot-stained fingers, felt renewed hope now that the Earl of Rycote was again in command. She was ashamed of her craven fear. Had she not escaped Walter without help and made her way clear to Durham while six months gone with child? Avoiding James Fenland with the help of two friends and two servants should be child's play in comparison. She straightened and marched toward the Three Feathers with determination.

"Now what do we do?" she asked when they had reached the inn's entrance. She stopped and looked to Dickon for guidance.

"We walk through the inn, climb the staircase, and repair to our chambers to pack," said Dickon. "Your friend Fenland will have gone to his own chamber by this time, God willing. I shall go on up to the attic to have a look at Elias and see whether he is able to travel. Would you ladies mind if he rode in the coach with you for a time? I can drive until he is feeling better. I do not believe it would be wise to let him drive yet—it looks like snow." Dickon scanned the sky, which was filled now with heavy gray clouds.

"Very well," said Ruth. She took Caroline's arm; Dickon took Caroline's other arm, and they entered the inn.

At the reception area an irate James Fenland was shouting at the innkeeper.

"I paid my shot at the White Horse!" he insisted. "I should not have to pay again! I tell you—"

The innkeeper tried to calm him. "You must take that up with the White Horse," he said smoothly. "You are fortunate, sir, that we can make room for you, but of course you must pay!"

Fenland made a face. "Just how am I to get my blunt back from the White Horse?" he asked. "Ain't nothing left of it! I ask you, why should a man have to pay twice?"

Dickon, Caroline, and Ruth passed by as if they were unaware of Fenland entirely. Caroline kept her glance on the floor, her head in its pink wool bonnet turned away from the innkeeper and his argumentative patron. Dickon had hoped for a good look at the man, but saw only his back.

Reaching the stairs without incident, they ran up as if shot from a gun.

Dickon was not entirely persuaded that Elias was fit to travel, but the coachman prevailed. "Duller up here than at Brancebridge," he reported. "Nobody but that Elsie to talk to, and she hasn't got two thoughts to rub together." He rose and started to dress as Dickon looked on. "I'd best see to the horses. What time are we leavin'?"

"As quickly as possible," said Dickon. "But first, you and I will walk through the inn and you will pay special note to the man I shall seek, if he is there. It is Mr. Fenland, Elias, the man who is after Miss Caroline—that is to say, Mrs. Makepeace. We will want to be able to recognize him."

"My Gawd," said Elias. "Has he seen 'er?"

"We do not believe so, but it has been a near thing."

As they descended the stairs, Dickon fought a desire to find and collar James Fenland and ask him his business. That would do nothing but lead to an altercation and let Fenland—and Not-John, eventually—discover Miss Caroline's whereabouts. A quick vanishing act was much to be preferred.

A trip through the common room and other public areas of the inn failed to produce anyone who might be Fenland. Dickon and Elias repaired to the stable to have the coach made ready.

While Caroline told Dossie of Fenland's presence and tried to calm her, Ruth arranged with the kitchen to have their hamper provisioned. No one had any desire to eat in public in the inn. By two of the clock they were ready to depart. Elias brought up the coach, climbed down to let Dickon take his place, and helped the ladies inside, then climbed in after them.

Their route took them past the smoldering ruins of the White Horse. Caroline pulled back the curtain to take a last look, and stared into the face of James Fenland. He stared back.

She slammed the curtain shut, but she was afraid it was too late.

"He saw me!" she cried. "Oh dear Lord, he saw me!"

Nine

Dickon, perched on the coach's box, had no knowledge of the encounter with Fenland and Caroline dared not signal him to stop so she could tell him. It was imperative they get away before Fenland could react. They had left Doncaster behind and gone a mile or two into the countryside before she pounded on the roof. Dickon pulled to the side and stopped, then hopped down and opened the coach door. "What is it?" he asked, scanning the frightened faces within.

"Did you see him?" Caroline, agitated, gripped her reticule as if it were a live thing trying to escape. "There by the White Horse? Did you see him?"

"You don't mean Fenland, surely?" said Dickon. He pulled himself together. After all their efforts, when things were finally going well . . . "I saw several men in the street, but I paid little attention, just so long as they were out of my way. Why would Fenland have gone back to the White Horse?" Then he answered his own question. "To ask for his money back, I have no doubt. Good God. Are you trying to tell me he saw you? Recognized you?"

"I am sure of it," said Caroline. "He looked directly at me, not more than two or three feet away."

Dickon pondered a moment. "I believe it is time we leave the Great North Road," he said. "There is a toll gate just ahead; we shall pay the toll, so if and when Fenland follows, as he surely will, he can ask and learn our direction. But we shall turn west at our first opportunity rather than continue toward Lincoln. With luck he will think us headed for Lincoln, and never find us. Agreed?"

His listeners nodded.

"How are you feeling? You look a bit downish," Dickon asked Elias.

"I ought to be on the box, sir, not you," said Elias. "It don't seem right, me ridin' with the ladies. Want I should come sit by you?" The coachman seemed distinctly uncomfortable.

Dickon laughed. "I shall let you suffer a while longer," he said. "Perhaps tomorrow."

He shut the coach door, prepared to remount the box, then hesitated. He returned and opened the door once more.

"Elias," he said, "I need your hat. Mine was lost in the fire, and it is blasted cold out here. May I borrow it?"

Elias produced his headgear and watched with interest as Dickon clapped it on his head. Too large, it settled around Dickon's ears and nearly cut off his vision. Dickon removed it, stared at it, and set it aside while he unwound his long scarf and wrapped the scarf around his brow. He added the hat on top. The effect was peculiar, to say the least, but the hat stayed out of his eyes.

"All set," he said. He shut the door, climbed onto the box, and cracked the whip.

The expected snow arrived, but it was light and intermittent, melting as it hit the ground. Dickon paid it little heed. He felt exultant. Now he knew their pursuer was real, not a maybe or a possible, but an actual flesh-and-blood man who had been seen and identified in Doncaster. It was up to him to outwit this knave. All kinds of possible plots and subterfuges went through his mind, occupying him so completely that he did not feel the cold and gave only minimal attention to his driving.

He had paid the toll and asked of the tollkeeper the distance to Lincoln, where, of course, he did not intend to go. Five mileposts beyond the toll gate he saw a lesser road leading to the west, and took it. This led through the hills to Conisbrough, where the majestic ruins of Conisbrough Castle stood on a knoll overlooking the countryside. Dickon searched his memory and realized they must be headed for

Sheffield; a signpost at an intersection confirmed it. He immediately turned west, knowing they would be wiser to stay on less-traveled roads and avoid the larger towns. From Conisbrough he continued west to Wath Upon Dearne, then south, and west, and south, and southwest. The roads twisted and turned, and as the afternoon progressed the dim gray light grew dimmer. Soon he was unable to read the few signposts. His sense of direction seemed to have deserted him, and there was no moon or stars to help. He could have been driving due north again without realizing it. He stopped the horses in the middle of the road, which was the only place he could stop since hedgerows closed in on either side. He lighted the running lamps and poked his head into the coach to confer with the passengers.

"I am not sure where we are," he admitted.

"Then we ask at the next farm," Elias said. He laughed. "I was wonderin' where you were headed," he confessed. "Let me take the box for a bit, your lordship. You could do with a spell inside." He lumbered out of the coach, retrieved his hat from Dickon's head, and held the door for his lordship to enter. Dickon climbed in, looking somewhat abashed.

It was good to get in out of the wind. Dickon made himself comfortable on the leather squabs, smiled at his companions, and relaxed. He was half asleep when the coach stopped sometime later and Elias opened the door to announce proudly, "Sheffield! We made it, your lordship! Happy New Year!"

New Year? No one but Elias had remembered the date. They had spent much of the day driving over half of Yorkshire, it seemed to Dickon, and still had landed in Sheffield despite his best efforts. He resolved to begin the year 1812 by making plain to Elias just where they were going, if he could figure it out himself.

They spent the night in Sheffield without incident.

James Fenland hardly knew which way to turn. He had been ordered to find Walter's woman, but he had also been reminded that a shipment was due by the first of January, and that he had better be in Kent when the shipment arrived. Well, he had found Walter's woman, right and tight in Durham, staying at the home of some dowager countess. That Fincaster woman, who was a real gabble-grinder, had informed him that the dowager's son and daughter were visiting through Twelfth Night, so it stood to reason that Walter's bitch would be there through Twelfth Night as well. She apparently was a friend of this son and daughter. Mrs. Fincaster's insistence that she did not know the identity of the woman visiting the dowager did not fool Fenland one bit.

Fenland had not even troubled to seek out the dowager's home to make sure Walter's bitch was in residence. Too chancey; he might be seen. Instead he thanked Mrs. Fincaster, assured her he would hire one of her girls to maid his wife just as soon as he could confer with his wife, kissed Mrs. Fincaster's hand, and took the next stage south, heading for Kent.

He had not intended to stop in Doncaster, but the caliber of his fellow coach passengers was such that he could not stand them another minute. A squalling infant, a drunken sot who vomited on the floor of the coach, splattering some of it on Fenland's boots, and a fat woman who squeezed against him so that he could hardly breathe—what was the world coming to? He decided to break his journey at Doncaster and hope for better companions on the morrow. If Walter refused to put up enough money for Fenland to take the faster mail coach, Walter could take the consequences.

Fenland still smarted over the Three Feathers landlord's insistence on money for a room when Fenland had already paid the White Horse. If he had not sought a refund at the White Horse, however, he never would have seen Walter's bitch, riding nice as you please in a fine black coach headed south. Damn! Where were they going? Had they learned he was after them? That fool Dossie must have tattled. He hadn't thought she'd known who he was; he had never paid her any attention, didn't think he'd ever even spoken to her.

What should he do now? Chase the bitch—who was

going who-knew-where—or hightail it to Kent, where the shipment, by God, was probably already in, and Walter would have his head. Damned if I do and damned if I don't, he thought morosely.

He'd paid for a room at the Three Feathers. The coach south was long gone; there would be another tomorrow. He would have a drink or two and think it over.

Though Elias's nose still ran and he coughed occasionally, he pronounced himself recovered and insisted on taking the ribbons the next morning. He and Dickon had conferred, and with the aid of a map supplied by the Sheffield innkeeper, they plotted possible routes. Dickon wished to avoid Bedfordshire altogether, but at the rate they were going, Bedfordshire was several days off.

He also conferred with the ladies. He was in charge of this journey; everyone acknowledged that, if silently. Years of receiving advice from his much older sister, however, had made him realize that sometimes the ladies knew what they were about. Their ideas often had merit. As a gentleman he felt he should listen to what they had to say.

What Caroline had to say was exactly what he expected: Go by way of Bedfordshire so she could see her brother Paul and learn whether he would offer her sanctuary. This Dickon was determined not to do. He asked Ruth for her thoughts.

"Your great plan to take the back roads and avoid the larger towns certainly gave us a view of south Yorkshire, did it not?" Ruth said, grinning at her brother. "I am sure it would be a glorious sight in summer, but in December? Dickon, we have been on the road forever. You must be back in the War Office soon after Twelfth Night. I for one believe we should head straight for London. Go to Peterborough and take the Great North Road again. We cannot roam all over England trying to avoid this Fenland person. I want to go home!"

"Very well," said Dickon.

And so, by slow stages, they journeyed to London.

* * *

By the time they reached the smart London townhouse shared by Lady Stilton and her brother, Caroline felt she had known the pair forever. She had had Ruth's life history from Lady Rycote, but that had been a mother's viewpoint. Ruth in person was a strong, self-sufficient woman who had little tolerance for fools and who had no delusions about the faults of her beloved younger brother. Caroline admired her tremendously and only wished she had Ruth's no-nonsense courage.

As for Dickon, Caroline began to believe he could do no wrong. When he and Ruth disagreed, as they often did, he never showed anger, but turned off her arguments with a joke. Sometimes he followed her advice; other times he smiled and did as he pleased. The arrogance he had displayed in the mail coach to Durham was as if it had never been.

"All your doing," Ruth confided to Caroline one evening before they reached London. "Dickon was too full of himself. Now he has something better to occupy his mind. I think your rescue will be the making of him."

"Oh, no!" Caroline colored. "He has been ever so kind, of course, but I cannot believe—"

"Take my word on it," said Ruth firmly.

Caroline began to feel apprehensive as they entered London. She was half afraid to look out the coach window for fear of seeing Walter stare at her in surprise, as had Fenland in Doncaster. For all her five years of living in London, nothing seemed familiar. Dickon and Ruth, she learned, lived in Mayfair on Golden Square. It was not far from Hanover Square, where she had lived with Walter, but she had never been in Golden Square before. Nor had she been anywhere else, she thought gloomily. The house in Hanover Square had been her prison.

She was determined that Lady Stilton's house in Golden Square should not become a new prison, though as prisons went it would be a luxurious one. She was quickly installed in a guest chamber decorated in cheerful yellow and cream, with windows that overlooked the back garden. It had a cream-colored marble-faced fireplace, a big, comfortable bed, and its own dressing room with a bed for Dossie. It even boasted a lady's writing desk complete with inkstand, quills, and writing paper.

Told to make herself at home, Caroline soon fell into a pleasant routine. "Morning" callers occupied many afternoons as word spread that Lady Stilton was in residence. Caroline, clad in the gowns ordered in Durham, was introduced as Mrs. Makepeace, an old friend from Durham making an extended visit. Lady Rycote had dispatched most of Mrs. Cutter's fashionable creations immediately after she heard from Ruth where to send them, and Caroline felt a new self-confidence wearing them.

She saw little of Dickon. His first order of business had been to see his banker and obtain funds to repay his sister for her loans during the journey, funds that Ruth then quietly slipped to Caroline. Caroline accepted them as a hedge against an unknown future. Dickon had then immersed himself in his work at the War Office, saying to the ladies only that reports had piled up during his absence and must be handled.

He felt a distinct letdown. Nothing at the War Office had changed; the war's end seemed no closer, and reading through hastily scribbled reports to make sense out of them was more stultifying than ever. He longed to be riding over the frozen acres at Ryfield, or guiding a coach down the Great North Road . . . His mind wandered. His immediate supervisor, Lord Avebury, more than once called him on the carpet for inattention.

He discussed it with Ruth one evening after Caroline had gone to bed. "You cannot believe how tempted I was to return to Durham with Elias," he confessed. "I kept telling myself it was because it was such a long journey for him to make alone, but in truth I cannot take the War Office much longer. I might as well be in jail."

"Now you must have an idea how Miss Caroline feels," said his sister.

"How do you mean?" Dickon asked, surprised. "She is not tied to work she despises."

"No, but she is tied. She cannot go anywhere for fear of being seen and recognized. Think about it."

How to free Miss Caroline? It was another problem for a man who believed he had enough problems already. Dickon had done everything in his power to save the lady—was she not free of her husband, of the man who pursued her, and now living a life of ease in Golden Square? Apparently that was not enough.

He had spent very little time with her since their arrival in London. He thought that best, for she affected him strangely. He knew she was forbidden territory, but that did not seem to quell his growing feelings for her. Just that morning, he'd had to conceal his desire to take her in his arms. Instead he resorted to light banter.

"You cannot want three pieces of toast," he said, nodding toward the rack. "You will get fat as a pig." He took the opportunity to study her figure. The painful thinness had given way to curves he found most interesting.

"Pig, is it?" she flung back. "And who is on his second helping of kippers?"

"You have something against kippers? No man should appear at his day's labors unless well kippered. May I kipper you, madam?" He gave her a hungry look.

"And just what does that consist of?" she asked, smiling.

"You have never been kippered? Egad. I thought every child learned of that in the schoolroom. Come closer, madam, and I shall demonstrate."

Dickon was sitting at the head of the table, Caroline at one side. She leaned nearer, laughing.

Dickon popped a kipper into her mouth. Instead of withdrawing his hand, he left his finger on her lips.

"You have to kiss the kipper-giver's fingers," he explained. "That is known as kippering." He smiled an innocent smile.

Blushing, Caroline complied.

"You see why I have kippers each morning," he said wolfishly, drawing his just-kissed fingers to his own lips.

Damn, Dickon thought, coming out of his reverie, I am playing with fire, and the flame is so hot it burns me. I want so much more. I think she does as well. Best I eat breakfast out from now on—and supper as well.

"Tell me again where I am supposed to live," Caroline said to Ruth over a cup of tea one morning. "Your friends Lady Robstart and Mrs. Hinkle seem particularly curious about it. I feel much as I did when Sir Harry began to quiz me at Ryfield—afraid I will put my foot in my mouth. It is difficult to remember a past that never happened."

Ruth laughed. "You are doing very well," she said. "Just describe the Durham countryside; I am certain those ladies were never there. What did you tell Sir Harry? I was not aware he had quizzed you."

"He asked about your sons, since of course I am supposed to know them," Caroline explained. "By the way, when will I meet them?"

"Any day now," said Ruth. "I had better tell you about them."

Will, the eldest son, who now lived in Dorset, at the Stilton family estate, arrived several days later. He was announced while Ruth and Caroline were entertaining a group of ladies that included Lady Robstart and Mrs. Hinkle.

Caroline was glad he had been announced, for she never would have known him to be Ruth's son otherwise. A man of four-and-twenty years, he was sandy-haired, with a bright smile and twinkling blue eyes. He was no taller than his mother.

Will greeted his mother, bestowed a kiss on her cheek, and turned to speak to the guests. Ruth made it easy for him, saying, "You remember . . . " and repeating each lady's name in case he had in fact forgotten.

Caroline saw the trap coming, but it was too late.

"You remember Mrs. Makepeace," said Ruth, smiling at Caroline.

Will frowned slightly and asked, "Have we met before, Mrs. Makepeace? Surely I could not forget you."

Caroline could hear the sudden buzz of conversation as Lady Robstart and Mrs. Hinkle digested this unexpected remark. She wished to sink through the floor. Instead she smiled bravely and said, "Will! You are funning me. Have I changed so much since last you were in Durham? Ruth," turning to Lady Stilton, "I have not changed that much, have I? Tell this silly boy I have not. Of course I have been ill, but now I am better."

Will appeared thoroughly perplexed, but at a glance from his mother, he seemed to realize something was afoot. He murmured, "Of course," and turned to the next guest.

Once the ladies had departed, Ruth explained Caroline's presence to her son. Caroline feared, however, that the damage had been done. The two ladies, each of whom had enough tongue for two sets of teeth, were certain to spread the story that Lady Stilton's own son did not recognize Lady Stilton's "oldest and dearest friend," a friend, moreover, who was closer to Ruth's son's age than to Ruth's own.

Caroline knew she must get away. She did not want to prove an embarrassment to her kind hostess.

January gave way to February. Caroline made the best of her voluntary confinement in Golden Square, helping Ruth give several small dinner parties and a musicale at which the newest Italian soprano sensation sang. She valued the experience. If she should decide to seek work as a housekeeper, she would know how to help her mistress plan entertainments. She had to continually remind herself of such things, knowing that though wonderfully pleasant, her current situation could not continue. She had gained weight and the worry lines in her face had eased. She took more trouble with her appearance, tried out new ways of arranging her hair, and began to feel more like her true age of two-and-twenty rather than two-and-thirty.

This was not lost on Dickon. The ugly duckling was turning into a swan, a graceful creature who haunted his dreams no matter how he avoided her when awake. His continued absences from Golden Square annoyed Ruth, who counted on him to provide a much-needed masculine presence at her entertainments. She refused to believe the War Office couldn't spare him for a spell.

"You say you are sick of the War Office, yet you spend all your time there," she upbraided him one Sunday morning when he announced he would have to miss church services again. "What is there to do on a Sunday? Surely no dispatches arrive on Sundays."

"They can arrive at any time," said Dickon, avoiding her eyes. "One never knows."

"Rubbish!" said Ruth. "You are avoiding Miss Caroline, are you not? You have developed a *tendresse* for her, I can tell. Dickon, you know this simply will not do. Why do you not take some time away from that infernal office and meet some young ladies? Young ladies who are elegible and *single*. A whole new crop is coming out this season." She paused, a gleam suddenly present in her eyes. "I know! I shall have a rout, and invite as many as the house will hold. You shall have your choice. You must promise to attend! Dickon, my boy, it is time you made your choice and settled down."

"I am much too busy at the War Office," Dickon said stiffly.

"Pah!" said his sister. "Go play with your dispatches. I must plan a rout."

Ten

Ruth set the date for her rout as February thirteenth, nearly two weeks away, and began preparations that had the house in Golden Square turned upside down. While Caroline, sitting at the desk in her bedchamber, wrote and addressed invitations, Ruth set the servants to turning out and cleaning all the first-floor rooms, polishing silver, ironing table linens, and laying in stores of foodstuffs.

Ruth had told Caroline the reason for the rout. Caroline could only agree that it was time Dickon took a wife, but the idea left her strangely bereft. That would mean he would set up an establishment of his own and she would rarely see him. Not that she saw him often as it was, but at least she knew he was available in case of need. What need? she asked herself. She needed no man. Her friendship with Ruth and Dickon would become only a pleasant memory kept alive with letters. She would start looking for a position immediately after the rout.

Seeing the fire was low and the coal scuttle empty, Caroline rose, massaged her cramped fingers, and went downstairs, scuttle in hand. The servants were so caught up in cleaning that she was not surprised her chamber had been permitted to run out of coal. One of the maids, polishing the stair rail, gasped when she saw Caroline with the empty scuttle. Without a word the maid took it from Caroline and rushed down to refill it.

Caroline found Ruth, wearing one of her oldest gowns with a mobcap on her head, discussing with a footman how best to rearrange the furniture. She wished to permit easy passage of the crowds from one room to another, yet leave chairs here and there for the older and infirm guests. Ruth drew Caroline into the discussion.

"Are you having older and infirm guests?" Caroline asked. "I had the impression they were all sweet young things to be paraded before the earl."

Ruth smiled. "It might seem so, but most of the sweet young things have mamas and papas," she said. "Then there are my own friends, who must not be ignored. Lady Robstart and Mrs. Hinkle, for example. At a rout one invites *everybody*."

"I do not believe I shall appear," said Caroline.

Ruth stared at her, arms akimbo. "Why ever not?"

"We must not forget I am in hiding. If you are inviting everybody, as you say, there could be guests who know 'John' and know his wife is missing. They might put two and two together, considering the suspicions your friends Lady Robstart and Mrs. Hinkle have put about."

"Can you see your husband letting it be known you have left him?" Ruth said. "Of course not. No one ever saw you, or so you say, so no one will miss you."

"Even so, I would prefer to keep to my chamber that day," said Caroline. "I am happy to help you, but I must decline to attend. Please understand."

Ruth believed she understood only too well. It would be difficult to watch while Dickon danced attendance on a bevy of young beauties. Her heart went out to Caroline.

Having set the rout for the day before St. Valentine's Day, Ruth planned to decorate the house with hearts. She had the servants scour the pantries and cupboards for any glassware and china in red or pink, and hired a seamstress to stitch serviettes of pink linen for the long tables where refreshments would be offered. Strings of heart cutouts were draped over mantels and hung from chandeliers. Pots of forced red tulips were distributed strategically around the house. The cook was swamped with making tiny heart-shaped tarts filled with strawberry preserves.

Finally even Ruth had had enough. Household routine had long since disappeared: meals were sketchy and late, furniture was not in its accustomed place, and the servants were weary and grouchy. Ruth pulled a heavy chair away from the wall in the library to set it back temporarily before the fire, and sank into it.

"Two more days," she mourned aloud. "By then I shall be ready for Bedlam." She rang for a pot of tea.

With the tea, brought by a clearly disgruntled maid, came her brother.

"Dickon!" she said, trying to summon some enthusiasm. "I have not seen you for days."

"This house is not fit to live in," Dickon grumbled. "I came only to tell you that I shall not be able to attend your fine party. I have just had word that the War Office—"

"Do not feed me that gammon!" Furious, Ruth rose and faced her brother. "I am doing this for you! For *you*! You will be here if I have to tie you down. You promised! Remember, you promised!"

"I did not promise. You asked me to promise, but I did not. The War Office—"

"Hang the War Office!" Ruth collapsed into her chair and buried her face in her hands. "Oh, Dickon, you must come," she sobbed. "First Miss Caroline, and now you. When I think of all the work—the time—the servants—"

"What about Miss Caroline? Has she begged off?"

"She lives in fear of being discovered," said Ruth, sniffing. "I cannot talk her out of it, though I doubt she is in any danger."

"Hmmm," said Dickon. "Very well. I shall petition Lord Avebury. Perhaps he will release me early so I can attend your rout for an hour or two."

February thirteenth arrived and everything was in readiness at the house in Golden Square except for bouquets of fresh flowers, obtained at the last minute, that Caroline was arranging under Ruth's eye. Ruth was so tired she was running on nervous energy.

Ruth surveyed the reception hall, the staircase, and the drawing room, its wide doors standing open. "It is too much," she said suddenly. "I have overdone it. I have a mind to tear down these hearts and remove half the floral arrangements. The *ton* will think I have gone mad! Oh, Caroline, I have tried too hard. I need to seek my bed and sleep for a month. My rout will be a disaster." She slumped into the nearest chair.

"There, there," said Caroline, who felt little better than Ruth. "The house looks beautiful. Your rout will be a great success. I could almost wish I were able to attend."

"It is not too late!" said Ruth eagerly. "Do come! You could wear your yellow-and-green gown—you have not worn it yet."

"How would that look with all your red hearts? No, thank you."

Despite her firm decision, Caroline could not help feeling lonely and left out as she repaired to her chamber. She had decided to have dinner sent up on a tray and spend time with a book before going to bed. Considering her fatigue, sleep would come early. She had worked nearly as hard as Ruth but would not be able to enjoy the results, she thought unhappily. She straightened. It was her decision and she would not feel sorry for herself.

The guests began arriving by late afternoon. Caroline could hear the musicians and the hum of conversation from her chamber, a hum that grew louder and more insistent. Ruth had hoped for a squeeze, and evidently she had it. Caroline tried to concentrate on her book with little success. Was the Earl of Rycote meeting a young girl who appealed to him? What would she look like? Blonde, no doubt, small and dainty, with blue eyes and a charming smile. Suddenly Caroline hated all small, dainty blondes.

A harried maid arrived with her dinner tray. "They said I was to get it here before they serve downstairs," she explained and dashed out again.

Not yet hungry, Caroline sat at the desk and ate as a means of passing the time. Half an hour went by. She was nibbling on a strawberry-filled heart tart when she heard a knock at her door. The maid come for her tray? "Come in," she called.

It was Dickon.

"Wh-what are you doing here?" she asked breathlessly.

Dickon had never looked finer. In the midst of her confusion at seeing him, she could not help but notice his dark-blue waistcoat, worn under a cream-colored coat that emphasized his wide shoulders. His pantaloons were blue, fitted snugly to well-turned legs. A froth of white ruffles from his shirt front peeped out beneath a perfectly tied cravat.

Caroline looked down at her shapeless gray gown, one of her old ones that she had donned to help with last-minute preparations for the rout.

"What are you doing here?" she repeated. Dickon just looked at her.

"Say something," she begged. Hastily, she dropped the remains of her tart on her plate, got up and brushed her skirt. She walked toward Dickon, an inquiring look on her face.

"You should be downstairs," said Dickon. He did not move.

"No! No. I explained to Ruth . . . You should not be here, your lordship. The party is for you, is it not?"

"You should be downstairs. Will you join me?" Dickon crooked his elbow and half-turned, as if to lead her out of the chamber.

"Do not be foolish." Caroline gave a nervous laugh. "Look at me, in this horrid old gown."

"Then we shall have to have our own party here," he said. "May I have this dance?" He held out his arms as if to clasp her for the waltz.

Caroline backed away. "This is not a ball," she said. "This is a rout. One does not dance at a rout."

"Excuses, excuses," said Dickon. He moved closer.

"Your lordship!" Against all reason, Caroline was frightened—terrified in fact, to the marrow of her bones. She had the strangest sense that nothing would ever be the same again, but she was powerless to intervene. She stood rooted to the floor, pinned by the dark eyes looking into hers. Her body seemed consumed by an odd, quivering heat.

"You have known this was inevitable," said Dickon. He

stood inches away, his hands rising as if to take hers. His eyes closed for a moment. "I know I must not," he said. "I am trying to contain myself." He stood immobile.

"I am losing," he said finally. "Oh, Caroline." Then his arms came around her, pressing her head to his chest, his fingers stroking her hair. He dropped little kisses where his fingers had been, then stroked again as if to rub in the kisses. After a few moments, during which Caroline stood motionless, he pulled back a little and tipped up her face.

"Tell me to go," he said. "Tell me. Or tell me that this is right, that we have been making this journey toward each other for many weeks. We cannot fight it any longer."

When she remained silent, only staring at him with wonder in her eyes, his mouth met hers. Warm and soft, his lips teased hers, seeking a response that she felt herself giving without a thought. She was conscious of the buttons on his coat, pressing into her ribs, and of the scent of wool, starch, and soap.

Caroline was like a rag doll with no will of her own. The kiss went on and on, but when Dickon ended it and drew away, she felt abandoned. Instinctively, she pressed her head against his chest once more and put her arms around him. Never had she felt so treasured, so desired.

This is what they mean when they talk about love, she realized for the first time. Oh, what she had been missing! Filled with a joyous exhilaration, she was consumed with a need to touch Dickon, to run her hands through his hair, to stroke his freshly shaven cheek, to trace the shape of his ear.

She did none of those things. She forced herself to pull away, walk over to the desk, and sit down, pushing away the tray holding the remains of her meal. Head in her hands, she stared at the inkstand.

"You know we cannot," she said in a tired voice. "Oh, Dickon, we cannot."

"Look at me and tell me we cannot," he said, standing behind her. "Turn around. Look at me."

"What do you want of me?" she cried. "God help me, I am a married woman. You wish me for your mistress, perhaps? I would be a sorry mistress." Her lip curled. "I am the original ice maiden. Did you not know?" She would not turn around, could not let him see her confusion.

"You are no ice maiden," said Dickon. He put his hands on her shoulders and slowly, slowly massaged her neck muscles. She broke out in goose flesh. It felt heavenly.

She knew if she listened to his voice, beguiling and warm as honey, or let him caress her once more, she would be lost. With enormous effort she turned to face him. "Ruth will be wondering where you are," she said. "She will expect you to help her receive her guests."

"The receiving line is all over," he said gruffly.

"But you are the guest of honor! You must be there."

"Ruth's boys are there. Let them do the pretty. Let her parade all the young chits for Will and Alfred. They are not married yet. No one will miss me."

"You know you should not be in my chamber."

"So you say. I rather thought you were glad to see me."

"Of course I am always glad to see you. You and Ruth have been nothing but kind—"

"You need not go through *that* again, as if I were a stranger who had helped you across the street. Let us face it, *Miss* Caroline. Something has developed between us." Dickon frowned. "We did not seek it; we have fought it— or at least I have. I am weary of the fight. Dash it, why do you think I spend so much time at the War Office? I can hardly bear the place. All those patriotic gentlemen pretending to be great statesmen who know just how to win the war.

"But that is neither here nor there. Can we not come to an understanding? I have little to offer you, my dear, but all I have is yours. We could flee London—live at Ryfield— my mother is fond of you; we could invent a tale that your Not-John is truly dead. Perhaps we could even go through a marriage ceremony of some sort for my mother's benefit . . . We would work it out somehow."

Caroline could not bear the yearning look in Dickon's eyes. His ideas were preposterous, as he must know himself. For them, there was no solution—but oh, how tempting he was! She must be strong. She rose and faced him.

"No, Dickon. I have seen enough of the married state to know I wish nothing more to do with it, and a sham marriage—or lack of it—with you or with anyone is quite impossible. I had already made up my mind to leave here immediately after Ruth's rout, and I shall do just that. Goodbye, Dickon." She paused, her voice breaking. "God be with you."

In response Dickon crushed her to him and covered her face with kisses. Caroline struggled feebly. He let her go for a moment, looked into her face, then gave her a searing, endless kiss on the mouth, a kiss that left her boneless and shaking.

When he let her go, she sank again into the chair, drained. Dickon turned on his heel and left the chamber, carefully closing the door behind him.

Caroline slept little that night. She relived every kiss, every caress, full of wonder that a man's attentions could be so soul-searing. Walter had been her only suitor, and Walter had never even kissed her; his intentions had been only to get her with child, and, she supposed, anything short of the ultimate act had seemed a waste of time to him. Any affection she had ever felt for Walter had disappeared on their wedding night.

After Walter's treatment of her, she had believed herself unable to respond to any man. How wrong she had been! And how hopeless was their situation. A divorce would be almost impossible, and Walter would fight the very idea even though he wanted to be rid of her. Walter wished to appear a pattern card of respectability, regardless of what he did in secret.

Worst of all, Caroline reminded herself, was the fact that Dickon would need an heir. Even if in some far-off, rosy future she should become free of Walter, she could never give Dickon an heir. Five years of failed attempts were proof of that.

Caroline tortured herself with hazy dreams of being in

Dickon's arms and thoughts of what might have been. The embers in her fireplace grew colder.

At last she mentally shook herself, rose, lit a candle, and added coals from the refilled scuttle to the fireplace.

I wonder if he realizes how much I love him, she thought as she drew out her portmanteau from the wardrobe and started to pack. I hope he can choose one of those fillies Ruth trotted out for him, live a happy life, and never have to know my heart is breaking through no fault of his.

It all came back to Walter. She had never loathed Walter so much.

Eleven

When Dickon came downstairs at eight the next morning, the house was eerily quiet. The first floor had been put back to rights as if the rout had never taken place. He made his way to the breakfast room. It was deserted. No food sat on the sideboard; no places were laid at the table. Dickon pulled the bell rope and sat down to a blinding sea of bare, polished mahogany.

At long last a drowsy maid appeared with a pot of tea on a tray with milk and sugar. "Tea, your lordship?" she asked listlessly. At his nod, she set the tray before him.

"Where is everyone?" he asked.

"Her ladyship said we was to take our rest this mornin'," she replied. "Said nobody'd be up afore noon." She gave him an accusing look. "You want breakfast, do you?"

"If possible," he replied. "How long will it be? I must go to my office."

"Dunno," said the maid, yawning, "—yer lordship," she added quickly.

"I shall not wait," said Dickon. Hastily he downed a cup of tea, set the cup down with a clatter, and left the room.

The butler was nowhere to be found, so Dickon gathered up his coat, hat, and gloves and departed, signaling for a hackney at the corner of Golden Square. He considered a hire preferable to awakening a groom and waiting while his horse was harnessed and his gig put to. The day would be over before he accomplished anything.

He had decided to resign his position in the War Office, and he wished to do it before he lost his nerve.

His tête-à-tête with Caroline the night before had had a

profound effect. He had been carried away, he admitted now. How could he have expected her to agree to such cork-brained schemes as he had offered? He could not afford to keep her; it was only by sharing with Ruth that he was able to live in a proper house, keep a proper carriage, maintain a proper wardrobe. His situation would not improve until he returned to Ryfield and ran it himself. That could not be accomplished overnight. Best he left the War Office, traveled to Durham, and began to recoup the estate's losses.

That would also remove the overwhelming temptation to capture Caroline and flee with her somewhere, anywhere. Not that she would agree, he knew. She would never go away with him willingly. Nor would she feel comfortable remaining under the same roof with him—though her discomfort would be no worse than his! "Discomfort" was a pale word for what he had felt when she suddenly became all stiff and proper, just as he thought he had her all soft and yielding. Damn, damn. He must leave so that she would feel able to stay. He could tell she was uneasy about visiting her brother Paul, and as for taking a post as a housekeeper, that was the most ridiculous thing he had ever heard.

He was among the earliest arrivals at the War Office. The stack of dispatches on his desk seemed even higher than it had been when he left the day before. He marched out again and sought a bake shop for something to eat while working.

At ten of the clock he asked for a meeting with Lord Avebury, who never arrived at the War Office before ten. He was told Lord Avebury had sent word that he would not be in for two days; he had been called to Oxford to extricate his son from some scrape.

Dickon sighed and returned to his pile of dispatches. Skimming them hastily, he found no mention of Captain Benjamin Richardson. Brother Ben, apparently, still lived to fight.

At one of the clock Dickon left his cramped office. He notified no one of his early departure, and no one asked where he was going. He stopped at a public house nearby, downed too many stiff brandies, and took a hackney home.

Ruth awoke at noon, noted the time on her mantel clock, and snuggled back into her pillows. She would not have to leave her bed all day if she did not wish to, and she was not sure she wished to. Thank all the gods in heaven that the rout was a thing of the past. It had been the most ambitious undertaking of her entire life, she was sure—perhaps because the reason for it had been so vital. She had never been so concerned about the success of one of her entertainments.

She made a wry face. Weeks of preparation, all to parade the most promising young ladies of the season before her stubborn brother, and with what result? Dickon had spent no more than an hour at the rout, presenting the same mechanical smile to each young lady, then moving on quickly to the next. To her horror, at one point Ruth had discovered him deep in an involved conversation with Lady Robstart— Lady Robstart, married and near old enough to be his mother! Soon after that he had disappeared.

If it had not been for her own dear sons, Will and Alfred, Ruth would have considered the rout a total disaster. George had been there as well, with his wife, Marian, but the unmarried Will and Alfred had outdone themselves. They had made any number of silly chits feel admired and special. She was proud of them.

Ruth would give Dickon a stern lecture just as soon as he deigned to come home from that poky office of his. Meanwhile, she decided to rise after all, and seek out Caroline, who would be agog to hear all about the rout.

Ruth walked down the hall to Caroline's door and knocked. No response. She knocked again, with the same result. Then she realized it was past noon; Caroline had not been at the rout, had not been up late. She would be downstairs, of course.

Ruth dressed and went downstairs. The breakfast room was vacant, a pot of cold tea and a used cup on a tray the only signs that anyone had been there. No servants were in evidence.

Ruth pulled the bell cord. When a footman appeared she asked where Mrs. Makepeace might be. The footman looked surprised and said he did not know. A canvass of those servants who were at their posts—several were not—produced no information. No one had seen Mrs. Makepeace that morning.

Ruth climbed the stairs in haste and opened Caroline's door without knocking. The room was empty. The wardrobe was empty.

A carefully folded note had been placed on the little writing desk.

"Thank you both from the bottom of my heart," it read. "I am going to my brother's; I have put it off too long already. You will hear from me once I am settled."

It was signed, "Caroline Makepeace."

"Oh, no!" Ruth was devastated. Caroline had not known her brother Paul's exact direction—how could she go off alone, with only old Dossie for company, when she was not even sure where she was going? It was the outside of enough, that was what it was, and Dickon was going to have to do something about it. If he ever came home from the War Office . . .

Ruth caught herself. What right did she or Dickon have to tell Caroline where to go or what to do? Caroline was a grown woman, capable of making her own decisions. Ruth would have to tell Dickon that Caroline was gone, of course, for he would notice her absence immediately. Perhaps she would try to restrain Dickon from following Caroline.

But even if he did try to follow her, Ruth realized with a start, they had no idea of Caroline's brother's last name, or where in Bedfordshire he lived. Could one travel all over Bedfordshire asking only for "Paul"?

When Dickon arrived at three in the afternoon somewhat the worse for wear, Ruth pounced on him.

"Thank God you are home early," she said. "Caroline has flown."

Two months we have known her, and we still do not know her name, her family's name, their place of residence, her husband's name, or his place of residence, Dickon grumbled to himself. Why did she never confide in us? We would have kept her secrets.

He was at the Bull and Mouth again, hoping against hope that Miss Caroline would take the mail coach to Bedfordshire. He looked down the stretch of St. Martin's-le-Grand upon which all the mail coaches traveled. The eight o'clock coach wasn't scheduled to depart for another two hours, but already passengers were gathering and coaches were being made ready. None of the nearly four hundred horses kept in the underground stables had yet been hitched. Dickon wandered toward the rough bench where he had first seen Caroline. It was vacant.

The weather had taken a turn for the worse. A cold wind whipped Dickon's coat and threatened to carry away his hat. Some of the prospective passengers in the inn yard sought shelter.

What, Dickon wondered, would a lone lady and her servant do all day? They had evidently left Golden Square that morning; it was now ten or twelve hours later. He made inquiries as to which coach would go to Bedford, found it, and settled to wait.

The wait seemed interminable. Tired of standing in the cold, Dickon leaned a negligent shoulder against the Bedfordshire coach until an irate guard shooed him off. He paced back and forth, from the Bedford coach to the King's Lynn coach and back again. He watched passengers enter, while others climbed on top, and the red-coated guard with his blunderbuss mounting up behind, ready to defend the Royal Mail from all comers. Before eight o'clock he heard horns and the cheers from the spectators, and saw the Bedford coach, third in line among a dozen or more, pick up its mail at the General Post Office and start north up St. Martin's-le-Grand. There was, however, no sign of Miss Caroline or her maid.

Cold, dispirited, and defeated, Dickon went home.

Maybe it was just as well that Lord Avebury was away, he decided as he warmed himself at the library fire. He did not confide his scheme to resign and remove to Durham to his sister, who pressed hot chocolate on him and insisted on hearing every detail of his search for Caroline.

He might as well face it: his desire to leave London had as much to do with removing himself from Caroline as it did with reclaiming and overseeing his estate. He knew if he and Caroline continued to live in the same house he would not be able to keep his hands off her, and he would be damned if he would continue to spend all his time at the dratted War Office.

Now that she was gone, his priorities suddenly shifted. He had to find her. In many ways she was an innocent; kept a virtual prisoner for five years, she was unaware of the dangers and pitfalls of life in the wider world. How was she to get on, with no help from anyone but an elderly maid? Dickon gave no consideration to her brother Paul or any other relative—obviously they cared little for her or she would have sought them out in the first place.

"Where could she have gone?" Dickon asked his sister, not really expecting an answer.

"Would she have taken a stagecoach instead of the mail?" Ruth wondered. "It would not be so dear, and she must be counting her pennies now that she is on her own. I never thought a stagecoach was safe, particularly for a woman alone! They are so crowded—people packed in like sheep in a fold—and often prey to highwaymen. Somehow I do not see Caroline in a stagecoach."

"Nor I," said Dickon, "but I shall endeavor to find out just the same. If I find no sign of her in London, I intend to travel to Bedfordshire and make inquiries. It may be for nought, but I feel I must take the chance." He sighed and examined the dregs in his chocolate cup. "I wonder whether she is warm, and whether some kind soul is offering her chocolate," he said softly. He shook his head. Rising, he prepared to leave.

"Just a moment," said Ruth. "You have not explained why you left my rout last night. The idea! After all my effort—I was humiliated, Dickon. A number of people remarked on your absence. You are not about to tell me you returned to the War Office, are you? That will not fadge, Dickon."

Dickon drew himself up and looked down his nose at his sister. "I was otherwise engaged," he said. "I never cared for your plan to parade a bevy of hopefuls past me in any case. I am capable of finding my own wife when I wish to marry.

"Admit it, Ruth. You had a splendid time at your own party and were able to introduce Will and Alfred to any number of young chits. You did not need me at all! So I left."

"Where did you go?" Ruth gave him a sharp look.

"Never you mind," said Dickon. He strode out of the library before she could say any more.

Dickon did not earn his keep at the War Office in the following weeks. He appeared each morning, scanned dispatches at lightning speed, and left after a few hours to haunt coaching inns that catered to stagecoaches as well as those that supplied mail coaches: he even inquired at stables that had post chaises for hire. He learned nothing of value.

Finally he asked for emergency leave (his mother again at death's door, he explained lugubriously) and drove his gig to Bedford.

The town of Bedford was tiny compared with London, which meant he had fewer coaching inns to investigate, but he had no more success. He remembered a remark of Caroline's, believing her brother Paul lived near Sandy, so one fine day when the sun shone and the spring bulbs hesitantly peeped out of the leaf cover he drove there.

Sandy was hardly more than a hamlet, a few houses and a shop or two on either side of a single street. He stopped before a bakery shop where delightful smells beckoned anyone within fifty feet. Now, he thought, what can I ask of these people?

He entered the shop, sniffing appreciatively, and bought two buns. As he dug in his pocket for change, he smiled in a friendly fashion and asked, "Do you get trade from a very large area?"

The shop assistant, a stout woman of uncertain years with a large white cap on her head, looked startled. "Sometimes," she said.

"I should think the good smells here would bring in customers from miles around," said Dickon.

The woman gave him a grim smile. "No different from any other bakery," she said. "Lots of 'em around here does their own baking. But we get by." She returned to her work, arranging small cakes in rows on a large platter, alternating white-iced cakes with pink-iced ones.

"Any big houses nearby?" Dickon persisted.

The woman hesitated. "Not what you'd call *big*," she said. "The biggest would be Sir Charles Lapham, I suppose. That would be down the road east. Then there's Sir Humphrey Smart, but his kind don't buy here. Too high in the instep. Why? You wanting to sell 'em something?" She looked at him curiously.

"I am looking for the home of a man named Paul," said Dickon, "but I cannot for the life of me remember his last name. Do you know any families nearby with a gentleman named Paul at the head? And no, I do not wish to sell them anything."

"Paul." The woman considered. "Only Paul I know of hereabouts is Paul Crask—he's the blacksmith's boy. 'Bout one- or two-and-twenty—would that be your man?"

"Thank you, no," said Dickon. He sighed. "Thank you for your help. I shall enjoy your buns."

He drove back to Bedford, gathered his belongings from the inn where he had been staying, and headed for London. He had never felt so frustrated. He could not search every inch of Bedfordshire when he did not know for whom he was searching. His journey had been for nought. At least he had been able to get away from the War Office for a few days.

He appeared at his office late the next morning, only to find that the stack of dispatches on his desk had reached monumental proportions. Some of his co-workers grumbled that the Old Man had suggested they might like to share Dickon's load, but they had their own duties, thank you.

Lord Avebury, the Old Man himself, appeared shortly, looking harried.

"Glad you're back," he said. "Your mother . . . did she . . . ?"

"Did she what?" Dickon said before he thought. He caught himself. "She is much improved, sir. Thank you."

"Glad to hear it," said Lord Avebury.

Dickon managed to lighten the load of papers on his desk in the days that followed, but his thoughts tended to stray. Where could Caroline be? Was she all right? Why had she not notified them of her whereabouts as promised in her note? Whenever it rained, he pictured her caught without an umbrella, her pink bonnet dripping and drooping, looking for shelter but failing to find it until she caught a fever. Invariably, the vision ended with her lying in a poor garret (it was never clear how she got to the garret), calling weakly for him with her dying breath. When the wind blew, he saw her shivering, dressed in rags with a thin shawl pulled around her shoulders, offering lavender for sale on the streets but failing to compete with the more experienced lavender sellers. When the sun shone, he envisioned her creeping from her garret to find a bit of warmth and cheer on a bench in one of London's parks. She was always pale, undernourished, sad, hopeless. She needed him. He was certain of it.

But he could not find her.

"Your mother ill again?" Lord Avebury asked Dickon one day in early March.

"Oh, no, sir. Thank you, sir." Dickon stood, making a muddle of his "read" and "unread" dispatch piles as he brushed against them.

"Something is eating you," said his superior. "Can't make head or tail of your last report." Lord Avebury rattled a paper before Dickon's eyes, a paper Dickon recognized. "See here," said Avebury. "You are talking about the Third Foot, the Buffs, and here you quote Lieutenant Colonel William Stuart, but at the bottom of the page, *here*"—he waved the paper wildly—"you are quoting someone named Makepeace! For God's sake, Rycote, you know as well as I do that Lieutenant Colonel Stuart commands the Third Foot. Who is this man Makepeace? Never heard of him."

Dickon turned red as a beetroot. "Sorry, sir," he said. "A slip of the pen. It shall not happen again."

Avebury gave him a doubting look. "See that it does not," he said. "Hmmm." He hesitated, glanced again at Dickon, and left the tiny office.

Dickon painstakingly reread the Stuart dispatch with the movements of the Third Foot, or what was left of them since their catastrophic encounter with the French at Albuhera in 1811, and wrote a new report. He wrote several more reports in the next days. He was very careful.

He arrived home after an exhausting day spent trying to decipher the impossible penmanship of an obscure captain—did the man mean "gun carriage" or "hen porridge"?—to find Ruth in a frenzy.

"She is found!" Ruth greeted him before the butler had taken his hat. "Dickon! You must go after her! Do not bother to remove your coat. I will go with you—I must get my cloak—oh, where did I leave my gloves? Mercy! There is no time to waste." Ruth, his calm, sensible sister, rushed about as if demented, choosing a bonnet only to cast it aside and choose another. She had a green glove on one hand and when she could not find its mate, snatched a gray glove instead.

Dickon knew how she felt. It seemed the day had suddenly taken on a warm glow, and he was filled with a furious excitement. At last! Caroline was found! "Where is she!" he demanded. "How did you find her? Is she all right? For heaven's sake, Ruth, tell me!"

"We must be gone," Ruth said, dragging him bodily out of the house. "I will tell you on the way. A hackney, do you think?"

"Yes, a hackney. Do come along!" A needless request on Dickon's part, for Ruth hurried toward the Upper John Street corner of the square well ahead of her brother.

Once settled in a worn vehicle, Ruth directed the driver to Charing Cross and then told Dickon what she knew.

"Dossie appeared this afternoon," she reported. "Said she

disliked seeking our help, but did not know where else to turn. Miss Caroline, she said, has been trying to make a living as a seamstress. They never left London! Caroline makes christening gowns, if you can imagine such a thing. Today she was to deliver some finished gowns to the shop, and Dossie took that opportunity to visit us. Poor old thing, she tried to walk to Golden Square, but lost her way and had to take a hackney. You may be sure I gave her the money to take a hackney back. I have Caroline's direction right here." She pulled a slip of paper from her reticule. "It is one of those mean little streets off Charing Cross. Oh, Caroline! Why did you do it?"

"A seamstress!" Dickon roared. "Wait until I get my hands on her!" He pounded the shabby squabs of the carriage in futile fury. "That is no better than her addlepated notion of becoming a housekeeper!"

"It seems she has had a deal of experience in sewing christening gowns," said Ruth. "Dossie reports she kept herself occupied thusly while awaiting the birth of her babes, always hoping . . . until it became something of a hobby, a sad one, I fear."

"She could hardly support herself and Dossie on such a pittance," said Dickon, somewhat calmer now. "Have they had enough to eat? A decent place to live?"

"Dossie gave me no particulars; she was anxious to get back before Caroline learned of her delay."

The hackney paused as the driver called out, "Charing Cross!" Ruth gave him further directions. They proceeded up Charing Cross Road for a short distance, then turned into a dingy alley lined with hovels and ramshackle buildings. The hackney stopped.

Ruth gazed in wonder at the disreputable building in front of them as Dickon helped her from the carriage. "Mercy!" she cried. "I never knew such places existed!"

"London has much worse," said her brother. "Surely you knew that."

The building, which might once have been a private home, was now evidently a rooming house. A flyspecked sign in a window read "To Let." They climbed the steps, littered with debris, and Dickon knocked on a door devoid of any knocker. A slatternly woman who reeked of gin finally opened it. She gave them an insolent stare.

"Seein' 'ow the other 'alf lives?" she asked. She spat on the landing, narrowly missing Ruth's foot.

"You have a Mrs. Makepeace here?" Dickon asked.

"Nay." She started to close the door.

Dickon quickly put his foot into the opening. "A young seamstress, who has an elderly companion," he elaborated. "She may be using another name."

The woman scratched her head, knocking her cap askew. "We got some seamstresses 'ere," she said. "I keep me a refined place, I'd 'ave you know. A group o' fine young leddies, they are." She opened the door another inch.

"Perhaps one of them is Miss Caroline," said Dickon.

"Miss Caroline. Hmm. I got Miss Maudie, and Miss Belva, and Miss . . . Ah. Miss Caroline. That must be the quiet one. We 'ardly ever sees her. Lives up top. Only been 'ere a few weeks."

"Yes," said Ruth eagerly. "May we go up?"

"Nuffin's stopping ye, is it?" The woman opened the door, drew back, and straightened her cap. "Up top," she directed them.

Dickon and Ruth climbed two flights of creaking stairs. The second flight ended at a door whose knob was nearly invisible in the weak light coming from below. Dickon fumbled until he found it. Then he knocked. If there was no answer, he would go in anyhow.

"Who is it?" came from the other side.

"Ruth!" said Ruth.

There was no response, but they could hear furniture being moved. The door opened. Caroline stood inside, her look of amazement turning swiftly into embarrassed confusion.

"Oh," she said. "C-come in." She moved back, nearly stumbling over the heavy old chair, its upholstery threadbare, that must have been shoved against the door. She pushed the chair farther away from the door in little fits and starts, intent upon her task. She did not look at her visitors.

Dickon's hungry glance took in the familiar old gray gown, which hung on her like sacking; the sturdy half-boots, her happy find in long-ago Doncaster; the rough, reddened hands, now making ineffectual swipes at the ground-in stains on the chair back. He checked an overwhelming urge to take her in his arms.

"How did you find me?" Caroline asked. She stood now behind the chair, her hands resting on its back. She seemed to need it for support.

Ruth wanted no blame to fall on the loyal Dossie. "Never mind," she said. "Caroline, this is folly. This is no place for you. Come home with us."

Caroline gave Dickon a meaningful look before she said, "I think not. I refuse to be a burden on you any longer. I am making out very well, Of course it is good to see you, but . . . Do come see what I am doing."

She led them over to Dossie, who sat quietly stitching by the light of a single candle. The maid was making tucks in a tiny garment of fine cotton. Caroline took the piece from her and displayed it proudly to the visitors. "It will have lace around the neck and sleeves," she said. "Fine, soft lace, of course, that will not scratch its wearer. This one has a row of tucks down the front. I had been doing smocking, but tucks are faster and of course speed counts in piece-work. That is a shame, for I would love to add some embroidery sometimes . . . You know that families often pass their christening robes down from generation to generation. I would like to think some babe will wear this fifty or a hundred years from now." She smoothed the little garment with loving fingers. "Dossie helps me. We are doing well. It was kind of you to come. I wish I could offer you some refreshment before you leave, but I—"

"Cut line, Caroline," Dickon bellowed. "Look at this place. A single room with a window so dirty I doubt the sun ever penetrates. The paper is peeling off the walls! No carpet! No fire in the fireplace! No fuel! Look at that furniture! A single narrow bed for the two of you! How you can—"

"Dossie and I keep each other warm," Caroline said, and smiled fondly at the old woman.

"You are coming home with us," Dickon said firmly. "We insist. Ruth, do we not?"

"Indeed we do," said Ruth. "This very night. May I help you pack? Dossie, where is Miss Caroline's portmanteau?"

The willing Dossie produced it from under the bed. It already held several gowns, for the room had no wardrobe. The two women's outer garments hung from pegs on the wall. Packing took only a few minutes despite Caroline's protests. She sat in the big, threadbare chair until Dickon picked up the half-finished christening gown and asked, "What do I do with this?"

"Take care!" she cried. She jumped up, took the little garment from him with reverent hands, and folded it into a bit of paper. "I must keep it clean," she explained. "They take off if a gown is soiled." She tucked it on top of her belongings in the portmanteau.

Dickon took her cloak from a peg and held it for her. "The rent is paid for the week," Caroline mourned. Nevertheless she let him wrap her in the cloak. As he snugged the collar around her neck, he kneaded her shoulders and upper back for a few moments with strong fingers, bringing forth such an incredible sensation that she wanted to sink to the floor. She felt herself back in her chamber in Golden Square the night of the rout. This gentlemen's very touch, now as then, stirred yearnings that she found increasingly difficult to suppress.

Dickon, she thought ruefully, was becoming as dangerous to her well-being as Walter. Nevertheless, she left the cold, shabby little room, going docilely down the stairs and out into the alley. They had to walk, single file, to Charing Cross before they could find a hackney. No hackneys frequented the alley by choice.

Caroline was silent during the drive to Golden Square, despite the efforts of Ruth and Dickon to make conversation. She was in turmoil.

What, she wondered, had she gained? She had not even supported herself and Dossie; they had lived on the remainder of the proceeds from the sale of her jewelry. And now they were to go back to Golden Square, where Dickon was. How was she to resist him?

She sat dry-eyed, dreading the future. Nothing was solved. She had no means of support. She would have to deny her attraction to Dickon. Was that not better than never seeing him at all? She could not decide.

Twelve

Dickon strongly suspected Caroline had not been eating adequately. Otherwise, why did she seem ravenous at the supper put before them soon after their return to Golden Square? When Dickon glanced at her plate, then at her face, she blushed.

"I must allow I have missed your cook's fine meals," she said. "Had you ever eaten on Porridge Island, you would understand."

"Porridge Island?" Ruth inquired. "Where is that? In the Thames?"

"Hardly," she replied. "It is a collection of food shops and the like, not far from where we were living. We had no means of cooking in our room, you see, except perhaps water for tea heated at the fireplace—and we rarely had a fire. Mrs. Hobbs frowned upon cooking in rooms. Attracted mice, she said."

"Mrs. Hobbs was that gin-soaked creature who let us in?" Dickon said.

"Gin? Is that what it was? I did wonder."

Dickon shook his head in wonderment. What an innocent she was! How could anyone live twenty-two years and not recognize one foxed by gin?

Pressed for an account of her life since she had left them, Caroline told of seeking out a shop that carried christening gowns and offering her services. She had been lucky; the shopkeeper had asked for a sample instead of turning her away. As she left the shop, she was joined by another young woman who, it turned out, also sewed for the shop. When Caroline asked where the other young woman lived and said she was in need of a room, the other young woman, Miss Maudie, took her to Mrs. Hobbs's rooming house. Miss Maudie lived below Caroline. They had become friends of a sort. Miss Maudie had led her to Porridge Island, had shown her the shortest route from the rooming house to the shop, and had advised her on the current rate for christening gowns so she would not be cheated. Caroline's sample had been accepted and she was in business.

"How did you explain Dossie?" Ruth asked. Few seamstresses had maids!

"Fortunately, I had thought of that," said Caroline. "I pretended she was my aunt. Maudie no doubt wondered why my aunt always addressed me as 'Miss Caroline' but I never explained."

"You never tried to find you brother Paul?" Dickon asked.

"No. I decided it was too dangerous. What could I do if Paul insisted on notifying 'John' of my presence? You had remarked once that London would be the last place 'John' would expect to find me, so I felt quite safe with Mrs. Hobbs. In all of London Mrs. Hobbs's rooming house would be the last place 'John' would look." Caroline smiled for the first time.

"I searched for you in Bedfordshire," Dickon told her. "It was useless, of course. I had no knowledge of your brother's last name."

"You did?" Caroline's heart warmed. He had done that for her? She loved him more than ever. She looked down at her plate to hide the tears in her eyes.

"Do you not think it time to tell us your brother's last name?" Dickon chided her gently. "I promise you I shall not tell a soul, never use it against you, never seek to learn more if you do not wish to tell us. For months now we have been in the dark as to who you are, while you know all about us. Is that fair? Surely, Caroline, you know by this time that you can trust us."

"Yes," said Caroline. "Of course you're right—I've not been fair. The family name is Lapham. I was born Caroline Lapham." She heaved a great sigh. At last it was out. She would not tell them her married name, however. Not that she did not trust them, but her fear of Walter ran so deep she had vowed she would tell no one his name. Somehow, some time, the wrong person could hear.

"Lapham!" Dickon pounded his fist on the table, making the cups jump in their saucers. "Lapham, by God! In Sandy I learned of a Lapham living nearby, but his given name was—let me think—Charles, I believe. Yes. Sir Charles Lapham."

"Charles is my third brother," said Caroline. "So *he* is the one living near Sandy! I knew one of them did, but I had believed it to be Paul. Just as well I did not go looking for Paul at Sandy, is it not?" She laughed without amusement. "Charles was in the army, but was injured and invalided home. He lost three fingers on his left hand and has a damaged knee, I was told." She sat back, lost in reverie. She had not seen Charles since he was a mischievous boy. He had loved to climb apple trees and toss green apples at unsuspecting passersby, including herself. He would not be able to climb apple trees now.

She roused herself and looked at Ruth and Dickon. Both wore expressions of loving sympathy. What good friends she had gained on that December mail-coach journey! "I hope you will continue to call me Caroline Makepeace," she said. "We must not confuse those of your friends who have met me."

"Of course," Ruth murmured. "Come now. Let us get you settled once again in your chamber."

Dickon grew even unhappier at the War Office. Lord Avebury seemed to doubt his accuracy in collating dispatches to give a broad picture of what was going on in any given battle zone. That was what Dickon had been directed to do, but it was not easy. Ten dispatches might concern ten widely separated areas, and it could be days or weeks before he received more information on any one of them.

Lord Avebury knew this, but Dickon suspected the Old Man had lost confidence in him. Two instances of a mother at death's door, the inadvertent quotation from one "Makepeace," the slipshod reports he had turned in while he was beside himself with worry over Caroline—they all added up.

Thus he was expecting the worst when he was summoned into Lord Avebury's office one day in late March. Perhaps he would be sacked; then he could repair to Durham with a clear conscience and get away from Caroline. Life in the same house with her was becoming unbearable. She treated him with the same casual friendship that she gave Ruth. But sometimes a look passed between them, a look that told him if she were not a married woman, if only circumstances were different, they would be more than casual friends.

"Yes, sir." Dickon had been ushered into Lord Avebury's office, a large, impressive room where Avebury sat behind an enormous polished desk. On the desk were pens, a pen knife, an inkpot, sand, miniatures of his wife and son, and a single sheet of paper. "You sent for me?"

"Sit down, Rycote." Lord Avebury waved toward the dark-green leather-upholstered chair facing him. "I get the idea you are not enamored of your work. Correct?"

"I try to do my best, sir," said Dickon.

"That is no answer. Your best has been slipping, my boy. Your mind has been elsewhere. Is it your mother? I recall she has been gravely ill."

"Ah—no, sir. She is much improved. May I offer you my resignation, sir?" Dickon tried to keep the jubilation from his voice.

Lord Avebury chuckled. "Hoping I would sack you for your sins, were you? Not bloody likely. We need you, Rycote, but I believe a change of scene would do you good. How would you like to leave London for a while?"

"You mean go on leave? That would most welcome, sir. I could repair to Durham, see to the estate, sir. It needs my—"

"Oh, no." Avebury stopped him. "Not that at all. Rycote, we want someone to look into a matter in Kent. Seems someone there is shipping arms and ammunition to France. That will not do, my boy. Good English guns going to

France to be used against us! We have very little information. Someone heard something and became suspicious, and thank God the word reached us. Can I interest you?"

This was so far from what Dickon expected that it took him a few moments to absorb it. The more he thought about it, the more he liked it. He would be away from the hated War Office—and from the temptation of Caroline—out in the fresh Kentish countryside, not tied to a stuffy office, and on his own, with no one to order him about.

"I am delighted to accept," he said. "Where in Kent do I start?"

"Romney Marsh."

"I might have known." Dickon searched his memory for what he knew of Romney Marsh. At the southeast tip of Kent, it was a vast, flat, mysterious area populated only by sheep and smugglers, from what he had heard. Only those who lived there a lifetime knew their way through the maze of water channels. Dickon had his job cut out for him.

"When do I start?" he asked.

"I have a mind to put young Bardsley on the dispatches," said Lord Avebury. "Explain your work to him, then go. Say Monday next?" He rose and shook Dickon's hand. "I will have Colonel Davenport in to meet with you before you go. He is the one who brought us the information."

Dickon returned to his desk, his head spinning. He had a deal to do before Monday.

Caroline had settled into the house in Golden Square almost as if she had never left it. Almost, because never before had she so appreciated a warm fire on a cold day, excellent meals that appeared without her lifting a finger, a pleasant, airy chamber that was twice the size of the one in Mrs. Hobbs's rooming house, and best of all, good friends. Maudie had been all that was friendly, but they came from two different worlds. Maudie had no acquaintance with the finer things of life. Caroline made a face at that thought. How holier-than-thou it sounded. Just the same, she was glad to be back to her accustomed spot.

She continued to sew the christening gowns. She had

always enjoyed the work and it gave her something useful to do. She intended to deliver a parcel of gowns to the shop, which had come to depend on her as one of several sources. Dossie did the plain sewing of seams and hems, but her eyesight was not sharp enough for the intricate trims or embroidery Caroline loved to add. She believed she could take more time on each garment now; a high volume was not so pressing.

Still she felt hopelessly indebted to her host and hostess. Ruth seemed to have plenty of the ready, though she did not display it. Dickon, she knew, did not. It took every penny he made to pay his share of the house, the servants, the carriage; very little came in from Ryfield. Caroline was privy to several of their financial discussions, though she tried to avoid them; she was too embarrassed that she was unable to contribute.

When she had completed six exquisite christening gowns, she decided to deliver them and collect the few shillings they would bring. A hackney to the shop and back would cost almost as much as she would make, but the shop was too far from Golden Square to walk. She would not ask to use Dickon's gig. That would require a groom, for she had no experience driving.

First, though, she wished to show her handiwork to Ruth. She found Ruth going through some old clothes she planned to donate to charity.

Ruth laid aside the gown she had been examining. "I seem to have put on some weight," she said ruefully. "Cannot fasten the buttons any longer."

"Can you not let it out?" Caroline asked.

"It has been let out already. What have you there?"

Caroline showed her. As Ruth exclaimed over Caroline's workmanship, they heard Dickon arrive downstairs.

"Ruth!" he called. "And Miss Caroline. I have news."

Soon they were settled in the library and tea had been ordered.

Dickon told them as much as he knew about his assignment. He tried to be calm, but here before his best audience he could not hide his enthusiasm and excitement. He paced up and down gesticulating.

"But Romney Marsh!" Ruth exclaimed. "It will be like finding a needle in a haystack. How do you plan to go about it?"

"I have been thinking. I shall probably make my headquarters at Dymchurch, which is said to be a hotbed of smuggling, and keep my eyes and ears open. Beyond that—how can I say?"

"Dymchurch. I have heard of that name somewhere," said Caroline. Suddenly it came to her. "I know! That is where this relative of my husband lives. The one 'John' visits regularly. I cannot recall his name; I have never met him."

Dickon pricked up his ears. No, he decided, there was no connection. Why should he think her aristocratic husband's relative had anything to do with smuggling arms to France? He would put that out of his mind. Just in case, however, he asked Caroline to tell him the man's name should it come to her.

"How long will you be away?" Ruth asked.

"Who knows? Be assured I shall write and keep you informed. I shall be in no hurry. What an opportunity to get away from the blasted War Office! I can hardly wait."

Caroline listened with concern. This was no country house party; Dickon would be in very real danger. Anyone involved in sending arms to the enemy would not hesitate to kill if discovered.

She could see, however, that he would enjoy the chase. It was much like their flight from James Fenland, a time when Dickon pitted his wits against an adversary and relished every moment of it. Dickon, she thought, was the perfect man for the assignment.

"Congratulations," she said heartily. She would not reveal how much she would miss him. "You can do it, I'm sure. Just be careful."

"Oh, I shall be," he said, smiling in anticipation.

On Friday Dickon had his meeting with Colonel Davenport. The old soldier was officially retired, but that did not stop him from taking a keen interest in the progress of the war. He had been in Kent observing the fortifications erected against a possible French invasion—strictly on his own, he assured Dickon, for he no longer held any official post—when he had heard the rumor.

"One of my old staff, Captain Ferris he was, before he lost a leg, met up with me in Rye," he said. "We had a drink or two for old times' sake and he told me about this rumor. Hopping mad, he was, that an Englishman would do such!

"After the third drink he admitted he was not above a bit of smuggling himself—he had a nice little job going in French brandy. 'Doin' no harm to anyone,' he said. 'What can a man do with but one leg?' He has a regular delivery route for his brandy. Someone else brings it in. Well, that is no matter. I shan't report him. He was a good lad.

"I asked him what he knew about this rumor, and he clammed up. Afraid to peach, no doubt, for fear of being caught. I had to buy him more drinks before he would say another word, and by then he was half-seas over, so who knows how good his information is? He muttered, 'Watch Carroway.'

"That don't tell you much, does it, lad? I never heard the name before, but there must be someone named Carroway living on the Kent coast. It is up to you to find him."

"I believe there is a Viscount Carroway living in London," Dickon mused. "Never met him myself. He cannot be the man, but perhaps it is some relative of his. The name is not a common one."

"Go to it, lad," said the colonel. "England will thank you. From what Lord Avebury tells me, you can do it if anyone can."

"He said that?" Dickon was inordinately pleased. He had believed Lord Avebury merely tolerated him. "Thank you, sir," he told the old colonel. "I shall do my best."

Dickon could hardly wait to tell Ruth and Caroline of his conversation with the colonel. The information he had was not to be divulged, of course, but he knew the two ladies who were his closest confidantes would not breathe a word. He wished for his old friend Harry Wadsworth. This was a man's undertaking and he needed to talk it over with a man. Failing that, he would talk it over with his sister and his . . . love. His love. Yes, that was what she was.

He had briefed his successor and cleared his desk; he had only a few last-minute notes to write on Saturday, so he went home immediately after his meeting. He found Ruth and Caroline in the back garden, exclaiming over the spring flowers now coming into bloom. He plucked a brilliant yellow daffodil and presented it to Caroline with a bow.

She grinned. "Trying to sweeten me up, are you?" she asked. "It will not do you a bit of good."

"I am devastated," he replied solemnly. So she wished to cast him as a harmless flirt, did she? He glanced at Ruth. She returned an enigmatic smile

"Send this heartless chit in to order tea," he said to his sister. "I have much to report."

Again settled around the fire in the library, they all drank tea while Dickon began a recital of the conversation he had had with Colonel Davenport.

"This Ferris chap was in Rye," he pointed out, "so maybe I should work out of Rye rather than Dymchurch. Perhaps I can find him—it should not be difficult to seek out a one-legged man—and get more details."

"What details did you learn?" Caroline asked.

"Only one—he said something about 'Watch Carroway,' whoever Carroway may be."

Caroline shrieked.

Dickon and Ruth looked at her in consternation. "Whatever is the matter?" Ruth demanded.

"Oh, my God," said Caroline. "Oh, my God."

The other two waited silently until Caroline could collect herself. Ruth fumbled for her little container of hartshorn and remembered it was upstairs in her chamber. She scorned the stuff, but Lady Robstart and other visitors occasionally called for it when repeating some particularly shocking bit of gossip.

"Walter Carroway, Viscount Carroway, is my husband," said Caroline. Her vow never to reveal his name meant nothing now; if Walter was a traitor, she would do whatever she could to bring him down.

She was greeted by dead silence.

Finally Dickon spoke. "Dear Lord," he said.

"That does not mean he is involved in smuggling arms to France," said Ruth quickly. "He is in London, is he not? I hardly see him in Kent—oh, no! You did say he had a relative in Dymchurch? Could that mean anything?" She frowned.

"He goes to see this relative regularly," Caroline reported. "I wish I could think of his name! Oh, yes, he sometimes takes James Fenland with him. Not always. Perhaps Fenland meets him there; I do not know."

"There, there," said Ruth. "We are condemning the man when we know nothing about it. Some other Carroway, I have no doubt."

Caroline's eyes narrowed. "Do not think to spare me," she said. "Walter is capable of it. He permitted me to know nothing whatsoever of his affairs, so I can tell you little. Oh, my God. I never suspected."

"Why would you?" said Ruth, all sympathy. "I still say, however, that there is no reason to believe your husband is involved. This Captain Ferris was jug-bitten when he mentioned the name, was he not, Dickon? One cannot trust the word of a man in his cups."

"There is truth in strong drink," Dickon muttered.

Viscount Carroway. Caroline, Lady Carroway. He repeated the names in his mind. Of all the nobility in London, Carroway was the last he would have expected to be Caroline's hated husband. He knew little of the man, who seemed to care more for sporting events and gambling dens than balls and parties, or so Dickon had heard. Not that Dickon frequented any of these himself. He did not even remember hearing whether Carroway was married. His wife had been hidden away in truth.

"I shall have to begin thinking of him as Walter rather than Not-John," he said, trying to lighten the pall over the gathering. "I believe I prefer Not-John.

"Caroline, I promise you, I shall learn whether your hus-

band is the man we are looking for. I hope he is not. If he
is . . . I cannot say."

"You will not kill him!" Caroline cried. "They might
have you up for murder!" Killing a traitor might be for-
given, but she did not want Dickon in any danger. Of
course, if Dickon or anyone else could accomplish it, she
and the rest of the world would be better off without Walter
Carroway.

"Oh course not. He surely deserves it for what he has
done to you, but I believe in letting the law take its course.
If he is the guilty one, and *if* we can catch him and prove it,
I fear it will be difficult for you, my dear, once it is known
you are his wife. Having a husband in prison is not good
ton. If he is convicted, he will probably be hanged or sent
to Australia."

"If he is guilty, he deserves it," said Caroline firmly. "I
shall survive, I assure you."

They talked of little else that evening. Caroline felt she
was living in a dream. This could not be happening. Walter
involved in sending arms to France! It hardly bore thinking
about. She racked her brain for any hints or clues he might
have dropped. None came to mind. Walter lived a life of
leisure, attending cockfights, races, mills; he gambled.
Often he was gone for hours doing she knew not what.
Once every month or six weeks, he would journey to Dymchurch to see his relative. After the first year or so they had
become so estranged that they rarely talked, exchanging
commonplaces at meals and little else.

As she prepared for bed, Caroline wondered for the first
time where Walter got his money. She had always assumed
he had inherited it; she had never asked, and he had never
told her. Perhaps, she thought darkly, it came from the sale
of arms to France. Had the food she'd eaten, the dismal
gowns she wore, the very coals in the fireplace, been
bought with money obtained from this despicable practice?

How could she have married such a man?

It was Monday, the day of Dickon's departure. He and
Ruth were friends again after a dispute over the clothes he

would take with him. When he burrowed through his wardrobe searching for certain old and shabby but favorite pantaloons and waistcoats—comfortable garments he believed appropriate for his mission—they were not to be found. He'd stormed out to confront his part-time valet, who looked blank, and then went to Ruth.

"Those old tats!" she said, affronted. "Not fit for digging in the garden. They are bundled with some of mine, ready to go to charity as soon as I get around to sending them."

"You had no right!" Dickon shouted. "You are not my keeper!" He muttered imprecations to himself. "Where are they?"

"In the scullery, I believe. For heaven's sake, Dickon, you cannot mean to—"

"I most certainly do mean," he said, glaring at his sister. He hurried down to the scullery to rescue them, and found them packed tightly into a bundle tied with a string. He tore off the string and surveyed the wrinkled assortment.

"Get someone to press these," he demanded of Ruth once he had brought them up to show her. "And never, *never* put your grasping hands into my wardrobe again."

They had been cool to one another all day, but now, on Monday, the incident was forgotten. The shabby old clothes were brushed, pressed, and carefully packed. The gig was being hitched. It was almost time to leave.

"I would feel better were you to take someone with you," Ruth said in a worried tone. "I dislike the idea of you all alone in that nest of thieves, or smugglers, or whatever. Should you not take a groom at least?"

"I believe I am old enough to care for myself," said Dickon, amused. Nothing would spoil his good humor today.

Caroline looked on, torn by conflicting emotions. If only she could go too! Dickon would not recognize Walter if they met face to face; he did not know James Fenland either. She could be such a help to him!

Repressing her feelings for Dickon had been as difficult for her as she believed it was for him. Not that he tried as hard to repress them as she did. She thought of the silly incident with the kippers. There had been a few others, some as innocuous as a smile for no reason at all, or an accidental brushing of hands as he reached for a teacup. He was plaguing her, and they both knew it.

Heavens, she thought. Many a married woman took a lover; why not she? It might cause talk, but it seemed to be accepted if done discreetly.

She could not bring herself to agree. She nodded and smiled and wished Dickon all success. She promised to write once they knew Dickon's direction. She waved until his gig disappeared around the corner of Golden Square. Then she set herself to cutting out another christening gown.

Head for Rye first in hope of finding Ferris, the informant, or go directly to Dymchurch? Dickon opted for Dymchurch. If Colonel Davenport, his old superior, could not learn more than a name after plying the man with drink, Dickon could not see himself doing any better.

He was not even certain that Dymchurch would yield anything. All he had to go on was Caroline's report that her husband visited a relative there. The visits could be entirely innocent. Already consumed with hatred for the man, he *wanted* Viscount Carroway to be his villain, but he tried to be dispassionate.

Spring was well advanced in Kent. Dickon took his time, drinking in the fresh air, the scents of apple, pear, and plum blossoms, the sights of farmers working in the fields. A colony of nesting fieldfares caught his eye in a garden along the road, their twittering songs in tune with his mood. Kent was not his beloved Durham, but it had much to recommend it.

He spent the night at Royal Tunbridge Wells and arrived in Dymchurch on Tuesday.

The last miles of his journey were an abrupt change from the fertile fields and gardens to which he had grown accustomed. No road led through Romney Marsh; he had to go around its edge and follow the coast to reach Dymchurch. He looked out over the vast seas of marsh grass, cut through here and there by waterways, and realized what an excellent hiding place it would be for anyone wishing to avoid the law. If the man or men he was after chose to conduct their business in the marsh, it was clear Dickon—who had never been in a boat in his life—had little chance of finding them.

Pegasus, his horse, seemingly had no love of marshes. The raucous calls of the water birds had the horse twitching his ears in nervous excitement and threatening to bolt. Dickon pulled him up, climbed down from the gig, and walked forward to the horse's nose to talk quietly in soothing tones. Pegasus looked around wildly until his master's murmured reassurances penetrated. Then he stood stock-still and refused to move. It took another quiet talk to get him going again. Dickon swore to himself. His light gig was not a good carriage for long travel in any case; it was more appropriate for Town use, but it was all he had.

That put an end to Dickon's optimism. He jogged slowly into Dymchurch and put up at a rundown inn.

Thirteen

Once Dickon had registered under the name of Daniel Richards, he settled into a room that boasted a bed, a washstand, a chair, a minuscule fireplace, and a grimy window—less appealing than even Caroline's room at Mrs. Hobbs's, he thought. He wandered down to the common room and ordered a brandy.

He considered himself somewhat of an authority on brandy—had he not sampled enough of it? At least he would be able to judge whether it was good French brandy—and therefore smuggled—or some inferior concoction.

It was French brandy, all right. It seemed out of place in this dingy inn, where patrons might be expected to call for beer, ale, or gin, not fine brandy. Dickon sipped it, consulted his pocket watch as if waiting for someone, and looked around him.

The common room was busy, with more jovial fellows pouring in every minute. Two barmaids were kept busy filling orders. The babble of voices soon became a roar, with men shouting at each other to be heard. Dickon's plan of eavesdropping on revealing conversations seemed hopeless.

At a table to his right, a bleary-eyed man wearing a knitted cap caught the arm of the barmaid setting a glass before him.

"Not so fast, my pretty," he said, smiling with blackened teeth. "Bide a while. I need a li'l company to 'elp me celebrate, don't I, Jimmy?" He turned to his companion, who nodded glumly. "Jimmy don't count," he confided to the girl. "He don't know how to celebrate."

"Sorry, sir, I 'ave me duties," said the girl, trying to pull away.

" 'Ere! Not so fast!" said Bleary-eyes. "Just for a minute, me pretty. Jest one drink. 'Ere, you can 'ave Jimmy's drink. He ain't drunk it yet."

The girl crouched slightly, pulled her arm abruptly downward, and left Bleary-eyes grasping thin air. She had wended her way past two tables before her admirer realized she had escaped him.

"God damn!" he said. "Jimmy, go 'ome. I cain't celebrate with the likes o' you. Not my fault yer old boat leaks. Show that sour puss to your wife!" He turned his back on Jimmy.

Jimmy gave him a mournful look, rose, and left the common room without a word. Dickon watched as Bleary-eyes tossed down the glass the barmaid had just left and looked around—whether for more drink or for a suitable companion, Dickon could not tell.

On a sudden impulse Dickon smiled ingratiatingly when Bleary-eyes' glance turned to him. Dickon rose, went over to the other man's table, and said, "May I buy you a drink?"

"What fer? I don't know you, do I?"

"No? You don't remember me? I heard of your good luck and wanted to help you celebrate. Girl!" he called to the barmaid, but his voice was lost in the din.

Bleary-eyes looked Dickon up and down. Dickon's clothes spoke more of Town than of a Kentish smuggling village, but they were worn and somewhat out of style. Others in the common room wore similar garments. Bleary-eyes apparently was satisfied.

" 'Ow's come I don't remember you?" he asked. "I ain't never sold you no brandy, 'ave I? I'd remember."

"Not yet you haven't," said Dickon. "We talked about it—oh, months ago now—but you didn't have any to spare. Don't you recall?"

"Hell, no," said Bleary-eyes. "Let's have a drink."

Dickon had brought his brandy glass with him, but he waved madly toward a barmaid and finally caught her eye.

It was the same one who had escaped Bleary-eyes earlier. She looked askance at Dickon.

"You with Bart, eh?" she asked. "Thought you was at that other table. Watch out for Bart. He's had a few."

"So I see," said Dickon, smiling. "I have just joined Bart to help him celebrate. Bring him another."

The barmaid pulled a face, but took Bart's empty glass. Soon she returned with a refill, making sure she kept out of his reach when she set it down.

"Now," said Dickon. "What are we celebrating?"

"Thought you knew!" said Bart. "Thought everybody knew! This is my lucky day!" He smiled widely. Dickon could see the tongue behind the blackened teeth.

"Of course I knew. I just wanted the details. By God, this *is* your lucky day, Bart, old man. Drink up."

Bart drank up. It took him some time—Dickon wondered where he found any more interior room for liquid—and in between, he talked.

He had made contact with a new supplier, a Frenchman with a boat at least twice the size of that of his old supplier, and his first delivery, during the night before, had gone off without a hitch. "Smooth as silk," he boasted to Dickon. The casks were neatly hidden in the marsh until they could be fetched, a few at a time to avoid arousing suspicion. "Not that them excise men can keep up with us," he said. "I could parade 'em right past the excise, bold as you please, and they'd look the other way."

"No danger, then, from the excise men?"

"Nay," said Bart. "I knows all their tricks. No excise man's gonna get the best of old Bart McBride. You say you was goin' ter take some o' my brandy? Want some o' this load? I might have a mite to spare."

"Be glad to," said Dickon, quaking inwardly. What would he do with kegs of brandy? He was interested in outgoing cargo, not incoming. He had a gut feeling that the two were related, however. It stood to reason that smugglers' craft bringing in brandy would be happy to have a paying load for their return trips.

"I will have to notify my customers," he told Bart. "They

are . . . er . . . over Canterbury way. Delivery in, say, a sen-night?"

"How many?"

"Three?"

"By damn, you kin 'ave six if you want 'em," said Bart. "For an old friend, y'understand." He smiled his blackened smile again, his head weaving unsteadily back and forth.

"Six next time," said Dickon. "Three this time. Have to line up the customers."

"Cain't remember your name," Bart fretted.

"Daniel," said Dickon. That was not hard to remember; he felt like Daniel in the lion's den. "Daniel Richards."

"By God, you're a right one," said Bart. "You goin' ter buy me 'nother drink?"

"By all means," said Dickon.

Later, in his room, as Dickon tried to go to sleep despite the din below him, he pondered the disposal of three kegs of contraband brandy a sennight hence. This was something he should have taken up with Lord Avebury before he left, but it was too late now. A daring idea came to him, but he doubted he would be able to carry it out. He was turning it over in his mind when he fell asleep.

The next day Dickon became acquainted with Dymchurch, such as it was. He paid particular attention to the seafront, which boasted vast stretches of sand. Not the best anchorage for smugglers' boats, he decided, but perhaps they stood off while small boats transferred their cargo to the shore. Or perhaps they landed elsewhere. He wished he knew more about the habits of smugglers. He would culti-vate Bart McBride if Bart, once he was sober, still felt kindly toward him.

Next he tramped to the other side of town to look over the marsh. It was as forbidding as it had seemed the day be-fore. Even though the sun was shining elsewhere, a thin mist hung over the vast expanse. He heard a riot of bird sounds—geese, ducks, moor hens, crakes, redshanks, curlews, and many he could not identify, birds not common to Durham, where he had learned what he knew of birds.

Periodically a flight of sandpipers or plover rose above the mist, wheeled, and settled down again.

Where the marsh met the edge of Dymchurch, he saw a few rowboats tethered, but no one appeared to be about. One day he would hire a boat and let the owner take him into the marsh.

His next objective was to inquire into anyone named Carroway. How to do this without arousing suspicion? He decided to put it off; an idea surely would come to him. He returned to the inn to change his muddy boots and have something to eat. Afterward he penned a joint letter to Ruth and Caroline, telling of his journey, his evening with Bart, and his direction so they could write him. That sent off, he returned to the common room to nurse a brandy and strike up conversations with the other patrons.

The barmaid who had served him the night before greeted him, but no one else paid him any attention. Bart McBride did not appear. Patrons were few. Last night must not have been a good smuggling night, he decided. He ate a late supper, gave up, and sought his bed.

Dickon's efforts the next day were fruitless, so much so that he almost despaired of finding an arms smuggler. Resolving to further his acquaintance with Bart McBride, he sought out the man's house—he was known in Dymchurch, so it was no hardship learning his direction.

The house, a surprisingly neat and sturdy structure, stood to the edge of the marsh. Apparently, fill had been brought in to raise its foundation a foot or two above marsh level, but Dickon wondered whether it would survive a season of heavy rains. Two young boys answered his knock, denied all knowledge of McBride's whereabouts, and pushed past him carrying fishing poles. They paid him no further heed as they walked along a muddy bank, looking for the best place to drop their lines.

Dickon's efforts at finding a boatman to take him into the marsh fared no better. He visited Pegasus in the inn stable, made sure he was properly treated and fed, and considered taking out the gig, but for what purpose? He decided against it. He wandered aimlessly around the village, greeting anyone who seemed at all friendly.

Finally his footsteps took him once again to the marsh, which held a strange fascination. He had never beheld such an enormous expanse of—nothing. Nothing? It was low, and flat, and seemingly endless, but it hid tens of thousands of marsh creatures, from fish to insects, and most especially birds. Dickon watched, fascinated, as a gray heron stalked a tiny fish, caught it, and flipping up its bill, swallowed it. He thought he could see the bulge as the fish traveled down the heron's long neck. A harrier—Dickon believed it to be a marsh harrier—quartered low over the land, its wings moving in lazy, graceful flaps as it searched for prey. As it flew by only a few feet above the heron's head, the heron, startled, let out a harsh *kaark* and rose into the air, high above the hawk, its long legs dangling.

The day ended with the finest sunset Dickon had ever seen, streaks of lavender, pink and orange glowing and shifting in the western sky, and reflected wherever there was open water.

The day was not a total waste. He wished Caroline had been there to see it.

Early next morning Dickon called for his gig and drove to Rye. There he inquired and was directed to an office where excisemen could be found. Establishing his bona fides with an impressive document Lord Avebury had given him, and which he kept in his left boot—he did not want it to fall into the wrong hands—he told his story.

The exciseman to whom he talked, one Harold Penney, threw up his hands.

"Be glad to help, boy, but you know what you're askin'?" said Penney. "The whole of Dymchurch is into smugglin', and what about New Romney? Little Stone? Great Stone? Camber? And all the places in between? There's only just so many of us, see, and we can't be everywhere at once.

"We have our spies, see, and we gets tips now and again, but we needs somethin' to go on, or no go. You see, what you're lookin' for is a man sendin' somethin' *out*, not bringin' somethin' *in*. No tax on somethin' goin' *out*. Not our problem."

At Dickon's crestfallen expression, Penney relented. "Now you just tie the two together and we'll be there," he said. "You're right. Likely the boat that brings in brandy or silk is the same one what takes out the guns, if your tale is true. We'll get 'em for the brandy or silk; then you can have 'em. But mind! They're all clever devils. How you goin' to catch 'em in the act, all by yourself? War Office too cheese-parin' to give you some help?"

"They thought I would attract less attention if I were alone," said Dickon. "I am posing as a buyer of smuggled brandy under the name of Daniel Richards. I have already arranged to buy three kegs from one Bart McBride."

Penney chuckled. "We all know Bart. Oh, yes, we know 'im! Good luck, lad. Send us a message if you ever get it fixed up to catch 'em. Daniel Richards, eh? Best I write that down. I'll tell the other boys, see, so they'll know who y'are.

"By the bye, son," Penney said as Dickon started to leave, "what you goin' to do with those three kegs?"

"If nothing else, I can drink them."

"King's evidence? It's Newgate for you, lad." Penney laughed uproariously as he showed Dickon out.

Dickon's journey back to Dymchurch was longer than his drive to Rye had been, for he went out of his way. He wished to appear to be coming from Canterbury, the location of his imaginary brandy customers, should anyone notice.

Although Caroline kept busy stitching christening gowns and helping Ruth plan an immediate At Home and a small dinner party to take place the following week, she still felt an aching emptiness. No one winked at her; no one sent her special looks. She had not gone out since Dickon had left, days ago now, for her only departures from Golden Square were journeys to deliver her sewing. Even though so much time had passed, she still feared discovery by her husband.

Surely he would have given up the search by now? She hesitated to risk it.

Lady Robstart and Mrs. Hinkle, as always, attended the At Home. Caroline wondered how they occupied themselves when not visiting Lady Stilton. They sat together, talking and nodding. Mrs. Hinkles's single ostrich plume, erupting from a scarlet turban, nodded with her.

"Come here, my dear," Lady Robstart beckoned to Caroline, who obediently walked over to them. "And where might dear Rycote be?" she asked. "I hear tell he has done a lope, disappeared, pulled it, gone. Can this be true?"

"I have no notion where he might be," Caroline answered. "Why not ask Lady Stilton?"

"Ha!" said Mrs. Hinkle. "We knew you would be the person to ask, you two being so *close,*" she simpered.

"Lord Robstart's sister's son-in-law is a clerk in the War Office," said Lady Robstart, "and he reports dear Rycote was *sacked.* Gone back to the wilds of Durham to lick his wounds, has he? Why did he not take you with him? You being so *close.*"

Thoroughly angered, Caroline thought briefly of stabbing Mrs. Hinkle, or both ladies, with the quill of Mrs. Hinkles ostrich plume.

She glared at them, said, "I *beg* your pardon," and walked out of the room.

The revelation that the gossips had her linked with Dickon, probably had her sharing his bed, came as a crushing blow. As if her actions had not been above reproach! Of course, she was thought to be a widow, thus quite able to receive the attentions of a gentleman. Even so, that anyone would believe they were having an affair right under Ruth's nose was insupportable. Perhaps the talk would die down now that Dickon was away.

Once the guests had departed, Lady Robstart and Mrs. Hinkle being the last to leave as always, she mentioned their remarks to Ruth. Ruth could only laugh. "If the world believes Dickon has gone to Durham, so much the better," she said. "I shall not deny it should anyone ask. Which reminds me, I am told we have a letter from Dickon, which I have waited to read until the guests left."

"Now we may write him!" Caroline cried once the letter had been read aloud. "Oh, I am so glad he is safe! I wonder what he will do with three kegs of brandy."

"If you have any ideas, tell him," Ruth said, grinning. "I cannot condone his drinking it all himself. Heavens!"

"I shall write him this very evening," Caroline said eagerly. "I have thought of the name of Walter's relative and I must tell him."'"

"Oh? What is it?"

"John Dunthorpe," said Caroline.

"John Dunthorpe," Dickon mused. "This requires immediate attention."

Only two days remained before he was to take delivery of his brandy, a situation that worried him excessively. His gig would not hold three kegs. He had already talked with a carter about hiring a tip cart, but where was he to send it?

He'd put that to the back of his mind upon receiving Caroline's letter. Now he had a name.

He had managed since his journey to Rye to ingratiate himself further with Bart McBride, though the man often scratched his head trying to recall meeting Daniel Richards before. Dickon had not yet penetrated Romney Marsh, but McBride seemed on the verge of allowing him to observe the loading of Dickon's brandy—where, Dickon was not sure. In the marsh? On the bank? Dickon tucked Caroline's letter away in a pocket, clapped on his hat, and set out for McBride's house.

McBride was at home, but did not appear happy to see his new customer. He did not invite Dickon in; they talked at the door. "What's up, lad?" he asked.

"I believe I have a better offer, McBride," Dickon said seriously. "John Dunthorpe can beat your price by nine shillings a keg. What do you think of that?"

McBride frowned. "You want good brandy? You get it from old Bart, lad. Now Dunthorpe . . . Where'd you meet 'im?"

"Here and there," said Dickon airily. "I have been getting around Dymchurch, and I have met a goodly number of people. Have to, in my business. The best brandy at the lowest price, that is what my customers want."

"Where was you gettin' it before you come here?"

Dickon thought quickly. "Little Stone," he said.

"What 'appened at Little Stone?"

"Too far. When you are wanting to sell it around Canterbury, you want the nearest source."

"Hah." McBride considered. "You was wantin' me to cut my price, was you? Not bloody likely. There's plenty what will take all I can give 'em. I was doin' you a favor, lad."

"You are certain your brandy is finer than John Dunthorpe's?" Dickon pretended to waver. "How do I know this?"

"By God, we'll give you a taste," said McBride staunchly. "Come in the 'ouse, lad. I might 'ave a bit laid by."

It was indeed fine brandy, smooth and mellow, though served in a pottery mug. Dickon sipped it with appreciation. It was better than he had had at the inn, and that had been excellent.

"You have convinced me," he told McBride. "But now I must cancel my dealings with Dunthorpe. Can you give me his direction?"

"You mean you don't know? Thought you'd talked business with 'im."

"But not at his house," said Dickon.

"Up the road, at t'other end of Dymchurch. One of those black-and-white 'ouses, two floors. Dunthorpe, 'e thinks 'e's high and mighty, livin' in that big 'ouse. Ha! Pushin' off cheap brandy, that's 'ow 'e made it. Give me me nice little cottage, and me self-respect anytime." He snorted.

"I am most grateful," said Dickon, shaking McBride's hand with enthusiasm. "I shall visit him straightaway."

Dunthorpe's house was, indeed, several cuts above those of his neighbors. Dickon did not visit it. He examined the immediate area for a good vantage point, settling for a low stone wall enclosing the front garden of a house across the

street. He perched on the wall and tried to look like a weary
pedestrian who had walked too far. The Dunthorpe house
faced the street; it had no front garden. It presented a blank
expense of half-timbering dating back probably to Queen
Elizabeth's day. It had sunk out of true over the years so
that the right half seemed slightly drunken, but it was
freshly painted and in good repair.

Dickon watched the door, which opened directly on the
street, and the two curtained windows on the ground floor.
He saw no humans, no sign of activity. The stone wall
where he sat became increasingly uncomfortable. He rose
and walked casually down the street, then back again.
Passersby, on foot or mounted, driving carriages and carts,
passed periodically. The afternoon wore on, and finally he
was treated to another spectacular sunset.

As darkness descended and Dickon at last prepared to
give up and leave, he thought he saw a dull glimmer behind
the curtain at one of the ground-floor windows. No one was
near; he crossed the street and tried to peer through the
window, but the curtain obscured his view. The light source
seemed to be some distance from the window. Why not go
around to the back?

For this he had to go the long way around, for the Dunthorpe house was cheek by jowl with the lesser houses on
either side. When he came to the end of the solid row he
turned left and then left again, finding himself in a mews
with stables and back gardens. He had failed to count how
many houses the Dunthorpe domicile was from the end of
the row, and, to his chagrin, discovered they all looked alike
in the gathering dark, and several had stables. He retraced
his steps. Dunthorpe's was the fourth house from the end.

Back now at the entrance to the mews, Dickon walked
quietly, hoping his dark clothing would render him incon-
spicuous. The white shirt! He paused to make sure his shirt
cuffs were hidden beneath those of his coat and his shirt
front was well-concealed. He tore off his neckcloth and
pushed it into his pocket. He moved quietly down the mews
toward what must be Dunthorpe's stable.

The nicker of a horse alerted him. He darted to the side,

creeping along the wall of a neighbor's outbuilding, until he came to the stable. It opened onto the mews, and he did not wish to appear in the opening. He stopped, intending to station himself at the end of the stable building where he could not be seen from inside, and turned toward the house. He ran headlong into a wall so hidden by rank growth that he had taken it to be shrubbery he could penetrate. He barked his right shin and skinned an elbow, besides making enough noise to waken the neighborhood.

Rubbing his elbow and muttering curses to himself, he stood unmoving for the space of two minutes. He could hear horses making small noises and oats being munched, but nothing that sounded human. Limping a little now, for his shin hurt, he sidled around to the doors of the stable. They were shut.

He carefully opened one door a crack. Its hinges creaked like a pistol shot. He stopped, his heart in his mouth, and waited. When nothing happened, he edged himself sideways into the stable, which was as dark as the inside of a coal mine. Surely, he thought, a door must open to the back garden so Dunthorpe could have access to the stable, but how to find it in the dark?

Feeling his way—he liked to think he knew the plan of the average stable—he crept slowly along its length, searching for a door. He felt the partitions between stalls; he ducked around the heads of horses, seemingly outstretched to investigate this stranger; he ran into halters, bits, and harness hanging from pegs, causing sudden jingles that stopped him in his tracks. Finally, at the far end, he felt rather than saw the lack of a horse and hoped he had found the door, and not an empty stall. There was no partition between the aisle and the back wall; that he learned with a toe. He inched forward, stretching out an arm to feel for the door.

He stumbled. Something large and limp was on the floor, in his way.

"That you, yer lordship?" said a low voice.

"Yes," Dickon said in a loud whisper. He froze.

"Good kick you gave me," said the voice. The man gave

a wheezing laugh, which soon became a cough. When he could speak again, he asked, "Where's yer horse?"

"At the inn," said Dickon truthfully.

"Master's not here," the voice reported. "Left me to tell you, you're to meet him an' Fenland here tomorrer, same time. Somethin's gone wrong and he's gone to see about it."

Dickon could hear the man sit up and rub some part of his anatomy, presumably where Dickon had kicked him.

"So Fenland is here?" Dickon whispered.

"Aye. He's been already. Told him to put up at the inn. Same as you. You'll see 'im there."

Dickon was aware when the man stood up, a giant of a man who towered over him, though Dickon could not see him. Nor could he see Dickon, and Dickon wanted to keep it that way.

"Thank you, I shall," he said. "Now that you have told both of us, you may go. The stable floor cannot be that comfortable." He edged gingerly toward the door at the other end of the mews.

"Didn't know you cared!" the man said, and broke into his wheezing laugh. Again it ended in a fit of coughing.

By then Dickon had reached the far wall and the welcome door. He edged through, shutting it behind him, and walked quickly back to the inn, pausing to brush some strands of hay from his pantaloons before walking through the door.

He went directly to his chamber, removed his boots, and sank on the bed.

What was he getting into? He heaved a great sigh. It was only by the grace of God that he had escaped the Dunthorpe stable. He had been so startled at finding a man there in the dark that he had not been able to think straight. Thankfully, when the man had asked if he were "his lordship," he had agreed automatically, for was he not indeed his lordship? Merely the wrong lordship.

He played some probable scenes through his mind. All his conjectures seemed to be true; James Fenland was involved, and that surely meant that Viscount Carroway was involved as well. He assumed the man in the stable had taken him for Carroway. But what would happen when the real Carroway arrived? Dickon had tried to urge the man in the stable to leave his post, which would mean Carroway would not get his message. What would Carroway do then? Should Dickon search out Fenland at the inn? How was he to get next to these people without giving himself away?

His head buzzing, Dickon finally roused himself, retied his neckcloth, brushed his hair, and went down to the common room. As he nursed a fine sample of smuggled brandy, he glanced around the room, wondering which man might be James Fenland.

Fourteen

After consuming a meager supper and retiring to his chamber to ponder his predicament, Dickon realized he had very probably put himself into a situation from which there was no escape. He'd thought through several possible plans, only to reject each one out of hand—none seemed good enough. The prospect of catching Viscount Carroway—for he was certain now that Carroway was his quarry—seemed slim, and the danger to himself, enormous. There was no backing out now, however, and he vowed to do all that he could.

Resolutely, he turned his thoughts from his own situation to Caroline's. It would be horrid for her, should her husband's misdeeds be spread upon the newspapers and tongues of everyone in England, but he hoped it would be possible to spare her most of that by keeping the secret of her identity. Would the fact that her husband was in prison be grounds for divorce? He did not believe so; he had never heard of such. And, of course, that would only make her situation more difficult, for she would have to identify herself to seek a divorce.

Whatever happened, he saw no way for her to be free of Not-John, and that meant he could never have her for his own . . . unless Not-John died—or perhaps was hanged? But treason no longer called for hanging; the prisoner would be divested of his land and, if additional punishment should be needed, he would probably be sent to New South Wales, on the other side of the world. Dickon vowed anew to expose Carroway, though he could not be assured that it would mean Carroway's death.

He sketched out dozens of possible lines of inquiry on scraps of paper. Each seemed more impossible than the last. He wadded them up and tossed them into the fireplace. One failed to reach the flames; he rescued it and was about to send it after its fellows when he reconsidered. He opened it. It was the same ridiculous scheme that had come to him the night he arrived in Dymchurch. Perhaps he had been given an omen. He smoothed the crumpled paper and placed it by his shaving things on the washstand, then settled into bed. That was the one he would try. If it did not succeed, he would think further—if he was still alive.

Dickon's first order of business next morning was to seek out Bart McBride and ask that his three kegs of brandy be delivered a day early. From his earlier conversation with the carter he was sure he could get a tip cart on short notice; if no horse were available he could use Pegasus. Pegasus as a cart horse! He had to laugh.

Accordingly, he sought out McBride immediately after breakfast. He had little doubt that James Fenland was also among those breaking their fast at the inn, but Fenland would have to wait. Fortunately, McBride was at home. Dickon could hear his raised voice, quarreling with a woman, before he knocked on the door.

One of the small boys answered the door and left him waiting. The quarreling voices wound down, and McBride soon appeared at the door, obviously full of venom.

"You again," said McBride. His head swiveled around to look behind him, apparently watching for the female. She was not in sight. He turned again and looked inquiringly at Dickon. "What is it now?"

"I have arranged for a tip cart, and I would be much obliged if I could take delivery today rather than tomorrow," said Dickon. "I am prepared to pay immediately, in notes."

McBride's belligerent expression faded. The prospect of immediate ready cash apparently tempted him.

" 'Ave to round up some of the boys," he said. "Can't unload or load your cart alone. Tell you what—bring the cart around here at one this afternoon. I'll get Jacky or Peter to 'elp."

"I would be pleased to help you unload and load myself," said Dickon. "I have handled many a cask, you may be sure. It is the least I can do, asking for delivery on such short notice." He smiled at McBride.

McBride sized him up, seemingly satisfied that this muscular young man could do his share, and agreed.

"It's donkey work," he cautioned. "Best get into your oldest breeks. There's mud and—"

"I shall indeed," Dickon agreed.

He set out quickly for the carter's, leaving McBride and his woman to resume their quarrel.

Dickon notified the carter he would want the tip cart a few minutes before one, asked for a horse—Pegasus was to be spared—and returned to the inn to change into the shabbiest clothes he had with him.

Breakfast was over and the common room vacant except for a pair of girls wiping tables and sweeping the floor. The innkeeper came and went, directing the girls' work and fussing over his receipts. When the disreputable-looking Dickon entered, the innkeeper looked him over and raised an eyebrow.

"Do you have a James Fenland here?" Dickon asked.

"Aye, he's back again," said the man. "Gone out now, I believe."

"I was asked to inquire for him," Dickon said smoothly. "I fear I would not recognize him."

"He was here for breakfast, I think. Wasn't he, Rosie?"

One of the girls nodded.

"How would I know him?" Dickon asked.

"Him? You look for a man you'd never notice. That'll be Fenland."

"He comes here often?"

"Aye. Comes to Dymchurch regular-like. He don't always stay at the inn, though. Don't know where he stays, but we sees him havin' a drink now and again when he ain't got a room here."

"Many thanks," said Dickon. "Please do not mention that

I was asking for him." Dickon gave the innkeeper a conspiratorial wink and slipped a sovereign into his hand.

"Never heard a word you said." The innkeeper grinned, pocketing the sovereign.

Dickon walked to the carter's and took delivery of the tip cart. He knew little about tip carts, and he was going to have to learn in a hurry. The cart produced for him was a heavy one, requiring two cart horses, and was intended, said the carter, for transporting seaweed to enrich farm fields. Wet seaweed was exceptionally heavy, the carter explained. What did Mr. Richards wish to haul? Whatever it was, the cart he produced would surely carry it.

"I do not need so heavy a cart," said Dickon. "Have you no one-horse carts?"

The carter did not at the moment. Dickon did not divulge what he wished to transport. For all he knew the carter could be one of the excisemen's spies.

The carter hitched a pair of cart horses and explained to Dickon how to open the tail board for loading and unloading. The tail board opened like a door rather than dropping downward from hinges on the rear shutter, a system Dickon was not familiar with. Ryfield had tip carts, but he had never driven one; that lot fell to the farm workers. He thought it odd that a cart intended for seaweed should have such an odd method of access. Perhaps that was why it was available.

He dared not try to ride in the cart, but settled for guiding the horses while he walked alongside. When he saw the deep ruts in the road and the lack of spring in the cart, he knew he had made the right decision. He guided the horses pulling the empty vehicle down the street, managed to stop them, and attempted a turn into a side alley so he could get back to his starting point. It was not easy. And he thought himself a whip! He found new respect for the carter.

He was still unsure, but it was nearly one o'clock, so he turned his pair toward Bart McBride's house.

McBride was waiting for him.

"My God," he said, "a seaweed cart!" He shook his head. McBride tethered the horses and indicated a path through the marsh grasses to a patch of open water where a small boat was tied. He motioned for Dickon to board. Dickon, unused to boats, found it tippy, and sat down suddenly before he lost his balance. McBride snorted, but said nothing. He untied the boat, leaped in, pushed off with a foot, and began to row.

Dickon had sworn to himself that he would note every change of direction or channel, but soon gave up. McBride seemed to know exactly where he was going and rowed steadily. It took no more than fifteen minutes to reach his cache of brandy.

As they neared a wooden boat that looked exactly like the small fishing craft that plied the sea, McBride grinned, pride evident in his eyes.

"Me freshwater fishin' boat," he declared, confirming Dickon's suspicions that that was indeed what it had once been. "Ahoy there!" McBride yelled. A tousled head appeared.

"Me son Abel," McBride explained. "He's me caretaker, like." McBride edged their rowboat alongside the craft and clambered aboard the larger vessel. Noting that Dickon hesitated, he gave Dickon a hand up. "Not used to boats, eh?" he said, and chuckled.

"Where's me victuals, Pa?" Abel demanded. "Cain't work without food!"

"Later," said McBride, striding toward the oak brandy casks, covered with tarpaulins, that ringed the boat's deck. "Give us a 'and here, boy."

McBride had a supply of sturdy rope nets to hold the casks as they were lowered into the rowboat. The transfer went smoothly and Dickon doubted his help had been needed. He wondered, however, why all these transfers were necessary. Why not hide the incoming brandy in McBride's house or some other safe place on land? He asked McBride.

"Are ye daft?" McBride demanded indignantly. "No safer place than Romney Marsh, no, sir. I do believe the Lord put it here jest for us poor folks tryin' to make an honest livin'. We'd be sawny not to use it."

The three kegs left very little room in the rowboat for Dickon's long legs, but he drew them up tightly against the seat and waited while McBride conferred with his son. Finally McBride tossed a packet of food to the boy, jumped into the rowboat, and they were off again.

Unloading the kegs when they again reached solid ground was considerably more difficult than the boat transfer had been, and Abel was not there to help. Finally, they manhandled them to shore and rolled them awkwardly toward the waiting tip cart. Dickon stood in the cart to receive them as McBride rolled them on, and, despite some blunders, they managed to latch the tail board door.

They repaired to McBride's house to complete the transaction. The quarreling female did not appear. McBride offered Dickon a mug half full of brandy, which Dickon accepted, and Dickon counted out the money owed. Thank heaven Lord Avebury had prepared for such an eventuality and had sent money with him.

"Six next time," Dickon reminded McBride, and directed his horses on a slow walk toward John Dunthorpe's.

Though by now it was late afternoon, it was not yet the hour that it had been when Dickon had run across the man in Dunthorpe's stable the day before. "This time tomorrow," the man had said. Dickon hoped he was not too early.

He drove the cart into the mews, stopping just short of Dunthorpe's stable. The cart took up most of the narrow alleyway so it would be difficult for anyone to pass in either direction. He tied the lead horse to one of the rank shrubs hiding the wall alongside the stable and walked boldly inside.

Thank heaven he had come early; there was still some light. He was able to see that only horses were in evidence. He walked to the other end, found the door to Dunthorpe's back garden, and went through it.

The garden showed signs of neglect, with only a half-hearted attempt at a flower bed near the back entrance to the house. A stone-flagged path was barely visible beneath a cover of moss and dead leaves. Dickon followed the path and knocked at the back door.

When a man with an overabundance of oily, coal-black hair, black eyes, and a small, thick-lipped mouth opened the door, Dickon smiled and said, "John Dunthorpe?"

"The same," said Dunthorpe. "What do you want?"

"I have a proposition for you, sir, that I do not believe you can afford to refuse. May I come in?"

"I'm not interested in any blasted propositions," said Dunthorpe. "Off you go." He retreated into the house and started to close the door.

"Oh, but sir, you mean to tell me you would turn down a proposition that would double your income, guaranteed? Very well. I shall have to offer it to someone else. Bart McBride, perhaps." Dickon smiled ingenuously.

"Bart McBride? That cawker?" Dunthorpe hesitated.

"It is entirely up to you. It can do no harm to at least listen, now can it?" Dickon waited, willing himself not to show his fear and uncertainty.

"Can't talk to you now. I have others here," said Dunthorpe. He frowned and started to withdraw again.

"Friends, are they? Perhaps they too would be interested in my proposition."

"What's it about? Trying to get me to invest in another canal? No, thanks. Some bloke was here last week selling canal shares, and I told him where to go. I got no interest in canals."

"This has nothing to do with canals, sir. The word here is *brandy*." Dickon looked hopefully at Dunthorpe.

"Brandy, eh? I know all I need to know about brandy. What's your game, young man?"

"If I may be permitted to come in and lay my proposition before you—and your friends as well, if you like—you will understand."

Dunthorpe seemed about to agree, then hesitated again. "Who sent you here?" he asked. "Why me? How did you get here? Through my stable?"

"Sir, I have been in Dymchurch for nearly a sennight," Dickon replied. "I have made it my business to learn something of the trade that goes on here," he said, carefully avoiding the ugly word, "and have had pointed out to me, time and again, the premier free trader of the town, namely yourself. While we have never met, I could see instantly that you, above all, were the man for my proposition. You have the good business sense, the reputation, the knowledge to take advantage of it as no one else seems to have."

"What's in it for you?" Dunthorpe demanded.

"Ah. I do not deny that I, too, hope to profit. That would be foolish, would it not? Let me explain." Dickon edged closer.

"Oh, very well," said Dunthorpe. "You might as well come in."

Aside from its low ceilings, the house seemed comfortable and well-appointed. Dickon followed Dunthorpe along a hall to a door on the left that opened onto what seemed to be a study, with desk, chairs, and a few books. Two men occupying the chairs looked up as they entered.

"Who's this?" one of them asked abruptly.

Dickon took in the speaker's appearance. A man in his late twenties, Dickon guessed, he was a handsome devil with dark-blond, curly hair, carelessly arranged, a straight nose, and wide-set eyes. The man sucked in his lips. Dickon noted the cruel mouth.

"Man's got a proposition for us," Dunthorpe explained.

"Look here, Dunthorpe, we've no time for propositions," said the second guest, a nondescript man with thinning hair. "Get rid of him."

Dickon immediately guessed who the two men were. He eyed Viscount Carroway narrowly.

"Not so fast, Fenland," said Carroway. "Let the lad have his say, now he's here. What's your name, lad?"

Lad? Dickon was older than this monster. He swallowed his indignation and replied, "Daniel Richards, sir. From over Canterbury way."

"And what's your game?"

"Sir, I can double your profits, guaranteed. I have contacts that can produce the finest French brandy ever, brandy such as the Prince Regent himself would swoon over. It is said that the Czar of Russia will have no other! The quantity is limited, of course, but because I have family contacts in France, I have been able to assure myself of an adequate supply. My only problem is in the shipping. My family contacts have no hand in shipping.

"Well, thought I, the answer is to find someone who already has shipping arrangements. No one, from what I hear, has transport already in hand better than Mr. Dunthorpe, here.

"The brandy is so far above the usual that it brings top prices, let me tell you. Double what you are charging, Mr. Dunthorpe. Is it possible that we can do business?"

"Pah," said Carroway. "Brandy's brandy. Most fools don't know the difference."

"Please permit me to offer you samples," said Dickon. "You must judge for yourselves."

"You have them in your back pocket, of course," Fenland sneered.

"Just outside," said Dickon. "If you will excuse me a moment?"

Carroway nodded, and Dickon hurried out to the cart. He had some trouble wrestling the awkward cask from the cart, through the stable, along the flagstone path, and into the house. He was panting with exertion when he rolled the cask triumphantly into the study. The men had not moved.

"You have glasses, sir?" he asked Dunthorpe brightly. It was evident that Carroway ran this operation, but he deferred to Dunthorpe.

"I will get them," said Dunthorpe. He hurried out.

Some time later the three men were sipping brandy while Dickon looked on, smiling.

"Have to say this is far superior to ours," Carroway admitted grudgingly. "What do you think, Dunthorpe?"

"Not bad," said Dunthorpe. "Fenland?"

"I agree."

Dickon nodded happily. "It would be my pleasure to give you two more casks," he said. "All I happen to have with me; delivery has been difficult, you understand. It may be that you would wish to offer them to your best customers. See what the reaction is, if you will. I can guarantee they will be surprised and pleased."

"That is kind of you," said Carroway. He did not look as if he thought it was kind at all. "We accept."

"Very well, gentlemen," said Dickon. "I will leave them with you as I go. Now, what delivery arrangements can we make?"

"Not so fast!" said Carroway. "We cannot set this up overnight; we have other . . . er . . . arrangements to make. A delivery is due tomorrow night. I will speak to the . . . boatmen when they come in. Perhaps we can do business next month. We get shipments about once a month, weather permitting."

"Might I be permitted to dicker with your delivery crew myself?" Dickon asked. "I would be happy to be of service tomorrow night. I can help unload, reload, whatever you wish."

"I think not," said Carroway. He gave Dickon a suspicious glance. "You could be a spy for the excisemen, for all we know. You just stay snug in your bed and we will take care of it."

"As you wish," said Dickon, pretending nonchalance. "May I meet with you Wednesday or Thursday to learn of your discussion with the crew?"

"Perhaps," said Carroway. "You are at the inn? We will find you."

"Very well." Dickon returned to the cart and laboriously unloaded his remaining two casks. He got them through the stable and left them in the back garden by the stable door. Let someone else dispose of them, he thought uncharitably.

He whistled as he urged his team, pulling a now empty cart, back to the carter's. He paid the carter for one day's hire and walked to the inn. He was rid of his three casks of brandy. All seemed well with his precarious scheme so far. He hoped his luck would hold.

That night he wrote another letter to Ruth and Caroline. He had missed Caroline dreadfully, but now he was grateful she was safe in London. That curly-headed monster who was her husband was in Dymchurch, and if Dickon had his way he would never get within miles of Caroline again.

In his letter he described his meeting with Carroway, Fenland, and Dunthorpe, trying not to let his loathing for the trio show. No need to belabor the point. As he wrote, however, a vision of Carroway and Caroline in bed together—a vision that he could now put an actual face to, rather than the blurred one his imagination had painted—made him clench his fists. Carroway was young and handsome, if one could overlook that cruel mouth. No wonder Caroline and her family had considered him a good catch.

How to learn where Carroway's shipment of smuggled brandy would be delivered the next night? It was imperative that Dickon be present. He would not wait an entire month until the May shipment should arrive. He sighed. His only source seemed to be Bart McBride. He prayed as he sought his bed that McBride knew, and would be willing to tell him.

"Bart, my friend!" Dickon greeted the smuggler next morning. McBride was not welcoming, but then Dickon doubted that he ever was. "You spoke the truth! I disposed of that load in no time, and have orders here for near a dozen more kegs when you can provide them. When is that likely to be?"

Dickon extended a list of inns and public houses that he had prepared in advance, but did not let McBride see them. They were all figments of his imagination.

"Most likely a fortnight," said McBride sourly. "Depends on the weather. Never can tell what the Channel will be like."

"Can you give me a dozen?" Dickon persisted.

"Guess I might. You stayin' in Dymchurch that long?"

"I am not sure. If not, I will be back. By the way, I had a rather unpleasant experience with your friend John Dunthorpe."

"No friend of mine!" McBride spat. " 'Im and 'is cheap brandy. Gives us all a bad name, 'e does. I wouldn't exchange the time o' day with that paperskull."

"He was downright nasty when I canceled my order with him," said Dickon. "I told him I had a better offer elsewhere, but I did not mention your name. He threatened me!

Said he would see to it that no one in Dymchurch would sell to me! Can he do that?"

"Nay," said McBride. "Gettin' full of 'isself, is 'e?" He laughed.

"I had an idea," Dickon said cautiously. "I would very much like to be present when his shipment comes in—tonight, I understand. I would not wish Dunthorpe or his friends to see me, but I could learn where he unloads. Then, if he *does* retaliate, cut me off from supplies—I could ship him to the excise."

McBride was horrified. " 'E's no friend of mine, but I wouldn't do that to me worst enemy," he said. "We don't tattle. No, siree!"

Dickon tried another tack. "I would not actually report him," he assured McBride. "Only threaten him. If I knew where he unloaded—I could say something like, 'Shall I tell the excisemen to look at such-and-such a place, about two in the morning, on such-and-such a night . . . ' Would that not do?"

McBride pondered. "I don't like it," he said at last.

"Do you even know where he unloads?"

"O' course. Up the coast a piece. Shan't tell you where. There's others that use it, too. Use it myself sometimes."

"The excisemen have not discovered it?"

"Nay. Not them! They ain't likely to, either." McBride laughed.

Dickon was desperate to learn the location. If he did not catch this trio tonight, it would be an entire month before he had another opportunity. He did not believe he could keep up his deception that long; a leak was bound to occur.

"Give me a hint," he said jokingly.

To McBride it was no joking matter. His face was closed as he said, "Not a chance, lad. Best you don't know." He put an end to the conversation by stepping back into the house and closing the door firmly behind him. Dickon was left standing on the stoop.

Dickon walked quickly back to the inn, greeted his horse, Pegasus, and had the gig made ready. He took off at a fast trot toward Rye.

Harold Penney was once again in charge of the tiny excise office and greeted him. "Mr. Richards!" he said. "What news?"

"Viscount Carroway and his friends expect a delivery tonight," said Dickon dispiritedly, "but I cannot learn where. Somewhere on the coast north of Dymchurch, I gather. Does that mean anything to you?"

"So you have learned it is Viscount Carroway? Congratulations, lad. That is more than we were ever able to discover. As for where the landing will be made—I wish I knew. Lord help us, there are dozens of places—and then they move the stuff into the marsh. Once it's in the marsh a thousand excisemen would never find it."

"Can I at least count on some help tonight?" Dickon begged. "Could we not get a lugger to sail near the coast and keep watch for suspicious fishing boats?"

"In the middle of the night, watching for a boat without running lights? Are you daft?"

"What about a moon?" Dickon asked hopefully.

"Past full. Let me see now. Full was two days ago. That means it will rise late—yes! We just might do it, see, if we have no clouds." Penney went to the window and peered out. "Cloudy out now," he reported. "Maybe it will clear, see, but if it don't, it's all for nothin'. May be all for nothin' anyhow."

He turned from the window and faced Dickon with a steady gaze. "You planning to come along, lad? If that bunch sees you you're done for. They'll never let you near 'em again."

"I know," said Dickon. "I will take the chance."

He and Penney arranged to meet at sundown at Globsden Gut, where a lugger would be anchored. Dickon left immediately. He had a long trip back to Dymchurch, with another shorter trip down the coast to the Gut after that. He wished to get something to eat and fetch his pistol, just in case.

In the end he had to guess at sundown, for a heavy gray cloud cover hid all signs of the sun. No spectacular sunset tonight. Dickon drove off the road into a grove of trees on the land side of the coastal road and unhitched Pegasus, leaving the gig hidden in the trees. He walked the horse to the single building at the Gut, a cottage by the stream that helped drain the marsh at this point. The surprised cottager agreed to stable the horse until called for, for a price. Dickon set out again, eating the bread and cheese he had brought along, for there had been no time for a meal. As he approached the lugger, he realized the Gut had no real dock and because of the broad expanse of sand and shingle, the lugger could not reach shore. Dickon hailed it, and Penney sent a small boat for him.

Penney swept his arm aloft. "Damned clouds," he complained. "Perfect night for smugglin'. Well, at least we'll get a bit of a run up the coast, won't we? Find yourself a corner, lad. It may be hours yet before anything happens. The other boys are below; they'll be up soon."

"How many?" Dickon asked.

"Two more, besides the crew. That's all we could spare."

Dickon found a coil of rope on deck and sat down. He checked his pistol, wrapped in oiled silk, and tucked it back into his waistband. He looked at the two masts of the lugger, whose sails were furled. He hoped he would be permitted to watch the sturdy old boat get underway. What a mass of sailcloth and rigging it took to move a boat!

As he glanced at the mainmast, wondering how tall it was, a drop of water splashed gently on his cheek. It had begun to rain.

Fifteen

Caroline never ceased to marvel at the speed with which the post was delivered. Her journey in a mail coach had only reinforced this impression. It seemed she had hardly finished writing to Dickon in Kent before a reply arrived, directed, as always, to Ruth as well.

The letter was delivered to her in the library where she sat alone, reading the newspaper. She was an avid newspaper reader, watching for any mention of Walter and trying to keep abreast of the war. When it was over, if it ever should be, she knew Dickon would abandon London for Durham. That did not bear thinking of.

When a footman offered her a tray bearing several letters, she did not wait for Ruth, who was changing her gown in preparation for another of her At Homes. Caroline broke the wax seal and read Dickon's message avidly. He was in good health—he was safe—he had run Walter to ground!

"Ruth!" she called, dropping the newspaper on the floor in her excitement, running out of the library, and up the stairs. "Ruth! Dickon has done it! He has found Walter! And Fenland, and Dunthorpe. Let me read it to you."

When it was done, the two ladies looked at each other. Though they did not say it, each thought of the grave danger Dickon was in, knowing intuitively that a false step could mean death.

"Oh, my dear," said Ruth. She clasped Caroline to her. "I know—I know how much you have come to mean to each other. This is not easy for Dickon, who is usually so blunt he embarrasses me sometimes, but he is clever and resourceful, and I believe he will win out. We must hope so and not let ourselves become blue-deviled."

"Yes," Caroline, sniffing, agreed. "We must."

So Walter, that hated man, was in Dymchurch. Caroline knew from experience that his trips to see his relative—was Dunthorpe truly a relative?—always took several days, rarely as long as a sennight. On this occasion she could be certain he would not return to London for two or three days, and Fenland was with him so Fenland would not be in London either. Now was her chance, a chance she had never expected to have.

"Ruth," she said a little later as they walked down the stairs together, "I believe I shall miss your At Home, if you do not mind. I have nothing to say to Lady Robstart or Mrs. Hinkle, and I have an errand I must attend to."

"Mrs. Hinkle will not be present. Mr. Hinkle has the gout and needs her to listen to his complaints, I imagine."

"I could not endure Lady Robstart even alone, I fear. I leave her in your tender hands, and Dossie and I shall go out. I should return soon after your entertainment."

Ruth looked puzzled—surely Caroline would not choose to deliver more of her christening gowns on a day Ruth was receiving!—but she did not demur.

"Dossie!" Caroline roused her napping maid in her chamber. "We are going home!"

Dossie looked bewildered. "We are 'ome," she announced.

"I mean we are going to Hanover Square," Caroline said impatiently. "Our old home. Come, Dossie. There is no time to lose."

"My gawd. Miss Caroline, you know what you're sayin'? You goin' back to that . . . that . . . back to 'is lordship?"

"He is in Kent, Dossie. He will never know. Where is my tippet?"

Caroline changed to her half-boots, and they left by the servants' entrance to avoid any early arriving guests of Ruth's. Dossie grumbled most of the way about the foolishness of certain ladies who insisted on dragging certain old women on wild goose chases. They took a hackney to Hanover Square, which was not all that far from Golden Square.

Caroline paused to look once more at the house where she had been a virtual prisoner for five years. It looked the same, neat and prosperous, its wrought-iron railing newly painted, its windows shining. It was easily the equal of any house on the square. Quelling a rising uneasiness, she climbed the steps to knock, but the brass knocker was missing. That meant the family—family? There was no family—was not in residence.

Caroline knocked anyhow, with her fist.

The door was opened by the butler, Jaynes, whose mouth fell open at the sight of her. "Lady Carroway!" he exclaimed.

"Yes, it is I," said Caroline. "How are you, Jaynes?"

"Very well, madam. It is good to have you back."

"I doubt that," said Caroline. She entered the familiar reception hall, Dossie cowering behind her, and glanced around. It looked the same. It was as if she had never left. She felt the walls pressing in on her, a feeling so intense she wanted to flee and never enter the house again, but she squared her shoulders and moved with assurance toward the staircase.

"I have merely come for some things I left behind," she told the butler. "I shall not keep you long."

"Y-yes, madam," he said. His arms waved uncertainly as if he wanted either to usher her out again, or send for a servant to help her. He did neither. He merely stared as Caroline, Dossie at her heels, climbed the stairs.

"I believe we have some satchels and valises in the attic," Caroline told her maid as they gained her chamber. "We cannot handle a trunk. Go to the attic and see what you can find while I look over my wardrobe."

She knew what she would find—more of those dismal, dark gowns. There were, however, the bride clothes she had brought to her marriage, no longer in style but of fine material that could be remade. There were stockings and undergarments. And there were four small christening gowns.

She had sorted the clothes into piles when Dossie returned with valises and satchels to hold them. In less than an hour they were packed.

Both hands full, they awkwardly managed the stairs. Jaynes was not in sight, but appeared from below stairs, seemingly alerted by the bumping and banging on rails and spindles as they descended.

Caroline set Dossie to watch over their hoard while she attended to the last matter that had brought her here. She walked toward Walter's private study.

Jaynes, aware of her intention, darted to stand before the study door, barring her way.

"His lordship has said you are not to go in there," he said.

"But he is not here, is he? I am in charge when he is away, you will recall. Stand away, Jaynes."

Jaynes did not move.

Caroline tapped her foot. "I do not have all day, Jaynes," she said. "You will move aside."

Jaynes still did not budge. He crossed his arms and glowered at her. "No, madam," he said.

In a sudden move Caroline ground the heel of her sturdy half-boot into Jaynes's right foot. Jaynes let out an anguished howl and backed away. Caroline darted into the study and closed and locked the door behind her, breathing a sigh of relief.

She went first to Walter's desk. The top was bare except for writing materials and its drawers were locked. She prowled the study to find some tool to pry the drawers open. She found nothing. Walter apparently did not leave useful bits of metal lying around. She scanned the bookshelves, as much curious about Walter's reading habits as in hope of finding anything useful. Most of the titles were deadly dull: law court proceedings, the annals of some obscure society for the betterment of poor potboys. They had never had a potboy; why would Walter be interested? She opened a volume and noted the name written on the flyleaf: David Winston Hargreaves.

In a book on a low shelf, a book whose cover was worn

until the gilt lettering was almost indecipherable, Caroline made out the word "*Lycee.*" French for school, she knew that much. Again a name on the flyleaf: George Hamstead. Walter had a library of used books! Chosen only for appearance! This one held no interest; its only notable feature was a bookmark left in the pages. The bookmark was leather, but it was rigid. Quite rigid.

Caroline soon realized it was a leather-*covered* bookmark, leather over a spine of metal—copper, she guessed from its weight. She had her prying tool.

She had made only one attempt to slip the bookmark between the center drawer and the desk frame when the leather covering slipped. It was then she discovered the soft leather was only a case for the metal. She worked the metal spine out, turning it over and over in her hand, and the truth came to her.

The metal piece was silverplate, not copper, and it bore an inscription.

> *Walter Carroway*
> Pour service méritoire à France
> *1809*

Caroline's eyes widened. Here was proof that Walter was a traitor, though she supposed he could invent some innocent reason for such a damning award, for an award it must be. She supposed he had left it in its protective case, put it in a book, and forgotten about it. Four years ago! He must have been providing "meritorious service to France" for much longer than that. She returned it to its case, which shielded her hand from the sharp metal edges, and set to work.

Still, her job was not easy. The desk drawers were tightly fitted, with no space at their margins for insertion of a pry bar. She worked feverishly, nicking and scraping the fine finish on the rosewood. Eventually she worked the center drawer out far enough to push in the bar, but it met resistance from the lock backplate. She looked around wildly, close to despair.

On a nearby small table was a silver candlestick holding a half-burned beeswax candle. (And he made me use tallow, she thought with disgust.) Caroline pulled out the candle stub, tossed it to the floor, and used the candlestick to pound at her pry bar. It was difficult to aim correctly; the candlestick slid off the smooth leather of the bar time after time. She narrowly avoided pounding her hand instead.

By now she was frantic. To get this far, and then fail! If only Jaynes were not so loyal to Walter . . . if only Dickon were with her . . . if only.

"If onlys," had never done her any good; they would do her no good now. She renewed her assault.

The lock did not give; the wood of the drawer front was solid. Caroline tried another tack. Sitting on the floor beneath the desk, she hammered at the drawer bottom with the candlestick. The drawer bottom was made of thinner, softer wood than the front. Hacking and gouging, pounding from below, she managed to split the wood and rip the bottom of the drawer out in pieces. Its contents fell to the floor.

Caroline rose and leaned back in the desk chair, pushing her hair out of her eyes and rotating her shoulders, which had become cramped. At last! Then she dropped to her knees again to examine the litter on the floor.

Most of the drawer's contents were of no interest: a supply of quill pens, a stack of calling cards, now spread over a large area of the rug, a neatly pressed and folded handkerchief. A gleam of metal caught her eye, and she found a ring of keys.

One of the keys fitted the other drawers of the desk. In a bottom drawer she discovered an account book, which she glanced at hurriedly. She was unable to decipher its entries, so she put it aside to take with her. Another drawer held sheaves of correspondence. She and Dossie could not carry all this, in addition to her clothes! She pressed a fistful of letters into the account book and left the others.

The ring held seven keys of various sizes and shapes. One, larger and shorter than the others, piqued her interest.

Somehow it reminded her of one of her father's, and it came to her: the key to a safe!

It took her no more than three minutes to discover the safe hidden behind a bland picture of a ship in full sail. The key fitted. The safe contained bundles of bank notes tied around with string and soft leather bags of gold sovereigns. Caroline left the sovereigns since they were too heavy to carry conveniently, and took a bundle of notes, which she pushed down the neckline of her gown. She now bulged in some of the wrong places, but she did not care.

Gripping the account book so the correspondence would not fall out, she left the litter on the floor, the broken bits of wood from the desk drawer where they lay, and the dented, battered candlestick set defiantly on the desk top. The leather-cased bookmark went into the account book. She listened at the door, and, hearing nothing, turned the key. Still nothing. She opened the door a crack and peered out. She saw not Dossie but a group of chattering servants, nearly the entire household staff, gathered in the reception hall.

They were firing questions at Dossie, who could be heard protesting, "I don't know nothin'!" again and again.

Caroline came to her rescue. "That will be all," she told the knot of servants in an imperious voice. Several looked at her in surprise. Not used to my raising my voice, she thought. Her control over staff had been minimal in the old days.

"You may return to your posts," she bid them. She edged her way through the knot and, tucking the account book firmly under one arm, picked up a valise in each hand. "Come, Dossie."

"Oh, Miss Caroline! I was wonderin' if you'd ever come back," said the relieved Dossie. "Are you all right?"

"Yes." Caroline turned to address the hovering butler. "Jaynes, you may open the door."

Jaynes sprang to his duty but looked angry. "Where can his lordship find you?" he asked. "He will wish to know."

Caroline glanced pointedly at Jaynes's right foot. "Tell him I am staying . . . *elsewhere*," she said. Heads held high, she and Dossie marched out of the house. The staff, who had made no move to return to their duties, watched in awed silence.

Not until they were settled in a hackney did Caroline begin to relax. She clutched Dossie's shoulders and gasped, "We did it! I cannot believe we did it! Oh, Dossie, I was so frightened."

"They'd never 'ave knowed it," her maid said loyally. "That Mr. Jaynes! Oh, I did like that, wot you did to 'im."

Caroline sat back, laying the account book, which she still held tightly, on the seat beside her. "Yes, I did rather well, did I not?" she said. "I did not imagine I could. I hope never to go back to that house again."

The two-masted lugger sat quietly at anchor off Globsden Gut, the water lapping softly at its sides. No other craft was in sight. Except for two of the crew, no one was on deck. They were below in the minute cabin, escaping the rain while they plotted the night's itinerary.

"If we don't get a wind, we aren't goin' anywhere," Harold Penney told Dickon. The other two excise men nodded solemnly. "With this rain we ought to have a wind. Damn!"

"Will you be showing lights?" Dickon asked. "If we are ever able to move, that is."

"Up to the captain," said Penney. "You sure McBride said north of Dymchurch? He could have been puttin' you off, see, when he really meant *south* of Dymchurch. The Dymchurch Wall runs on up north a bit, which means there's a lot o' sand and shingle to cross, just as there is here, and besides, there's hardly a track to the shore up that way. Can't get horses in, see? Horses to haul the stuff to the boats they got hidden in the marsh."

"What is the Dymchurch Wall?" Dickon asked.

"Sand, shingle, runs all the way from about Hythe down to near Denge Ness. You didn't see it at Dymchurch? All that sand? Can't bring a boat in close."

Dickon tried not to show his disappointment. He had been so certain the landing point would be north, as Bart

McBride had indicated. He brightened. Perhaps McBride was wily enough to think "Mr. Richards" would not believe his story of a landing point north of Dymchurch and would look south, when north was right all along.

He suggested this to Penney.

"McBride's a downy cove, he is," said Penney. "You may have the right of it, lad. We'll try north if the wind ever picks up. Don't have much hope for tonight, though. Rain, no wind, no moon. Damn! 'Excise luck,' we call it."

The men sat morosely in the cramped little cabin for an hour, awaiting developments. Dickon wished he had saved some of McBride's brandy for the occasion. It would go down very nicely right now.

At last they heard shouts and activity above, the rattle of the anchor chain, and finally, creaks and groans as the lugger got away. Dickon climbed on deck to watch. Sailors were hoisting the sails, which caught the freshening breeze and drove the old lugger northward. It carried a single running light at the stern. The rain still came down, but Dickon believed it had slackened.

Someone gave him a waterproof and he repaired to the stern to watch the wake, more of a sound than a sight in the dim light of the single lantern. Around him, wavelets kicked up as the sea grew restless. His rising feeling of excitement soon became a feeling of another kind.

Seasickness! This was a possibility that had never occurred to him. As they sailed north past Dymchurch, he leaned over the side and gave up his bread and cheese.

Surely it must be morning by now, Dickon thought dimly. He had stretched out on deck near the stern, out of the crew's way and as far as possible from the wheelhouse where the captain reigned, chatting with the three excise men when he had the time. The rain had stopped, but Dickon was wet through. The deck was not the best place to lie. He was also chilled. April in the Channel was hardly high summer.

Considerate of his condition, the other men had left him alone. Probably laughing their heads off, he thought morosely. He sat up, fumbled with cold fingers for his pocket watch, and learned it was just past midnight. He felt better. The lugger rode more smoothly.

He rose and, holding to the gunwale, lurched to the wheelhouse, where he was greeted by Penney.

"We have gone to the end of the Wall and are starting south again," Penney reported. "Haven't seen a thing suspicious. You may have got wet for nothin'. How d'you feel?"

"Better," said Dickon, pushing his wet hair out of his eyes. "But most definitely wet. No dry clothes available, I trust? I apologize for my unseemly . . . er . . . behavior."

Penney laughed. "You ain't the first, lad. Have a tot of rum to warm your insides. Duty's been paid, mind! The navy's been runnin' on rum for centuries. Wish we could offer you some dry clothes, but . . . " He held out a half-full bottle.

Dickon took it gladly. One gulp and it was running down his throat like fire. It stayed down, though. He believed it helped.

By one o'clock the wind had dried his outer clothes and he felt much improved, though his undergarments were still damp. His enthusiasm had departed entirely. What in God's name did he, the Earl of Rycote, born and bred in Durham, a landlubber to the core, think he was doing? Telling a bunch of His Majesty's excise men where to go and what to do? Thinking he could catch Viscount Carroway in the act of smuggling brandy into England and smuggling guns out? How jingle-brained could a man be?

A soft whistle cut into his thoughts. The captain looked up as one of the crew raced to alert him to a dark shape in the water ahead, presumably a boat without lights. The captain motioned for silence and ordered the sailor to douse the stern light and trim sail. This could not be accomplished without noise, but the captain hoped the occupants of the boat were too busy to notice as the lugger lost speed and crept toward them.

"We'll wait until we're right on 'er," the captain said in a low voice. "We'll have to go about or we'll ram 'er, and you don't want that, do you? If we can slip alongside, quiet-like, maybe you can board 'er." He squinted at the shape ahead.

"Where are we?" Dickon asked.

"Just off Brock Farm," said the captain. "Track goes from there to Butters Bridge. Gives 'em a way in an' out."

"They're using *that* again?" Penney burst out. "Hellfire! When I think of all the times we surrounded that spot, and nobody came . . . I could have sworn they'd abandoned it."

The lugger arced around, intending to come in alongside the dark boat, and was not more than twenty feet away when the moon peeped through the broken clouds. It revealed a trawler almost ready to capsize from the number of men and kegs gathered on the side away from the lugger, the men striving frantically to lower their cargo into a pair of longboats. They were using nets, but in no sense of order. Apparently, pandemonium had broken out.

"Ahoy there!" the captain called. "State your name and nationality."

He got no response. The large fishing trawler flew no flag.

The captain repeated his command. A flippant voice replied, "What business is it o' yours?"

Penney strode out of the wheelhouse and leaned over the lugger's side. "Excise!" he boomed. "We're about to board you."

"Not bloody likely," the voice answered. Those in the lugger could see the men in the fishing boat flinging themselves over the side into the two longboats, a chaotic collection of nets, kegs, and men piled upon men. In short order the boats began to move toward shore, the remaining kegs on board abandoned.

Penney swore softly. "They'll be hard to catch now," he said. "About all we can do is impound their boat as evidence. Captain, can you have a couple of your men board 'er? Are they armed? May be that their crew is still there, hiding."

"Mr. Penney!" cried Dickon. "Sir, you are thinking only of the brandy. They will need the boat to load the arms! How will they get the arms to France without that boat?

How can we catch them red-handed if the boat's gone? Please, sir. Let us land. Let them think we know nothing of any guns and hope to catch them on land before they can get the brandy into the marsh."

"They'll never load no arms as long as this lugger's sittin' here," the captain pointed out.

"Then sail a few miles away and come back for us later," Dickon begged.

"You tetched? With 'alf my crew off to board that other boat? Can't do it alone." He looked at Dickon with scorn.

"Hurry!" Dickon watched the two longboats, now not more than thirty feet from shore, move forward in fits and starts. The oarsmen did not appear to be coordinated. The fitful moon revealed their efforts, picking out the flash of oars wielded in haste.

Penney evidently agreed that no time should be wasted haranguing. "Don't board," he directed the captain. "We'll try what the lad suggests; can't do no harm. Take your crew and disappear for a while, will you? Give us two, three hours."

The crew members who had expected to board the other boat had not done so. They were not eager to take it by force, and who could blame them? They were not excise men, but hired crew not in the habit of pirating. When they heard the new orders, they efficiently lowered the small boat from the lugger and stood by to help the excise men and Dickon into it.

"Come along, Richards," said Penney. "Did you check your pistol? Is it wet?"

Dickon smiled and patted his midriff. For once he had done something right. "Wrapped up tight," he reported.

Penney did not even suggest Dickon help row. The other two excise men grasped the oars and the boat shot through the water. It scraped bottom well before it reached the shore, which did not seem to bother the excise men in the least. One hopped out, took the painter, and waded in, pulling the boat behind him. The water was only a couple of inches deep when he stopped and everyone got out.

The two longboats were drawn up not fifteen feet away.

They still held a jumble of kegs, but not a smuggler was in sight.

"After 'em," Penney ordered. He sounded discouraged. "Seems like I've done this a few times before."

Dickon, his feet wetter than ever, felt no more optimistic. He scanned the beach in both directions. The only sign of life other than their own small party was a trail of footprints leading inland, and in the dark they were difficult to follow.

One of the excise men produced a lantern, and after he had managed to light it the group set out to follow the footprints. Very soon they found themselves on the edge of the marsh with a stream or canal alongside that emptied into the ocean. The footprints, now that they had left the sand, gave way to flattened grasses. At the bank of the stream they stopped entirely.

Someone was going to have to pick them up again on the other side. Dickon sighed. "I will do it," he offered.

It was only the first of four. Dickon waded them all, roundly cursing Viscount Carroway, James Fenland, John Dunthorpe, Romney Marsh, and the French nation. There was no clear path between streams, only the evidence of trampled grasses.

After the fourth stream, the ground rose a little and seemed dryer underfoot. Dickon was making good headway when he stumbled on something that uttered a startled "Baaa!" It was a sheep, and then it was a dozen or more sheep, who roused and trotted away.

Dickon looked down at the trail he was following. It had been obliterated by the bodies of sheep, resting in the night. It took him a good ten minutes to pick it up again.

They had been on the trail of the smugglers for nearly an hour now, and seemed no closer. Dickon began to worry that the lugger would return too soon; the smugglers must have a base at some distance from the shore, and it might be several more hours before they brought out their guns and ammunition in hopes of loading them onto the longboats and sending them off to France. This would never happen if the lugger was in sight. Dickon hastened his pace and the others followed.

When they came to a cottage standing alone on a slight rise of ground in the marsh, Penney let out an oath.

"Brock Farm!" he cried. "We've been had."

The others looked at him in surprise.

Penney clenched his fists. His expression was ugly. "They've led us astray," he said bitterly. "Brock Farm is not more than a mile from the coast—less, if I recall. There's a cart track between the shore and the farm. If we'd known where we were going, we could have been here in a quarter the time. You can be sure some of 'em took the track and notified the receivers that we were followin' them, while the others led us 'round Robin Hood's barn. Kept us sloggin' through the cursed marsh while they did their nasty business. I'll wager we won't find a sign of 'em here."

Penney was half right—no men, but plenty of tracks. They found trampled ground all around the cottage, and evidence of a horse and cart, seemingly having arrived from the direction of Butters Bridge and then proceeding along the track toward the shore.

"To the shore!" Penney yelled, and the little group broke into a trot, all they could manage with their sodden boots. An excise man relieved Dickon of the lantern and took the lead.

"At least they'll have to unload the longboats before they can reload 'em," Penney said breathlessly to Dickon, who trotted beside him. "That may give us time."

Suddenly the marsh petered out and the shore lay ahead. They had gone less than a mile since leaving the farm. The group stopped, panting, and the excise man extinguished the lantern. They spoke in whispers.

As they crept forward they could see the longboats, darker shadows against the water, and six or seven men with a single shielded lantern, grumbling in low tones as they hefted brandy kegs from the longboats. Again, there seemed to be little sense of order to the operation, but the kegs tumbled out anyhow, some on end, some on their sides. Two of the men left the kegs and began removing a series of crates from a nearby cart, quickly loading them into the longboats.

Dickon described as best he could the three men in charge of this operation. Dunthorpe was known to the others, but Carroway and Fenland were not. Penney deployed his small force. Each man checked his pistol. They advanced.

The smugglers had posted a lookout, who stood far enough away from the longboats to be in complete darkness. His silhouette was apparent against the dim light cast by the smugglers' lantern, however, and it took but a moment for one of the excise men to put him out of action. A hand over his mouth prevented his squawk. Penney quickly gagged the man with his neck scarf and tied him up to be dealt with later.

"Six left, I believe, or is it seven?" Penney whispered. "Remember, we want 'em alive. If you have to shoot, don't aim for a vital spot. We're outnumbered, but we have surprise on our side, I hope!"

Chaos broke out when the smugglers realized they had been discovered. Those loading crates stopped what they were doing and shoved violently at one longboat, which now sat on the shingle, for the tide had ebbed. The other longboat still held a few kegs. Those unloading the second boat dropped their loads; two ran off into the marsh, leaving three men. Using the second longboat as a shield, they ducked low and let off a shot. Meanwhile the first longboat, now clear of the shingle, was being rowed toward the smugglers' own craft. The lugger was not in sight.

It should have been easy, four men against three smugglers, but it was not. The longboat and the kegs gave protection to the smugglers, while Dickon and the excise men were out in the open, easy targets despite the dark. The smugglers' lantern had been doused. The shot spooked the horse harnessed to the cart and it tried to flee, but was hampered by a lead weight to which a tie-down rope was fastened. The horse dragged the weight a few yards and stopped, too far from the smugglers to offer them protection, but also too far from the excise men to be of any help.

At Penncy's command, one of the excise men ran in a zigzag course while Penney covered him, finally reaching safe shelter alongside the cart. Luckily, a shot intended for him went wide. The other three, crouched in the dark, then fanned out to approach the smugglers from three different directions, hoping the darkness would keep them safe until they were within firing range.

"Carroway, come out," Dickon muttered to himself as he approached the longboat from one side. He knew the three remaining smugglers had to be Carroway, Fenland, and Dunthorpe—they would not be likely to flee, leaving their brandy and remaining crates, not to mention the horse and cart, behind.

Carroway evidently believed the crates to be evidence more damning than the brandy. Before Dickon or the others could reach the longboat where the smugglers hid, a figure that Dickon took to be Carroway leaped over the longboat and dashed for the cart. He was madly trying to lift the heavy hitching weight into the cart when the excise man hiding on the other side rose and announced calmly, "Give it up. Lay down your weapon."

Carroway, sneering, disregarded the pistol aimed at him and quickly pulled a gun from his pocket, shooting the excise man in the right arm. With a startled grunt, the man dropped his gun and sank to the beach.

Dickon was too far away to make sure of his target, and he did not wish to hit the horse. He ran after Carroway, hoping his quarry would have to stop and reload. Carroway, however, seemed more intent on getting the cart going with himself in it than in shooting anyone; he bent once more to the task of freeing the horse. Holding the reins with one hand, Carroway searched in the cart, came up with a scythe, then in a wild and poorly aimed swoop he severed the tie-down rope and one of the reins as well. He leaped into the cart and urged the horse onward.

The two other smugglers, their bemused expressions clear in the flickering light of the fickle moon, watched Carroway's flight. When it became apparent that their leader intended to escape without them, they yelled after him but did not leave their refuge. Penney and his remaining excise man, who had made a wide circle, managed to creep up behind them and subdue them without much difficulty.

Dickon ran on after the cart, hampered by sodden boots that sank into the wet sand. What chance did he have, trying to outrun a horse? All Carroway had to do was turn and fire; he could hardly miss. Breathing heavily, near exhaustion, Dickon refused to give up.

Then the horse swung in a wide arc back the way it had come. Dickon could not imagine why, unless Carroway hoped to find the cart track and head back to Brock Farm and Butters Bridge. Dickon altered his course to cut off the returning cart.

It did not head for the cart track. It continued the arc. It was going around in a circle. Dickon tried to puzzle it out as he set one foot before another. The only explanation seemed to be that Carroway was driving with a single rein; he had cut off the other too close to the horse's head. In his agitated desire to escape he was pulling on the one rein, and the horse continued to turn.

Carroway could be heard roundly cursing the horse, the cart, and all England's excise men. Finally, as the cart's circular path took him near the edge of the marsh, he leaped out, fell to the ground, picked himself up, and ran toward the cover of the marsh. Dickon was right behind him.

Dickon could hear him thrashing through the tall grasses. His feet made sucking sounds as he hurried through the mud. Dickon got a good look at him as the moon made another appearance. It was Carroway, all right.

"Halt!" Dickon cried.

Carroway turned. "You!" he said. As he reached for his gun, Dickon aimed his pistol at Carroway's leg. The shot hit home, and it was all over.

Sixteen

Dickon's letter, hastily written, informing Caroline and Ruth of Viscount Carroway's wounding and capture, and of the capture of Fenland and Dunthorpe as well as the smugglers' lookout, got to London long before Dickon did. He was involved in corroborating Penney's account of the capture. He also wished to wait and see whether the fishing trawler, which had escaped with only a partial load of crates, could be overtaken and captured. It was not.

Most important, he was eager to learn just what and how much were in those crates. He, Penney, and the uninjured excise man had broken one open at the scene. It held ammunition. Presumably some of the others held guns, but they did not investigate immediately. They had an injured man who needed a doctor's attention; they had another, more seriously injured prisoner; and they had three grumbling smugglers who were bemoaning their fate. They also had a cart with a horse that had but one useful rein.

The lugger had returned for them more than an hour after the trawler had disappeared. The prisoners—all but Carroway, who was moaning and nearly unconscious—were encouraged at gunpoint to load the crates into the lugger, but there was no room for the horse and cart. The uninjured excise man was left with them, to be rescued when someone could return with a new rein.

The lugger sailed back to the Gut, where Dickon left it to retrieve Pegasus and his gig. Penney arranged to meet him next day in Rye, where the prisoners would be held temporarily. By now it was daylight. Dickon wearily got his horse, paid the man who had kept it, hitched the thoroughly wet gig, and drove to Dymchurch, where he went to bed and slept for thirteen hours.

He ate an enormous supper in the common room after his refreshing sleep. The room was abuzz with rumor and conjecture; it was clear that word of the smugglers' capture had reached Dymchurch, but his part in it apparently had not come out. He was grateful that only the three principals could identify "Mr. Richards" as one of their captors. Talk in the common room had an ominous quality; he could picture himself being beaten, or hanged, or something equally fatal should they learn of his part.

Next day, after posting the letter home, he drove to Rye with all his baggage. He had no desire to see Bart McBride or anyone else in Dymchurch again. In Rye he learned that the injured excise man was doing well and would recover. Carroway however, was another matter. It appeared Dickon's bullet had damaged a most vulnerable spot.

"But I shot him in the leg!" Dickon insisted.

"So ye did, lad. Maybe your aim was a mite high? Maybe he moved just a bit at the wrong time?" Harold Penney asked.

"Possibly. Will he recover?"

"No doubt. He's a tough one. We aim to keep him alive until they question him, at least. He's to go to London so the War Office people can have a look at him. Plenty they'll want to ask him, see."

"What about the brandy smuggling? I thought you wished to clear that up first."

Penney grimaced. "That's the lot of the excise, lad. Nobody likes us. We break up a big smugglin' operation, and do we get thanks? No, we got to give up our prime smuggler—a viscount at that!—and let the War Office have 'im. Excise luck, it is."

"May I see the viscount?"

"Ho! I suppose so. Best do it today; he's to go to London tomorrow."

Dickon found Carroway in a cell in the Rye jail, lying on a cot with his eyes closed. His right hip and thigh bulged with bandages. He did not open his eyes when the warden, opening the cell door with a clang, announced he had a visitor.

"Lord Carroway," Dickon addressed him. The man on the cot did not respond.

"My lord," said Dickon, "may you rot in hell for what you have done to Lady Carroway." He turned to go.

Carroway immediately revived. "What did you say?" he asked in a harsh voice. "Lady Carroway?"

"She is well, but no thanks to you," said Dickon. "She knows of your arrest; she knows the whole sordid story. I have made sure of that."

Carroway stared at his visitor. "Did she have the babe?" he demanded.

"It did not survive," Dickon said shortly.

Carroway did not seem surprised. "Who are you, 'Mr. Richards'?" he asked. "You and your 'double your profits' scheme? What have you done with my wife?" He sneered. "My dear, barren wife?"

"Nobody," said Dickon. "I am nobody. Good day, your lordship."

Dickon rattled the door of the cell until the warden came to release him.

An inventory of the crates had revealed enough guns and ammunition to annihilate an entire regiment. They too were to be shipped to London for inspection and action by the War Office.

Finally, having shaken hands all around with the excise men, he pointed Pegasus toward London.

"A thousand pounds? Mercy! How brave of you!" Ruth was all agog to hear the details of Caroline's visit to Hanover Square.

"But let me show you what else I found," Caroline said excitedly. "Look at this." She held out the silver bookmark in its case, now shredded and torn.

Ruth turned it over and over, mystified. "What is it?"

"Remove it from its case."

Ruth did so. "Oh!" she cried, noting the inscription.

"Wait until Dickon sees this! And what else have you there?"

Caroline produced the accounts book stuffed with correspondence. The letters were carefully worded, referring to "deliveries" or "loads" or "goods." She believed them to be from Walter's brandy customers. They were signed with single names only, Jem or Roger or, in one case, Billy One-Eye. They would be of little use as evidence. None could be tied to a trade in guns, for the writers were ordering, not selling.

Caroline then turned to the accounts book. It seemed to be in some sort of code—something for Dickon to handle.

But the thousand pounds and the clothing she had rescued were all hers. She had enough money for the foreseeable future, clothes, and her self-respect. It was a heady feeling.

She and Ruth marked time until Dickon returned a few days later. Caroline tried to work on another christening gown, but her attention wandered. Several times she had to pull out her embroidery stitches and do them over again; finally she lost patience and put the garment aside. What was the hurry now, when she had a thousand pounds in reserve?

She was full of uncertainty. What should she do about Walter, now lying seriously injured somewhere? According to Dickon's last letter, he had been taken to the Rye jail, but she assumed he would be brought to London to face charges. Would he be held in Newgate? In his present state he could do nothing to her, and with Fenland in custody, she believed herself safe. What about her wedding vow, "in sickness and in health"? Must she hold herself to that, now that Walter was injured?

In her heart of hearts, she wished Dickon had killed him.

She chastised herself for such a thought. Surely he would be hanged if convicted of treason. Surely there was enough evidence to convict him.

Dickon's final arrival was almost an anticlimax. Ruth and Caroline had spent hours planning a fitting celebration, and could think of nothing more festive than an elaborate dinner.

"It must include all his favorite dishes," Caroline decreed.

"Nearly any dish is his favorite," said Ruth, laughing. "Had you not noticed? Put food before him and he eats it with relish."

Ruth conferred with the cook, and they settled on a menu built around a roast of beef and ending with gooseberry fool. Their only problem was when to schedule it, for they did not know when to expect Dickon.

He arrived late one morning while the ladies were reading the day's mail. They were quietly discussing the pros and cons of attending Lady Lacroix's musicale when Dickon sauntered into the sitting room and said, "Good morning."

"Dickon!" Ruth shrieked. She flew into his arms for a big hug. "Oh, Dickon, you are home safe! We are so proud of you!"

Caroline rose, too, but stood, hesitant.

"Do you not wish a hug?" Dickon quirked a smile at her. "I have plenty to spare, I think—wait just a moment." He turned and looked behind him. "Yes, several there in reserve." He held out his arms.

Caroline laughed in delight and went into them.

Dickon smelled of the outdoors, of faraway places, but that was forgotten now as her world became encompassed by his arms. Caroline could not look into his face for fear of what she would see there: an invitation she could not accept. She pressed her cheek against his chest. She was so glad to see him—and yet she was not. The old tension, the old longings, were back.

"Welcome home," she said, her words spoken into his coat. She hugged him, hard.

Caroline tried to act as if nothing had happened when Dickon released her. She felt embarrassed at the display of affection before Ruth, but Ruth gave no sign of having noticed. She spoke brightly of the festive dinner to come and begged to know whether Dickon would prefer trifle to gooseberry fool.

"Fool, by all means," said Dickon. "Now that we have covered the most important decision of the day, would I be amiss in asking how you two have managed without me? What mischief have you been up to?"

"You shall see," said Caroline, a gleam in her eye. She hurried from the room and soon returned with the bookmark and the accounts book. She pulled the thin strip of silver from its case and laid it before him.

Dickon stifled an ungentlemanly expletive. "Where did this come from?" he demanded. "Oh, will this ever put the cap on Not-John's case! Well done!" He squeezed Caroline's hand.

Caroline related details of her visit to Hanover Square. "and here is the accounts book," she said eagerly. "I also took a thousand pounds in notes, as payment of five years' pin money."

Dickon scarcely heard the reference to the thousand pounds, he was so fascinated with the accounts. The figures he could read; they marched down the pages in straight rows, income and outflow. The notations next to them could have been in Greek or Sanskrit for all he knew. In any case, it was apparent that Viscount Carroway was a major figure in the smuggling game. If his code could be broken, here was enough evidence to convict him twice over. The bookmark was the crowning touch.

"I must go to the War Office immediately," he said, refusing a cup of tea. "I am delighted to know of this extra evidence; Lord Avebury must be told at once. Perhaps someone on the staff is good at breaking codes. I shall inquire. But Caroline! How should I explain my having these? Are we to tell Avebury that Viscount Carroway's wife is living under an assumed name with my sister and me?" He frowned. "That will set the tongues to wagging!"

Caroline considered. "Must you tell how you came by them?" Informed that it would be odd if he did not, she agreed to his revealing the truth. "But do ask him not to spread it about," she begged.

"I shall do my best," Dickon promised. He left, taking the accounts book and the bookmark with him, and promised to be home in time for the festive dinner.

They had not even had time to hear Dickon's own story.

Ruth riffled through the pile of invitations remaining on her desk. "Lady Lacroix's musicale? I think not; we shall be exceedingly busy for a time. Ah. I see Lady Robstart is to have a Viewing Tuesday next, and you and I are both invited. What are we to view, I wonder? Ah, yes, here it is—we are to admire her portrait, just completed. Full-length, it says here! You will wish to go, of course?"

"Beg pardon?" said Caroline.

"Lady Robstart's Viewing! You did not hear I word I said."

"No," Caroline agreed.

Her mind was with the gentleman now on his way to present to his superior the evidence that would likely send her husband to his death.

Cook fussed over the soup, the roast of beef, the jellied eel, the carrots, the savories, the gooseberry fool, and all the other dishes she had lovingly prepared for his lordship's return.

He did not return.

Ruth sent one message after another to the kitchen, setting dinner back fifteen minutes, then half an hour, then another half an hour. She and Caroline had donned their finest and sat waiting impatiently.

"He is usually on time!" Caroline said in a worried tone.

"When at the War Office? You jest! One never knows when he can or will tear himself away."

"I hope nothing has happened to him," Caroline went on. "He promised . . . What can be keeping him?"

"Who knows?" Ruth said lightly. She would not let Caroline know that she too was worried. "Shall we continue with the invitations while we wait? We must let Lady Robstart know . . . I suppose I should attend her Viewing, considering all the visits she has made here. May I hope you will go as well?"

"Hang Lady Robstart," Caroline said inelegantly. "To see her portrait, *full-length,* as well as to see her in person is a double dose I doubt I can countenance. No, thank you."

"It is my cross to bear that she is a relative of my late husband," said Ruth. She sighed. "Very well."

Conversations died as they sat waiting.

Dickon did not return until near ten of the clock. Cook had long since despaired of him. She sent word to Ruth that the roast was too brown and dried to a crisp, the vegetables were tasteless puddles, and she would not answer for the gooseberry fool. Still, the two ladies refused to dine without him. What was a celebratory dinner without the honored guest?

Dickon looked haunted when he came in, unlike the cheerful Dickon of the morning.

"He has killed himself," he announced without preamble.

"You mean Walter?" Caroline cried. She felt cold all over.

"Yes, Walter."

Dickon would remember that grisly scene to his dying day. He had spent the day with Lord Avebury, filling in details. He had presented the bookmark and accounts book; Avebury had set one of their more educated lads to puzzling out the accounts. The bookmark was received with delight and would go into evidence. Avebury and Dickon were concluding their talk when a messenger arrived with news of Viscount Carroway's death. They hurried to the prison.

The prisoner, who had arrived from Rye earlier in the day, had paid for a decent meal but had eaten only part of it when he apparently decided to end it all. His cot stood under a high, barred window; a very tall man standing on the cot could just see out. Carroway was not that tall. He had unwound the bandage from his bullet wound, fashioned it into a noose, placed it around his neck, then had managed to stand on the cot long enough to fasten the noose to a bar of the window. A kick at the cot with his good leg, and it was soon over.

Dickon had seen dead men before, but never a sight so appalling as Walter Carroway, his wound bared, his tongue out, eyes staring. He had been the lone prisoner in the cell, whether at the War Office's orders or through his own payments to the warden, Dickon did not know. He probably had been dead for some hours before he was discovered.

I brought this on, Dickon thought in wonder. I shot him. How do the men fighting on the Continent ever get used to this? For them it must be an everyday occurrence, seeing their comrades as well as their enemies die. Perhaps one gets used to it.

He did not dwell on the unpleasant details in his recital to Caroline and Ruth.

"Walter must have been quite determined, to have raised himself on that cot with that wound," he concluded. "The bullet had been removed, of course, and I am told he was healing quite well. Probably would have recovered completely, except for the loss of . . . ah . . . certain manly parts."

"Now there will be no trial," said Caroline. Perhaps, then, word of the whole affair would not get out, unless some journalist got wind of it. It seemed almost too much to hope that her own name need never come up. But there would have to be a funeral, and who would arrange it but herself? She thought dismally of the black gloves, the wreaths, the cortege. And she would have to go back into her blacks. It was too much to be borne, all for a man whom she despised.

Perhaps she could persuade his solicitor to take on those burdens. The solicitor, however, knew very well of her existence. She did not see old Mr. Lamburton doing this for her.

"I wonder why he did it," Dickon mused. "I must confess I am at a loss. To hang himself! The penalty for treason is forfeiture of lands, not hanging. I had forgotten that. That traitor could have lived to a ripe old age! Scorned, yes, and landless, yes, but he would have managed. Lord Avebury was astonished. He expected Walter to deny everything at his trial, and it is possible he could have got by with paying a fine, slippery eel that he is, er, was. Fenland and Dunthorpe, however, were happy to peach on him. Both insist they are model citizens who were forced at gunpoint to do Carroway's bidding."

"I have an idea the 'gunpoint' was blackmail," said Caroline. "If Fenland ever was a model citizen, he would have

outgrown it by the age of two. He made me shiver every
time he visited."

"I suppose we shall never know the straight of it,"
Dickon mused. "Shall we go in to supper?"

"I know! Of course!" Caroline burst out. "You say he
was shot in the . . . in the . . . "

"He was."

"Then he could never sire an heir." An enormous weight
seemed to fall from Caroline's shoulders. Walter's death
had not begun to remove the guilt she still felt at failing to
provide him with an heir. By some convoluted reasoning,
the fact that he could not have fathered a son had he lived
freed her of that guilt.

"Dickon!" she cried. "I am free!"

"Yes," he said. "You are just beginning to realize that?
At last you are free."

But at what a cost. His elation at bringing Walter down,
at breaking up the man's treacherous arms trade as well as
his brandy smuggling, had dissipated, to be replaced by
cold disgust. Walter had been only one of the many oppor-
tunists profiting from this protracted war with France.
When would it end? How much longer would young Eng-
lishmen be called to defend their country and die, or be
brought home with limbs missing? What chance did his
brother Benjamin have to survive?

His face was set as they went to supper, a lady on each of
Dickon's arms—although he held Caroline's arm more
tightly than necessary.

"I should like to accompany you when you visit your
man of law this morning," Dickon offered at breakfast. It
was still early. Caroline, dreading what lay before her,
wished to get it over with as soon as possible.

"Oh, would you?" she said with relief. "I cannot think
what to do about Walter's funeral. I am likely to agree to
anything Mr. Lamburton suggests, as much out of igno-
rance as anything else. I suppose I should be seeing to
black armbands for the servants—black gloves—a service

with the reverend extolling Walter's supposed virtues . . . I am not sure I can face it."

She was looking pale and careworn this morning. It was almost as if she truly mourned the blackguard, Dickon thought.

As if she had divined his thoughts, Caroline said, "It is not that I am sorry he is gone. I only wonder whether I could have prevented all this, or perhaps stopped it. I should have sought to take more interest in his affairs. Instead I wallowed in my misery and sewed christening gowns and felt sorry for myself. Surely I could have learned what he was about; James Fenland often visited, and they would shut themselves up in Walter's study. Somehow I could have eavesdropped, or paid one of the servants who was not in Walter's pocket—not all were completely loyal to him—and learned of Walter's business. But I did not! I never suspected! I thought too much of my own f-f-failure to b-b-become a mother . . . my own unhappiness . . . "

Caroline put her head in her hands and sobbed.

Dickon asked gently, "What could you have done had you learned what Walter was doing?"

"I don't know!" she cried. "Surely I would have thought of something. Dossie could have smuggled out a letter to my father perhaps. I could have written to the prime minister!"

"Possibly," he said. "I rather think the accusations of an unhappy wife, denied of course by Walter, would have carried little weight."

"Yes," she said in resignation. "You are quite right, I suppose. Who would listen to a mere female?" She bit her lip.

"Let us be off to see Mr. Lamburton. The gig is waiting." Dickon sent a glance of understanding to his silent sister and ushered Caroline out.

Mr. Lamburton advised Caroline to have as small and quiet a funeral ceremony as possible, but agreed that it would be difficult. Already word of Walter's treason and his death was spreading throughout London, thanks to the newspapers. Dickon was not mentioned by name. Nothing was said about suicide, however. It was given out that he had died in prison from his wounds while awaiting trial. There was nothing to prevent his burial in hallowed ground.

Feeling guilty of deceit, Caroline agreed. She did not really care where Walter was buried, but a straightforward funeral would be easier. She supposed she would be expected to receive mourners afterward at the house in Hanover Square, a task she dreaded, but it would be over in a few hours.

"And now, about the will," said Mr. Lamburton.

"Yes?" said Caroline. "I suppose he left his estate to a society for the improvement of potboys?"

Mr. Lamburton frowned. This was no occasion for levity. "You are his sole legatee," he said, "unless"—he looked pointedly at Caroline's slim waist—"there is issue from this marriage?"

"No issue," she said.

"The will is dated November of 1807," Lamburton continued. "That would be, I believe, soon after your wedding?"

"Yes."

"His lordship mentioned to me a time or two recently that he wished to change his will, but he never did," said Lamburton. "I have no notion of what he planned. This, then, is his last will and testament. I bring it up today because there are no other heirs to notify; you are the only one. If I recall, he had no near blood relatives who might be expected to challenge. Am I right?"

"You are," said Caroline.

"It will take time to learn of all his investments. As I recall, he owns—owned—property in Kent and elsewhere as well as the house in Hanover Square. These are certain to be confiscated by the Crown as happens when a man is convicted of treason. However, your ladyship, you should receive—ahem—in the neighborhood of two hundred thousand pounds, give or take a bit."

Lamburton did not look happy.

Caroline was stunned. Two hundred thousand pounds! She was not aware so much money existed. Her memory turned to that wall safe in Walter's study. The bank notes and gold sovereigns left there probably did not figure in Lamburton's estimate, so the amount she would inherit probably would be even higher. And the house—and the property in Kent, whatever it was ... How much of it was the profit from smuggled brandy, smuggled arms? She was sure most of it was illegally acquired, but how was one to tell?

"Will I be held liable for ... for Walter's illegal gains?" she asked Lamburton.

He frowned. "It is quite possible that a fine will be levied as well," he said. "You must be aware that I knew nothing of his lordship's—ah—trading activities until I read the newspaper. Nothing at all! Naturally I am shocked. *Quite* shocked."

"Thank you," said Caroline. "My lord Rycote, shall we go?"

Dickon, who had been introduced to the solicitor as a family friend, rose and took Caroline's arm. He gave Lamburton a rueful smile. It was intended to convey to the solicitor the impression that Lady Carroway was a helpless female who understood little of this matter, and needed a man at her side for support. Dickon had no doubt Lamburton knew every devious path Walter Carroway had taken. He intended to see that the man's greedy fingers got no more of Caroline's inheritance than absolutely necessary.

They left amid pleasant and wholly false thanks and good wishes on both sides.

The funeral was much like a performance at Astley's Amphitheatre and drew a larger crowd. Caroline's wish to have it as small and brief as possible went for nought. Curiosity-seekers surrounded the church and later, the house in Hanover Square, where she offered refreshments to the mourners. She had long since run out of the black-bordered handkerchiefs and mourning rings she gave as mementos. She wore black bombazine, a gown taken from her own old supply.

What she found hardest to bear were remarks made by well-meaning people offering sympathy. Many of Walter's good-time friends did not seem to know she existed and had difficultly hiding their surprise. No one seemed to know quite what to say without referring to the reason for Walter's death.

Ruth and Dickon offered their stalwart support, though they were known to few of the mourners; they and Walter had moved in different circles.

Ruth attempted to waylay a pair she had been certain would attend: Lady Robstart and Mrs. Hinkle. They had even brought their husbands. The two ladies gave Ruth perfunctory kisses on the cheek and moved on toward Caroline despite Ruth's efforts to distract them.

"Lady Carroway!" cried Mrs. Hinkle. "You could have knocked me over with a feather! I simply could not believe it when I learned you are not Mrs. Makepeace at all." She giggled. "Lady R. and I wish to offer you our deepest sympathy. I *know* you must be devastated at the passing of your beloved husband." She cast a telling glance at Dickon, standing nearby.

"Oh, yes," Lady Robstart gushed, "it is such a pity, to be widowed at such a young age! You have no children, I gather? They can be a comfort at a time like this. But of course you have dear *friends* to comfort you." She glared at Dickon.

The last several days had been so full of stress and demands that Caroline was not certain she could hold up until this dreadful ordeal was over. The cutting remarks made by these two harpies seemed the crowning blow, but she rallied one last time.

"Thank you for your condolences," she said as calmly as she could. "They are much appreciated." She turned away to speak to someone else, subtly dismissing the ladies and their husbands, who trailed behind and said nothing.

When the guests were gone and only she, Ruth, and Dickon were left, Ruth said, "Now let us go home. It is all over, thank God."

"I shall go with you, but tomorrow I move back here," said Caroline. "This is my home, at least until I can arrange for another. Surely the government will permit me time to find a home."

"You shall do nothing of the sort," Ruth said firmly. "What nonsense! Someone will be along any minute to throw you out!"

"You cannot do that!" Dickon cried. "You belong with us!"

"Thank you both, dear friends. This is my house for the moment and I mean to make some changes. Jaynes, the butler, must go, and I shall sack some others. There is much to be done, and I must be about it."

Seventeen

The parting was bittersweet. Caroline packed and did not allow herself to think of the coming lonely days. She expected to be so busy she would not have time to miss Ruth and, particularly, Dickon. She tried to make clear to both of them that they were to call often; she owed them more than she could ever repay.

Dickon refused to let her go without a private talk. The morning of her departure he motioned her into the library while Ruth was conferring with the cook.

She walked into the library ahead of him. He closed the door firmly, leaning against it. "Come here," he said.

Caroline looked up, startled. Since that light-hearted hug the day he returned from Kent, they had never so much as touched. No secret smiles or looks had passed between them; Dickon had been grave and preoccupied. She could understand that. Walter's treason and death overshadowed everything.

"Come here," Dickon said again. At her hesitation, he went to her instead and took her into his arms.

"God! It has been much too long," he murmured between kissing her and stroking her cheek. "Dear Miss Caroline!" He kissed her under her right ear. "My adored Mrs. Makepeace!" He switched to the left ear. "My beloved Lady Carroway!" He kissed the tip of her nose. "Do you not think it time to change your name once more? To Lady Rycote, perhaps?" The next kiss was on the mouth, and it was by far the best of all.

Caroline felt her heart ready to burst. Oh, if only she could! Enfolded in Dickon's arms, with kisses that grew in ardor, she was ready to agree to anything he asked. But it was, of course, impossible. She must mourn the regulation year. Dickon would understand that. But would he understand that she could never give him the heir that he would surely want, perhaps as keenly as had Walter? Let him choose some young girl who could give him a son, a raft of sons. She now had enough money to live comfortably the rest of her life; she could travel, perhaps become reacquainted with her family, undertake good works.

Somehow the future looked bleak.

"Oh, Dickon," she cried in despair. "You know I cannot."

"Why is that?" He teased a curl behind her ear.

"I must observe a year of mourning. I dislike to think what is being said about me already. You may be sure it is all over town, if Lady Robstart and Mrs. Hinkle are aware of it. I dare not add insult to injury by failing to mourn properly."

"What is being said?" Dickon kissed her fingers, one by one.

"You know as well as I! That I fled my husband, hid under an assumed name—it is actually my grandmother's maiden name, did I tell you that?—that I am said to be *close* to a man not my husband, a state that existed long before his death. Is that not enough? The next thing you know, they will have me mixed up in Walter's smuggling!"

"Who is this man you are said to be close to?" Dickon ran his fingertips lightly up Caroline's arm.

"As if you did not know! You, of course! And to think how proper we have been, always! But there are some who must believe the worst."

"I see nothing *worst* about it," he said, giving her a heart-stopping smile. "I think it sounds perfectly delightful. I can think of nothing finer than being close. Quite close." He hugged her again, then framed her face with his hands. "Caroline," he said, looking into her eyes, "I need you close for the rest of my days. I love you, and I want you for my wife. Forget what 'they' will say. Marry me, and we will show them who is *close*."

Almost undone by Dickon's caresses and his warm proposal Caroline burst into tears.

"Oh! If only . . . " she cried, twisting from his embrace.

If only. There it was again. She had vowed never to wallow in "if onlys." She straightened and wiped her eyes.

"I cannot, Dickon. You know I cannot. Please, let us not speak of it further. It is time I left. Do you wish to drive me, or should I take a hackney? I seem to have rather a lot of baggage, and there is Dossie to consider."

"Then I shall make two trips," Dickon said. He kissed her lightly. "You have not seen the last of me," he warned.

"I should hope not! I want you and Ruth to come to dinner the moment I am settled."

"Madam, your wish is my command." Straightfaced, Dickon gave her an elaborate bow. He swept open the library door with a flourish to usher her out. As she passed him, he winked.

Caroline had her hands full coping with the situation at the Hanover Square house. The staff was at sixes and sevens, with ill feelings between those loyal to Viscount Carroway and those who had disliked him, though never before had they dared show it. Caroline knew fairly well which were which, but some of the lower servants' loyalties were a mystery, and some she had rarely dealt with. The grooms, for example. Beyond knowing their names, she knew little of them. She did not wish to turn off good workers who sorely needed their positions.

In the end she sacked Jaynes and two footmen who seemed to be his cronies. Through an agency she hired a new butler named Crubbins, and a single footman. As a widow living alone she did not need another.

She lived in perpetual fear of being turned out of her house, and she had done nothing about buying another; she could not afford to until she came into her inheritance. Mr. Lamburton advised patience. He had acted to delay the forfeiture by submitting to the court that no trial had been held; Walter had not yet been convicted. That seemed to Caroline a mere formality, but she accepted Lamburton's explanation and the bill that accompanied it. He would not receive his fee until the will was proved.

She went out every day. June had come to London, and June that year was better than average, with many beautiful days. The air was clearer, now that fireplaces were allowed to grow cold. Her real reason for leaving home regularly was to assure herself she was free to come and go at will. All it took was a message to the stables to have the carriage and groom ready, and she could drive anywhere she liked.

To her surprise this eventually palled. By July she had lost interest in going out with no destination in mind. She feared leaving the house and finding herself dispossessed when she returned.

She busied herself deciding which items she would keep and which would be left for the Crown. She supposed the Crown had a right to all of them, but surely her clothes, her personal possessions, would not be forfeit? What about the new, small desk she had bought to replace Walter's damaged one? She had found his hoard in the wall safe untouched, and removed most of it to the bank. There was plenty to pay for her new desk and keep her, she hoped, until she gained her inheritance. She had found nothing else of interest in the old desk. The sheaf of correspondence she had discovered earlier consisted of more seeming orders for brandy and wines. She burned them.

One day she was called upon by Lord Avebury, who found her in the study that was now hers. She was astonished to receive a call from Dickon's superior, the Old Man himself, and when Crubbins announced that Lord Avebury awaited, she quaked inwardly. Did he think she knew something of Walter's business? How long was she to be tangled in this mess Walter had created? She wanted only to have done with it.

"Show him in," she told Crubbins.

After the usual pleasantries, Lord Avebury came to the point.

"There is a matter of a fine," he said. "The case would come up in the Exchequer if you chose to dispute it. You will be notified, of course, but I thought it best to warn you."

"Am I to be held liable forever for something Walter did?" she asked. "They are already going to take this house, I am told. And whatever properties he had elsewhere."

"Oh, yes. The fine will be levied against his estate; perfectly legal, I assure you. You have not yet come into the estate, have you?"

"No," she said. "I am told that it takes time. How much is the fine likely to be?"

"The Crown is seeking fifty thousand pounds. If you wish to contest it, it will be up to the judge—the baron, as he is known."

Caroline's dream of a long life free of financial worries vanished abruptly. "Fifty thousand pounds!" she cried. "That is beyond anything! How can they do this to me? Why such a monstrous sum, your lordship?"

Avebury gave her a sympathetic look. "Because they know he had it," he said. "You are fortunate that they are not taking everything he owned, leaving you with nothing. I was able to intercede on your behalf, considering the evidence of that silver bookmark you found and gave to Rycote. Not to mention that accounts book; our cipher expert is still working on it. We hope it will lead us to the supplier of Carroway's arms. It may be highly irregular, but I have managed to persuade them that you knew nothing of your husband's activities, that in fact you have done the Crown a service, and that you should not be left penniless. Do you mean to fight the fine? I advise against it, for it is not likely you would win, and it could drag through the Exchequer for years, then go to the other courts, and eventually to the House of Lords.

"Think, my lady. Where do you suppose his funds came from? I never heard that the Carroways were particularly plump in the pocket. He probably inherited this house"— Avebury glanced around the finely appointed study—"but little else. Did you not know anything of his circumstances when you wed him?"

"No," she whispered. "No, nothing."

"Did your father not inquire of his prospects? Did you not think to ask your father? From what I hear of you from our mutual friend Rycote, I gathered that you are awake on every suit, not an empty-headed fribble. In fact, I must congratulate you; can't think why I have not done so before. Finding that telltale bookmark! That was a stroke of luck, I tell you! Would have done in the viscount even had Rycote not caught up with him."

"Thank you," she said faintly. "Thank you for all you have done for me. You have been most kind! As for knowing of Walter's prospects, sir, I was but sixteen, and I did not worry my head overmuch. My father was all for the match; Walter was handsome and most attentive . . . "

"Of course," said Avebury. "Bowled you over, did he?" He smiled. "We all make mistakes, my lady. I trust you do not intend to make another one and break poor Rycote's heart."

Caroline's face grew scarlet. "I am in mourning," she pointed out.

"For that traitor? Oh, madam, I know you are trying to put the best face on it, but who would wish you to mourn for him?"

Avebury obviously believed he had said too much. "Beg pardon," he muttered. "I am pleased I see you well, madam. Do call on me if I can be of assistance." He left abruptly.

Caroline thought long and hard after Avebury's departure. He had made sure she would have enough to live on to the end of her days, a bounty she had never expected to have until her visit to Lamburton. She could manage nicely on a hundred and fifty thousand pounds. She would notify the solicitor that the fine should be paid.

Still, she felt a need to talk it over with someone, but had no one to talk to at all, other than servants. How had she lived five years in this house with no one to confide in? Not very well. Then those wonderful months with the Dowager Lady Rycote, Ruth, and Dickon had followed, when she could and did talk about anything that was on her mind, and they had listened; she in turn had listened to them. Her only acquaintances in London were those she had made through Ruth and Dickon. She had depended too heavily on those two. It was time she cultivated some friends of her own. To put a fine point on it, she was lonely.

She tried to imagine herself discussing a fine of fifty thousand pounds with anyone she had met. Lady Robstart? Ha! It was unthinkable. Her thoughts turned, as they invariably did, to Dickon.

She sent him a note by her footman, hoping he did not read too much into the invitation.

When he appeared next afternoon as requested, she greeted him formally and led him into the study. Taking his cue from her, he asked, "What can I do for you, my lady?"

How to tell him she longed for a friendly conversation such as they had had innumerable times in the past? How to tell him she had been hungry for the sight of him, for his smile, his touch? For the meeting of minds, when they seemed to communicate without saying a word?

"I wondered how your work at the War Office is progressing," she hedged. "Are you still involved in preparing reports from the front for Lord Avebury?"

"I have been eased out of that," he said, laughing. "My successor, who took over when I left for Kent, is so eager to make a good impression with the Old Man that he takes pains I never took. I say, leave him to it. The Old Man seems to believe I have talents in other directions, and he is having me meet with certain informants to see if we can unearth a few more traitors. I may have to do some traveling as a result.

"But that cannot be why you asked me here," he continued. "What is it, Caroline? You know you can tell me."

"Lord Avebury called on me yesterday," she said.

"He did? Whatever for?"

"It was about my inheritance, actually, and the fine they are levying on Walter." She explained what Lord Avebury had told her. "Imagine, Dickon! He interceded on my behalf, so I shall not be left penniless! I have the money from Walter's safe, but I had not realized the Crown would wish to take everything. They may have the fifty thousand pounds. You are working for a good man, Dickon."

Dickon chuckled. "He has his good days," he said. "Do you plan to stay in London?"

"Why, yes. Where else would I go? I have thought of returning to Bedfordshire, but somehow . . . "

"Durham?" he suggested. He held his breath for her answer.

"Durham? Whyever would I—oh. Dickon, you are impossible. I know what you are after! I have asked you not to mention this again. Please!"

"Are you happy now, Caroline?" he asked seriously.

"Indeed. I am perfectly happy. Would you care for tea? Let me just ring." She hurried over to the bell rope, her face averted.

Dickon looked at the woman he loved. She was wearing a horrid, shapeless black gown, the duplicate of so many he had seen on her before. It did nothing for her. A black riband was twined in her hair. She had blossomed in the months he had known her, but now the sparkling eyes were dulled, the healthy bloom in her cheeks fading. She was no happier than he was.

"Caroline, you are living a lie, mourning for that monster," he said. He rose and went to her as she stood, still holding the bell rope. He took her face in his hands, forcing her to look at him. "You may be in mourning, but it is not for Viscount Carroway. Look at you! Living alone in this house, worrying about your money, about where to live, about paying Walter's fine, and, I'll warrant, seeing no one. Why not give up this pretense and marry me? For God's sake! You have never given me a single sensible reason for refusing. You are free, remember? You love me, do you not? Or have I been deluding myself?"

He would not take her in his arms and kiss her senseless until she agreed. He would *not*. It took every bit of his self-control.

A maid answered the summons and took the order for tea. Dickon stood motionless, holding Caroline's head, until the maid had gone.

"I do love you! You know I do!" Caroline said, looking

up at him with tears in his eyes. "That is why I cannot do this to you!"

"Do what?"

"Dickon, I cannot bear a healthy son. Lord knows I have tried hard enough. I cannot go through that again! You can have no idea of the crushing blows one feels when one loses another and another . . . You are the Earl of Rycote, descendant of I-do-not-know-how-many Earls of Rycote, and you deserve to have a son who can carry on the name. I cannot give you that son. You must find a wife who can."

Dickon's face became thunderous. "Is *that* your reason for refusing me?" he roared. "I would have you know, my lady, that my sister has *three* sons, any one of whom is welcome to the title of Earl of Rycote. More important, I have a brother, and though he, too, has not yet taken a wife, he can be expected to do so assuming he survives the war. There are heirs in plenty!"

"But they are not your sons," she said.

"Madam, I am no Walter Carroway. Getting an heir is not the prime goal of my life. My dearest wish at the moment is persuading you to become my wife. If we have no sons, so be it."

They were interrupted at this point by the maid bearing a tea tray. Caroline remained silent as she poured for them both. Dickon wished he knew what she was thinking.

Never had she been so tempted. She believed him to be more interested in having a son than he let on; what man would not be? What she could not bring herself to tell him, however, was her fear of the marriage act itself. He would, of course, expect his marital rights, and that meant that she would inevitably find herself with child—a child she would lose, or who would be born sickly, only to die in infancy. She could not face that again. Not even for Dickon would she face that again. It would be as devastating to him as to her.

"No," she said. "I cannot do that to you. I am so sorry, Dickon. You must find someone else."

"Is that not *my* decision to make?" he cried. "If *I* do not mind if I have no sons, why should *you* play the martyr?"

He ran his fingers through his hair in agitation. "By God, madam, I have had enough. I bid you good day." He set down his still-full teacup with a clatter and stalked out.

Caroline looked about her, at her newly purchased desk, the small Sheraton table on which she took tea, the heavy blue draperies, the wine-red upholstered chairs, the bookshelves, the handsome Axminster carpet on the floor. All mere things. Things, not people. Yet they were things she stood to lose.

Now she had no one to talk to at all. She had driven off Dickon, and she doubted Ruth would be in charity with her either.

She was too dispirited to cry. She sighed and drank her tea.

Caroline saw almost no one in July. The London season was drawing to a close, she told herself; most anyone who was anyone would be leaving the city. She was on no one's invitation list, for she was the widow of a traitor, and thus beneath notice. Old friends might have rallied to her, but she had no old friends. She thought of Ruth's frequent informal At Homes and considered having one of her own, but knew she would feel worse than ever if no guests arrived.

One evening at dinner she took stock of herself. There she sat, alone, at one end of a long, polished mahogany table, with a uniformed footman standing at attention behind her. A dozen candles blazed in a silver candelabrum. Crystal goblets were lined up before her, and at least a hundredweight of silver flatware bracketed her plate. Her end of the table was laden with side dishes, condiments, and a salt dish, all in polished silver. Beyond this collection the bare mahogany stretched on and on; an endless row of empty chairs lined either side.

Caroline looked at the setting, looked at herself, dressed in her usual funereal black, and laughed. She laughed until tears came. Then she dabbed at her eyes with her serviette.

The footman, concerned, said, "My lady? Are you all right?"

"I am not certain," she told him. "What else is to come? I forget."

"You have had only the soup course!" he said, horrified. "Was the soup unsatisfactory? What may I get you, ma'am?"

"You may get me the carriage. Tell Haskell I wish to go out. Then you may clear the table, Oliver. I wish no more dinner."

"Yes, ma'am," said Oliver, looking frightened. "Right away, ma'am."

Caroline hurried from the dining room to her chamber, where she instructed a startled Dossie to lay out her yellow-and-green gown, the one she had had made in Durham.

"No more blacks," she said through clenched teeth. "This atrocity is to go into the dustbin. Toss all the others after it, Dossie. I have just emerged from mourning."

"Yes'm," said Dossie, beaming.

In twenty minutes she was on her way to Golden Square.

"Caroline!" said Ruth, Lady Stilton. "Is it really you? We had given you up. Come in, do. Hawkins," she said, turning to the footman who had admitted the visitor, "will you fetch the earl?"

Hawkins disappeared while Caroline said hesitantly, "I just happened to be passing—I know it is late—have you finished dinner? I do not wish to disturb you—"

"Nonsense, child," said Ruth. "Two of my sons were here for dinner, but it is over and they are sitting around the table with their drinks. Will is no doubt boring Alfred with tales of his conquests at Almack's. Come into the sitting room."

Caroline followed Ruth up the familiar stairs, along the familiar hall, and into the familiar sitting room. This cozy house seemed more like home than her own, where she had lived for five years and was now living again.

Ruth immediately took note of Caroline's gown. Her eyebrows up, she inquired. "No more blacks?"

"No," said Caroline. "No more."

"Good girl," said Ruth. "How have you been keeping?"

"Very well," said Caroline, "And you?"

Ruth laughed. "One would think we had only just met," she said. "We have missed you, Caroline. We do not hear a word from you, or about you. Even Lady Robstart and Mrs. Hinkle have noted your absence. If they do not know of your activities, no one does."

"They could have called," she said. "I would have received them, I believe."

"Lady Robstart was hurt that you did not attend her Viewing. You may recall it was several months back, right after Lord Carroway's . . . ah, um. Her portrait fills most of one wall in their Yellow Drawing Room, which has sixteen-foot ceilings, I swear. She is shown holding a black-and-white puppy. The puppy is quite true to life, though he is nearly grown now. I cannot say the same for Lady Robstart."

Caroline laughed obediently. Where was Dickon?

"Dickon has had to be out of town a great deal recently," Ruth went on. "Looking into some suspicious doings in Essex, I believe. He came home only a day or two ago. I am delighted you chose to visit us while he is here. Where can the boy be? He asked to be excused from my sons' prattle over the wine. Said he had some papers to go over."

"You wished to see me?" said Dickon, suddenly appearing in the doorway. His face stony, he looked only at Ruth as he walked into the sitting room, chose a chair, moved a cushion, and sat down. "Oh, Miss Caroline, is it?" He seemed to be speaking to a stranger as he turned to her.

Ruth looked from one to the other, these two determined people who could not seem to settle whatever differences had arisen between them. Now that Caroline was truly widowed, Ruth had no desire to put a series of young chits in Dickon's way. These two were meant for each other and Ruth wished only to further the match. And then, suddenly, Dickon refused to mention Caroline and had told Ruth in stronger language than she thought necessary that their friendship was at an end; he never intended to speak to Caroline again and suggested Ruth follow suit. Ruth had thought it a temporary misunderstanding, but it had gone on for many weeks. Dickon refused to discuss it.

Looking at them now, she knew her own presence was *de trop* and that the best she could do for these two miserable specimens was to disappear.

"I have some things to say to Will and Alfred," she said into the silence. "Do pardon me." She hurried out.

"What brings you here?" Dickon said baldly. Caroline had not responded to his greeting, if greeting it could be called.

"I got to thinking," said Caroline. Now that she was here, her bravery deserted her. She looked down at her lap and smoothed the skirt of her gown. So much for breaking out of mourning; Dickon did not seem to notice.

"Yes?"

"I fear I have been selfish, Dickon. If—if you still wish it, I will agree to become your wife." She looked up at him uncertainly. Had he found another woman in the weeks since they had seen each other?

Dickon did not look as joyful as she had hoped. Her heart plummeted.

"An interesting decision, madam," he said. "May I ask what brought it about? Some circumstance has changed, perhaps?"

"No," she said. "I have changed."

He looked at her more closely. She looked the same to him—the same dear, kind, and caring woman he had fallen in love with, the same beautiful face and tall, graceful body—but he suddenly realized she had shed her horrid blacks.

"You are out of mourning!" he said in surprise.

"Yes. I no longer wish to live a lie."

"I commend you. It takes courage, but I know you have courage. Let the harpies make of it what they will."

"Do you not want to know what else has changed?" she asked. Surely he did not believe she had come here solely to show she had come out of mourning?

"There is more? Am I to guess?"

She laughed, a bitter little laugh. "No. As I said, I have been thinking. Dickon, this is quite difficult for me to say. I assumed that if we were to be married—if you still want me—you would wish your husbandly rights."

Dickon's interest had been piqued. He watched her closely. "I would, of course," he said. "I love you, Caroline. Are you trying to tell me that you are willing to marry me only if I promise to leave you alone? Good God, woman, what kind of marriage would that be?"

Now she was coming to the most difficult part, a part she had hoped never to have to explain to anyone. She steeled herself. It was now or never.

"Dickon, I would never wish to do that to you. It did occur to me, however, that if—if I let you have your conjugal rights—and I would! Oh, for you I would!—I would inevitably become with child. I know I would; it always happens. Then we would both hope, and pray, and take the best care, and still I would lose the baby, or it would be stillborn, or it would be weak and sickly—and we would lose it. Dickon, I did not believe I could live through that again, and it would be so tragic for you as well.

"That is why I have refused your offer in the past. Then, tonight as I was eating a lonely dinner in that monstrous big house, it came to me. Am I to suffer—and you, too, perhaps—for the rest of my life, years and years and years, because I am afraid to try to give you an heir? I would be the proudest mother in Christendom if I could give you an heir. It will not happen, I fear, but I am willing to take the chance."

She had hardly got the words out when she was lifted from her chair by Dickon's strong arms and enveloped in his embrace.

"My dearest dear!" he cried, kissing her madly. "Why did you not tell me this long ago! I wanted you, heir or no heir. I still do. What will be will be. We shall take our chances.

"But Caroline! What makes you believe it be your fault that you have had such a sorry time bearing children? Could it not have been that monster Walter's fault? Have you though of that?"

Tears glistened in her eyelashes but the smile she gave him was wholehearted. "Of course I have, but Walter as-

Anne Douglas

sured me that such a thought was nonsense. He was a healthy and well-made man, Dickon; truly he was. He pointed that out to me, and reminded me of my own short-comings. I was prey to morning sickness, and megrims, and I lost weight—I was the veriest hag when you first saw me, was I not? He complained bitterly that he was cheated when he chose me—me, from a family of good breeders!

"You, too, are a healthy and well-made man. If I cannot birth a healthy child, we can be certain it is my fault."

Caroline hid her face in Dickon's shirt front. She felt terrible misgivings about the step she was about to take.

Then she remembered her resolution to avoid "if onlys." Should she refuse to become Dickon's wife and try to bear his children, she would live with "if only" for a long and lonely lifetime.

"We will accept what fate has in store for us," Dickon murmured, once more wrapping her in his arms. "Oh, Caroline. My dearest Caroline!" He showered her with kisses.

When he finally pulled away, he said, "We must tell Ruth without delay. She has worried her teeth on this for weeks."

He called for his sister, who guessed the happy news the moment she saw their faces. "You will be my sister-in-law!" she cried. "Welcome to the family!"

Because Dickon was to leave on another trip for the War Office in a few days, he obtained a special license and they were married quietly with only Ruth and Lord Avebury in attendance. Dickon removed to the house in Hanover Square, which he admired but in which he did not feel at home. While he was away on the track of a man believed to be sending large sums of money to the French, the house was claimed by the Crown. Caroline moved back to Golden Square, having rescued only her clothes and her new small desk. Eventually she received her inheritance of one hundred fifty thousand pounds, minus a stiff fee from Lamburton.

Fenland and Dunthorpe were sentenced to Australia.

Dickon's new position was discontinued soon after the nineteenth of October, when Napoleon was defeated at

Leipzig in what came to be called the Battle of the Nations. Though Bonaparte did not abdicate until the eleventh of April, 1814, the worst was assumed to be over. Dickon was permitted to resign from the War Office and took his bride in triumph to Durham. There the Dowager Lady Rycote greeted them both with open arms and put on a gala ball in their honor, with Sir Harry Wadsworth and his bride as special guests. Caroline and Maddy, Lady Wadsworth, soon became bosom friends.

Never had Caroline imagined such tender lovemaking as she enjoyed with her beloved Dickon. The conjugal act she had so dreaded bore no resemblance to her grim relations with Walter.

She was bursting with well-being one night as they went to bed after a long and busy day. Her marriage had done that to her, she thought happily. She was energetic, eager for each day to begin, and filled the hours with activities that had the dowager shaking her head in wonder.

"I do not believe I have ever felt so well," she said lazily to her husband as he shed his shirt. She was lying in bed, admiring the handsome man she had married. "I give you full credit. I am well because I am so happy. Come here." She opened her arms.

"Ah, a kiss you wanted, was it?" he said, obediently leaning over her and planting a hot salute on her lips. "I always try to oblige."

"Well, yes, that, but do you know, I am hungry. I can see in my mind's eye the grapes that were on the table at dinner, and they are calling to me. Dickon, I must have some grapes. Would you be a dear and go after some? I promise not to leave the seeds in the bed."

Wondering at this sudden need for grapes, Dickon did her bidding. A plateful of grapes soon appeared and disappeared, leaving nothing but seeds. Finally, it dawned on him.

"My dear, would you possibly be increasing?" he asked. "Why did you not tell me? We must take the greatest care of you now, you know." A worried frown appeared on his face.

"Increasing? Why should you think so? Just because I wanted some grapes?" She laughed.

"Has this never happened to you before—a need for some particular food? I remember Ruth telling me, when she had Alfred—and George as well, I believe. It was hot cross buns with her. Difficult to find after Lent. I wonder whether we can keep you in grapes."

"Truly? I never heard about that! But I cannot be increasing, can I? I feel too well!" She counted back, however, and it could be true. She had not had her monthly course, but it was sometimes irregular.

It turned out to be true indeed. After an uneventful pregnancy, in June of 1814 she gave birth with no difficulty to a healthy boy, who was named Richard after Dickon's father. If his parents watched and worried over him in excess, it was understandable, but his no-nonsense grandmother, the dowager countess, counteracted that with brisk efficiency.

After the Battle of Waterloo on the twenty-second of June, 1815, Benjamin Richardson came home to Ryfield, bearing an ugly scar across his shoulder, but otherwise whole.

The advent of a daughter, Ruth, born to Caroline and Dickon in 1816, caused rejoicing to equal that of Benjamin's return. Caroline's biggest problem now was with the jealousy her young son showed toward the new arrival.

Then came Harry, and Peter, and last, John, healthy babies all. Caroline surveyed her growing family with pride.

"Were you aiming for a cricket team?" she asked her husband one day as she put baby John down for his nap.

Nanny often complained that young Lady Rycote spent too much time with her children, but Caroline disagreed. She and Dickon were their parents, perhaps too doting, but they never tired of watching their brood's growing accomplishments. She *always* put John down for his nap.

Dickon laughed. "Too much difference in their ages," he said. "Do you see John, here, holding a cricket bat for years yet? Richard is already determined to be team captain. And what about Ruthie?"

"Mayhap we should have a female team as well," said Caroline.